TURNING (THIRTY)

A NOVEL BY NAT CUDDINGTON

Turning Thirty
© 2023 Nat Cuddington

You can visit Nat's website at **natcuddington.ca**

Find Laura Kulson, the cover artist at **etsy.com/shop/SirenBayStudio**

Also by Nat Cuddington:

For anyone who feels like they need to pretend sometimes
(or all the time) to get through the day.

It's okay, I'll pretend with you.

PART ONE

TURNING (THIRTY)

|

I know my friends are throwing me a surprise party. They've actually been doing a pretty good job at making me think nothing is happening, and I have to commend their acting and improv skills surrounding the whole thing, but it's all just a little convenient. My birthday's on Tuesday and it's the Saturday night before, and no one can come to the get-together I tried to plan. As if everyone has plans on my birthday weekend, except for my best friend, who feels bad that no one else can come. She invited me to her place so that she can at least do all the work for a quiet hang out, you know, rent the movie on Prime, order the food, and do the cleanup herself after I go home. She even said that she wanted to do a fun birthday photoshoot, so I should wear something cute. That's her way around me not showing up to my surprise birthday party in sweats, because everyone knows I would if I thought it was just the two of us hanging out.

So I put on the new dress that I bought for the occasion - when I thought it would be a non-surprise party planned by me.

Thirty. I can do this. I can turn thirty and not freak out. Absolutely I can. Plus look at me in my sexy dress. It's dark purple and has thick straps that just run over the edges of my shoulders, threatening to fall off. It's got a cute, sweetheart neckline, and my rose gold necklace holding a little round pearl sits just below my throat. Also I just got new glasses and the frames are so cute! They're big and sort of a rounded square shape with a dark tortoiseshell design, and they make me feel really cute.

The hemline of my dress sits a few inches above my knees, and some of the watercolour splashes around my childhood dog's paw print tattoo are visible. I do a French twist with my bangs, watching in the mirror as I grab and twist my dark brown hair along my forehead, and down to my ear. I tie it in place and let the rest mix in with my shoulder-length waves.

Thirty.

My best friend, Angela, texts me and tells me that I can't come over yet. Her friend from high school has had an emergency and needs to Skype. In other words, they're not ready for me yet. I smile and take a deep breath. I wonder how many people will be there. I don't have that many close friends, but I had invited a bunch of people from work, so I wonder if they'll be at the party. I wonder where everyone's going to park. If I show up at Angela's house and see ten cars lining the curb, I'm going to laugh.

I stick some facial tissue under my armpits while I wait; the spring air is nice, and it's a comfortable temperature in my apartment, but I'm still getting all clammy. I don't want to show up to my own surprise party with sweaty armpits.

After about twenty minutes, Angela texts me again and says I can come over any time, and that the door is unlocked, so to just let myself in. I grab my purse and slide my phone into it, and almost grab my keys without taking the tissues out from under my armpits. I decide to throw on some more antiperspirant and then head over to my surprise party.

Oh I hope they're actually throwing me a surprise party. I'll feel like an idiot showing up in a dress with no change of clothes if we're actually just watching movies and eating Thai takeout.

Everyone jumps up and yells surprise before I'm even fully through the door, but the front door opens right into the living room, so it's not like they needed to wait for me to turn a corner or something. I thought I was going to have to pretend to be surprised, but my reaction is genuine. I throw my hands to my mouth and immediately start crying because I was not expecting this many people to be here. There are at least fifteen people in the living room and a few more in the kitchen, and there's streamers across the ceiling, a table of snacks, a birthday cake, a collection of booze, even!

"Oh my god," I finally say. "I wasn't expecting all of this."

"Were you... expecting some of it?" Angela asks. She's let her hair out of her usual braids and has her now big, curly hair pulled onto the top of her head.

"Yes, you guys were so obvious," I laugh. "But I must say, playing along was the most fun I've had in a while." I make my way to Angela in the middle of the room and give her a hug. "I love your hair, by the way."

She smiles and tilts her head to the side a little. "Why thank you."

"This is amazing," I say to everyone. "Thank you guys all so much."

I'm definitely the most fancy dressed here, but Angela probably figured her "wear something cute" comment might make me go all out, so she's got on a flowy knee-length dress with thin straps, showing off her dark brown shoulders.

Everyone says happy birthday and I hug most people, and most people tell me that I look amazing in my dress, and then Angela turns on some music and we immediately start doing shots.

"Happy birthday, Reese," someone I've never met says to me. He's paler than I am, if that's possible, and his black hair is short, but still long enough to be a bit messy. It's sticking up in some spots, and poking out around his ears.

"Thanks," I say.

"I hope it's okay that I'm here. Um, I just started working with your friend Claire, and she invited me so I could meet some people."

"Yeah of course. Did you just move to town?" I ask.

"Yeah. I actually lived here a few years ago, well, more than a few years ago now. But everything's so different now, it feels like a new town."

"Well, welcome back," I say with a smile.

He smiles and nods a little, looks away as if he's nervous.

"You have to do a shot with me," I say, grabbing a bottle of Jack Daniel's. "Have you ever had a Snappy Jack?"

"You mean an Apple Jack?"

"No, I mean a Snappy Jack."

He shakes his head. "What's in it?"

"I can't remember!" I laugh. "Obviously Jack Daniel's, but I don't remember what it's mixed with."

"Apple liqueur? I think you're thinking of an Apple Jack."

"No, it's not apple," I say. "Let's just do a shot of Jack on its own. I can't remember what it's mixed with."

"Or we could do a shot of something that burns a little less going down." He raises an eyebrow at me, but before I can answer, Claire comes over and puts her arm around me.

"Heeeey girlie!" she yells happily. "Are you drunk yet?"

"I'm getting there!"

"I think she's there," Black-haired-paler-than-me guy says.

"Excuse me, you haven't met me before. You don't know what I'm like when I'm drunk."

"Whatever you say," he chuckles.

"Okay, Jack Daniel's-shot-know-it-all, you just..." I point my finger at him and wiggle it a little, as if I'm going to say something, but really I have nothing. Also I'm totally drunk. "You just…"

"Yes?" He seems incredibly amused by this entire interaction, but I'm just annoyed that I can't remember what's in a Snappy Jack.

"You stay there. I have to go have a conversation with my good friend Claire."

"No shots then?" he asks.

"You decide on a less burny shot, and we'll do it together when I come back."

"Okay," he says with a laugh and a tilt of his head.

"I saw that," I say. "You're very condescending, you know, with that head tilting."

He looks at me with one of those flat smile things and raised eyebrows, you know, when someone thinks you're being ridiculous and so they give you this look that tells you they think you're being ridiculous.

Claire grabs my arm and pulls me away and we make our way around the kitchen counter and towards the fridge.

"I think Emily's going to ask me to marry her," she blurts out.

I gasp. "Oh my god, no way! Why, what's she been doing? Do you want to marry her?"

"Yes, of course I want to marry her. I just… I sort of wanted to ask her."

"You're cute," I say. "You still could. You could do your own proposal later. I bet she'd think it's sweet."

"You think?"

"Yes! Hey, do you know what's in a Snappy Jack?"

"Do you mean an Apple Jack?"

"Not you too."

"Anyway, Emily's off talking to Isla on the phone, which is totally weird, right? She's gotta be asking her for advice or something."

"Yes, that's definitely what's happening," I say with a smile. Isla is Claire's best friend who moved to LA a little while ago to live with her celebrity boyfriend. Sometimes I'm sad that I wasn't friends with her earlier, so I could have gotten a chance to meet him.

"So you think I should do my own proposal later?" Claire asks.

"Yes, it would be the cutest thing, and also she would never suspect it!"

"Oh yes, that's true! You're smart."

"Only the smartest."

Angela comes over and puts her arms around both of us. "Hey there's some cute guy over at the booze table asking about you, Reese."

"The guy who looks like he's never seen the sun?"

Angela hits me in the arm. "Reese! That's rude."

I shrug. "It's just an observation."

"Well anyway, I think he's cute, and I think *he* thinks *you're* cute."

"What if I don't think he's cute?" I ask, narrowing my eyes at her.

"Well it doesn't matter, it's not like you have to date him. But he's waiting for you."

"Okay, I will go."

I make my way through the kitchen and back to the booze table where Whitey is waiting for me. Maybe I should come up with better nicknames for him. Maybe he's sensitive about how pale he is.

"Hello new friend," I say.

"I've decided that we are going to have Polar Bears."

"Delightful."

I watch him pour the two liquors into a mixing cup with ice and he shakes it like he's a professional. He smiles before pouring it into two shot glasses, and then he hands one to me. I clink my glass against his and we both knock them back.

"That was fun," I say. "Let's do another."

There's still some in the cup so he pours us each another one, and we cheers again before drinking them in one go.

"So how's your birthday going so far?" he asks after we do our shots.

"Well technically it's not my birthday yet. It's my birthday on Tuesday."

"Ah. And how old are you going to be?"

"Thirty."

"I remember turning thirty. It'll be fun."

"How old are you?" I ask.

"274."

I laugh and hit him in the chest. Yes, I am very drunk. I never touch men's chests unless I have a major crush on them or am in love with them.

"Okay but really," I say.

"Thirty-two," he says with a grin.

"You made it sound like you turned thirty so long ago."

"Sometimes it feels that way."

We stare at each other for a few seconds and I sort of get lost in his eyes. They're such a light blue that they're almost grey, and blend in with his pale skin in this weirdly attractive way. Plus his dark hair just pops and is like, 'Wow! That's some nice hair!'. Don't judge me, I'm drunk.

"Anyway, I'm Felix," he finally says, breaking our staring contest with a blink and a glance down at his hand. Ah yes, he wants me to shake it.

I grab onto his hand which is a very unusual temperature in that it doesn't have one. It's not cold but it's also not warm, and I don't know how to explain it except that it definitely makes me think that's a little weird. Like, it's like I'm shaking hands with a couch. Except it's his hand.

"Nice to meet you, Felix. Thanks for coming to my birthday."

||

Felix is the first person to text me on my birthday. I wake up on Tuesday morning to see that he has sent me a string of birthday related emojis and then an animated emoji of a unicorn with his voice singing Happy Birthday. He actually has a really nice voice. I smile and text him back.

Thanks, Snappy Jack. Also you should be a singer when you grow up.

He replies with a voice clip. "That's the dream."

Are you working today? I text.

He finally replies via text this time. **Yeah. You should come get pizza.**

Maybe I will.

Angela meets me at my work fifteen minutes before five, and my boss lets me duck out a little early. She drives me to my apartment so I can get changed out of my stiff office clothes, and she waits in the living room as I put on a pair of skinny jeans and a flowy, striped t-shirt.

"So this Felix guy," she says with a grin as I emerge from my room.

"Is very nice," I give her. "But I'm not necessarily looking to date anyone right now, so we're currently nothing more than friends."

"Currently," she emphasizes.

"He hasn't said anything about wanting to date me anyway. We texted a little bit over the weekend and he sent me a happy birthday message this morning. That's it."

"And invited you for pizza."

"Where he works, Angela. He's going to be working."

"Well I think this is very promising."

I sigh and open my rats' pen door. "I'm not really looking for a boyfriend. You know I don't like the idea of dating."

"Ah," she says, holding her index finger up. "You don't have to date per se, to get a boyfriend. This is one man, Reese. Who you don't even have to date-"

"Per se," I finish for her as I lift Hazel Grace out. "Yeah. I get it. But I still don't like the idea of hanging out with someone just because they could potentially become something more than that, you know? He *could* potentially become more than that, but he also couldn't, and I'm not using either of those possibilities as a factor in my reasons for hanging out with him."

"Fine," she huffs. She walks over to me and pets Hazel Grace with her index finger and then scoops out April May. "You win this time," she adds. "But you know I just want you to have someone."

"But I have you, Angela. You and your wonderful husband. And my rats. I don't *need* someone."

"But it would be nice."

"Yeah. But so would going to Cuba."

Carter's is busy when we arrive, but Felix reserved us a table and he shows us to it right away. We obviously don't get to talk much while we're there because he's working, but he smiles at me every time he passes by, and lingers a little when he takes our order and brings our drink refills. I watch him as he brings other tables their food and it looks like he's moving in fast forward.

Like, he's not jogging, he's definitely just walking, but he's going too fast for a regular walk. Even when he puts people's plates down, his movements are really quick but very precise, and I'm in awe at how he does it. He must have been a server before moving here.

We stay until the restaurant dies down and Felix gets a chance to sit with us for a bit.

"Good birthday?" he asks.

"Yes, except I didn't get any cake."

"Oh shit, I totally forgot!" He immediately gets up and leaves.

"Oh," I say to Angela, slightly confused. "He didn't have to leave…"

But then he comes back with a slice of Reese's Cup cheesecake with a sparkler in it. I clap my hands softly in front of me as I watch him place it on the table, and then I look up at him and smile. Back to the sparkler in my cake. Back to Felix.

"Sorry, I didn't know it would take this long to go out," he says.

"That's okay," I reply. "But you have to stay here and awkwardly watch it with me."

He huffs and sits down again, and Angela smiles, raising her eyebrows at me.

"So, it's still going, eh?" he says.

"Yeah, sparklers will do that," I say.

"At least it's pretty."

"Yes, it does have that going for it."

"You should take it out and wave it around," Angela suggests.

"Don't-" Felix holds out his hand to stop me before I even move. "Don't do that. Sparklers are for outdoors if you're going to wave them around."

"Yeah, Angela," I say. "They're only for cakes if you want them indoors."

The sparks finally get to the bottom and fizzle out and the three of us clap and say yay together.

"That was fun," I say with a smile. "Thanks for the magical sparkler and the cake that's also sort of my name."

We go back to Angela's for about an hour for Bingsu, which is a Korean version of shaved ice. It's a dessert made of shaved frozen milk, fruit, and sweetened condensed milk. Her husband's family is Korean and he made it for us the first time I met him, when they first started dating, probably to try and impress me. He said it was the way his grandma makes it, and I always bug him to make it again but he says he's too lazy to make the ice for it. I guess he isn't too lazy to do it for my birthday! Ha! We put strawberries and kiwi pieces on our desserts and drizzle the condensed milk over top, but what I can't get over is how Josh gets the frozen milk shavings to be so *fluffy*. It's so delightful.

Angela drives me back to the office since my car is still parked there, and she waits with her lights on until I'm in my car with the doors locked. I drive home with a smile. Usually something disappointing happens on my birthdays, and I end up crying at some point, but today was good. My coworkers got me a card and a box of Reese's Pieces (everyone thinks they're being clever when they do this, but I don't mind because yum), so that was fun, and nothing annoying ended up happening workwise. All the clients I dealt with were pleasant and the work day went by fast. Even the weekend leading up to it was good. The party was so much fun, and I hardly even had a hangover on Sunday. Maybe thirty will be super excellent.

Felix and I text back and forth throughout the rest of the week, but nothing big. Silly little things, like funny things people say at work, or random thoughts that pop into our heads. But on Friday night, our random little texts turn into a conversation and it's almost two in the morning before I realize how long we've been texting for.

I should go to bed I finally say. **I didn't realize how late it was.**

Or we could go for a walk.

A walk at 2am? I ask.

What's wrong with walking at 2am? I much prefer the moonlight anyway.

Alright then. Where should I meet you?

I'll come to you. I don't want you out on your own this late.

I tell him my address and he's buzzing my apartment in less than fifteen minutes. I run to the washroom and look in the mirror to make sure my hair isn't a mess, which it is, so I run to the intercom and tell him I'll be down shortly. I brush through my hair quickly and grab a Qtip to fix my raccoon eyes. Should I brush my teeth? Do I have horrible breath? It's 2am, I probably have horrible breath. I brush them really fast and then head down to the apartment lobby to meet him. He's got jeans and a blue pullover hoodie on, and he's standing with his hands in the kangaroo pocket.

"Oh shoot," I say, "I should get a sweater."

"Oh sure."

"You can come up if you want."

He grins and follows me to the elevator. We're quiet as we wait for the doors to open and we're quiet when we step inside together. I'm not sure why I suddenly feel awkward around him, but I hope he doesn't feel it oozing out of me.

"So," I finally say.

"So."

But then the lights flicker and there's a big screeching sound, followed by the elevator coming to an abrupt halt. I almost fall over, and reach my arms beside me, grabbing for the wall, and well, Felix, I guess. I grab onto his bicep and he immediately reaches out and grabs my hand.

"Oh my god," I say, already feeling like I'm out of breath.

"We're okay," he says calmly.

"What if the elevator plummets?" The panic is crawling up my throat.

"It's not going to plummet."

"What if we're stuck in here and no one knows we're here? What if we run out of air?"

"We're not going to run out of air."

"How do you know that? You don't know that, Felix!"

"Okay, I'll stop breathing if you want. I'll let you have all the air."

"Right, and then I'll be in here with a dead body. Sounds fun."

"Oh you have no idea." He grins, but I'm just confused. Maybe he's confusing me on purpose to make me stop panicking. But then the idea of him trying to stop me from panicking makes me panic more and now I can't breathe. My chest is closing up and my heart is thumping against my ribcage and I'm dizzy and I can't -

"Reese," Felix says quietly. "Reese, it's okay. Look at me."

I look into his grey eyes but I'm still trying to catch my breath and I can feel tears stinging my eyes. He reaches over and grabs my other hand and spins me so that we're completely facing each other instead of standing side-by-side.

"Take in a deep breath," he whispers.

"I can't-"

He nods. "Yes you can. I'll do it with you. Okay? Come on, deep breath in." He breathes in through his nose and I watch his chin raise a little as he does it, so I try my best to match him.

"Good," he says. "Hold it for a few seconds."

I hold my breath and keep looking into his eyes. They're so calm and soft, and I don't want to look away.

"Okay, out through your mouth," he says.

I let my breath out and am glad that I decided to brush my teeth. He lets his out too, and he smiles.

"Again," he says gently, taking another deep breath in.

We stand in the elevator breathing together, and I don't even feel weird about it. I feel safe. We take about five more deep breaths together, and each time we exhale, I feel a little better.

"Good," Felix says. "Your heart isn't racing so much anymore."

"How do you know?" I ask.

"Uh- Because you're calmer." He quickly lets go of my hands and leans towards the door, where he pushes a red emergency button. He steps back and huffs a little, then presses the button again. "Is something supposed to happen?" he asks.

"I don't know, I've never been stuck in an elevator before."

"I feel like there should be an alarm, or a beep or something so that we know it worked."

I shrug at him, trying to stay calm, but my nerves are just coming back at full force. A whine comes from above us, and I swear the elevator drops us a bit. It moves and then shakes and I almost fall over again.

"Oh my god we're going to die!"

Felix pulls me into him and wraps his arms around my back. "We're not going to die. Here."

He lets go of me and turns back towards the doors, puts his fingers in between them, and starts prying them open! With his fingers! He hardly even grunts as he does it, it's like he's opening a sliding door into someone's backyard! We're just under a floor, so there's concrete in front of us, and the floor above our heads.

"Great, we can just climb out," he says.

"Excuse me? No way. With my luck, I'll be pulling myself up and the elevator will plummet and cut me in half."

"That's not going to happen."

"How do you just know things?" I ask. "Huh? You know that Snappy Jacks aren't a real shot, and that my heart rate slowed down, and that the elevator just isn't going to plummet? How?"

"Okay, I guess I don't *know* that the elevator won't plummet, but it probably won't. And in the time we've spent discussing it, we could have climbed out. We'd be out by now." He reaches his hands up to the floor above us, and pulls himself up and out of the elevator like he's climbing out of a pool. He lies down on his stomach and comes close to the opening, putting his hand in for me to grab onto.

"Um, no," I say. "I'll just stay in here until it's working again."

Felix sighs and looks down one end of the hallway, down the other, and then gets up. But then he puts his hands under the frame of the elevator, between the doors, and starts *lifting* the elevator. He just lifts it like he's lifting a box of pillows over his head, and I stare at him in wonder, horror, I don't even know, until the floor of the elevator is close enough to the actual floor for me to get out really easily. He wipes his palms together a few times to get the dust off and then grabs my hand, helping me step up and out.

I stare at him.

He stares at me.

We're still holding hands.

The elevator dings behind me and I hear the doors finish opening and then shut. The elevator dings again and I turn a little to see the doors opening again, to reveal the now normal, working elevator.

I turn back to Felix, my hand still in his. "What the fuck was that?"

|||

Felix drops my hand and runs his fingers through his hair, messing it up. He looks at the ground and then back at me, and then he just. Shrugs. He just shrugs! He pulled an elevator up with his hands and he just *shrugs?*

"That wasn't nothing that just happened," I say. "You can't just shrug. What the fuck? What the actual fuck, Felix?"

"Shh." He grabs both my hands and pulls me a little closer to him. "It's late; people are sleeping."

"Then you have to tell me what the hell that was," I whisper.

"It was me lifting the elevator so you could get out. I don't know. It wasn't as heavy as I thought it would be."

"Excuse me? It wasn't as heavy as you thought it would be?" I pull my hands from his grasp and start making my way to the stairwell.

"Where are you going?" he asks, following me.

"To my apartment." I slam the stairwell door open and let it shut behind me, but Felix grabs it before it's completely closed.

"Oh we're taking the stairs, are we?"

"Well I'm not getting back in that death trap!"

"Fair enough. What floor do you live on?"

"The eighth."

"Cool."

He stays a few stairs behind me the whole way up, and the entire time I try to think of something to say. I can't think of anything to say. He doesn't even look that built; there's no way he did what he just did. He is a little taller than me, but height has nothing to do with strength!

I imagined it. That's what happened. The elevator was working before I stepped out, but I was so delirious with nerves that I thought he was the one pulling it up, but really it just did it on its own. And he's not making a big deal out of it because … I don't know why. If he didn't actually pull the elevator up, he would have said "I didn't pull the elevator up, Reese, you're imagining things." Unless he's just going along with what I saw because he doesn't want me to feel like I'm losing my mind, or because he doesn't want me to be embarrassed about thinking I saw him lift the elevator with his bare hands.

Oh my, this is a lot.

I have to stop near the top to grab onto the railing and put a hand on my knee. I suddenly can't breathe again. Felix comes up beside me and puts a hand gently on my back.

"Are you okay?" he asks.

I shake my head, but say nothing.

"I don't know what to tell you, Reese. I don't know what happened, either. I just thought I would try it, and I could do it."

I take a couple deep breaths, nod once, and continue up the stairs.

"Why are you mad at me?"

We make it to my floor and I exit the stairwell and start making my way down the hall.

"Reese."

"It's late, Felix, people are sleeping."

I want to say he jogs to catch up to me, but he just walks faster, somehow with it still looking like he's walking at a regular pace. Like you know when someone walks faster than normal, they actually move differently. But Felix doesn't. He just goes on fast forward, like he was doing at the restaurant.

"Reese," he says. "Reese, I don't understand what's happening."

I make it to my apartment and unlock my door. I turn to him before opening it and sigh. "Neither do I. I'm not mad. I'm just. I don't know. That was weird. Don't you think that was weird?"

"Yeah, for sure. But I mean... Like I said, it wasn't that heavy. Or maybe it was already working and it just looked like I lifted it."

"No, it would have lifted faster than that if it was working."

"I don't know, but maybe the mechanisms helped me somehow."

"I don't really feel like going for a walk anymore," I say quietly. "But you can come in for a bit if you want. I have peanut butter butter tarts."

"That sounds amazing."

We take our shoes off once we get inside and I grab the butter tarts from the fridge. I put one on a little plate for each of us, and walk into the living room to find Felix admiring the rats.

"These little guys are cute," he says, turning to me and taking his butter tart.

"They're girls," I correct. "Hazel Grace and April May."

"Why do they each have two names?"

I put my butter tart down on the coffee table and lift both of my rats out of their little home and place them on the floor to run around.

"Don't you need to put them in those little ball things?"

"One question at a time, Felix," I say with a laugh.

"Okay but seriously."

I shrug. "If I had a bigger place or other pets I might put them in those ball things, but they're fine."

"Well they're really cool."

"Of course they're cool," I say with a bit of a grin. "That's why I named them after two cool girls written by two cool men."

"Um. Okay?"

I wave him off and try to change the subject. "So, you much prefer the moonlight, eh?" I ask.

Felix smirks. "It's quieter."

"The light is quieter? Or you just think nighttime is quieter?"

"Both. But no, I mean the light. It's a soft glow instead of a bright light, I dunno." He shrugs. "I like the soft glow of moonlight. It's calming." He sits on the couch so I do too.

"Okay," I say, nodding. "And do you like working as a server?"

"I like the tips. And I like that most of my shifts start later in the day. I actually used to work at a bar so I would start much later. I wouldn't get home until close to four in the morning. That was the best."

"But the night is over by the time you get home."

"Almost. But on my days off I have the whole night. I mean most people prefer the day, right? And they all work during it. The day's almost over by the time they get home."

I smile at him. "That's true."

He finally takes a bite of his butter tart and his eyes widen. "Wow, this is amazing. Did you make these?"

"Yeah," I say. "It's kind of my specialty."

"Really. Is it like, your thing? Do you want to open a bakery or something?"

"No, I just like doing it for fun. And for eating." I take a bite of mine. "But butter tarts are my favourite, which is weird because there's no chocolate in them. I mean unless I make ones with chocolate, but you know what I mean."

"So chocolate's your weakness, then? Chocolate and butter tarts?"

I smile and nod. "What's yours?"

"I'd tell you, but then I'd have to kill you," he says with a grin.

My eyes bulge a little but then he continues talking. "Sorry, that wasn't funny. Maybe I'm a little nervous. The pastry is amazing, by the way. It's probably the flakiest, most amazing pastry I've ever had."

"Like I said. My specialty." I smile at him and take a big bite of my butter tart. "But also thanks." I can feel myself blushing so I look away.

Angela comes over on Saturday night and we put on a movie but just end up talking the whole time.

"So what's going on with you and that Felix guy?" she asks.

"The same thing as the last time you asked." I grab some popcorn out of the bowl we're sharing.

"But do you like him now?"

"Angela, I've known him for a week."

"Right."

I feel the corner of my mouth curl up. "I know you're worried about me."

"I'm not worried about you," she says quickly. "I'm just…" she sighs. "I want you to be happy but I also don't want you to avoid possibly having a relationship with someone who could be really good for you just because of your exes."

"I'm not doing that," I assure her. "Yeah, I'm a little wary about starting a new relationship, but I don't think that's a bad thing. I want to get to know him before I jump into anything. Build trust. Friendship. You know?"

"Yeah, I know. I get it. I'm sorry if it feels like I'm pushing this on you. I don't mean to. You've just been very avoidant of dating for so long and I don't want you to be alone just because someone else fucked up your relationship."

"Being alone doesn't have to be a bad thing," I say. "As long as I'm not lonely."

"Are you lonely?"

I smile at her. "No."

"Okay. Good."

"I have my-"

She cuts me off. "Your only reason for not being alone can't be your rats named after book characters."

"Why not? I love them."

"What are you going to do when they die in a year?"

"Cry," I say quietly. "And then maybe get a chinchilla."

"Reese," Angela whines.

"Angie," I whine back.

"Fine," she huffs. "As long as you promise you're okay."

"I promise I'm okay." I lean into the couch behind me and curl up on my side so I'm facing her completely. "Ugh, but I do miss having someone to cuddle with on the couch. Or having someone to sleep next to. Someone who isn't a dick, I mean."

Angela nods in a super serious way that it's almost funny. "Right, of course."

"I'm totally happy just being me without a boyfriend, but I do miss having someone to be close to."

"You can be close to me!"

"Okay!" I move closer to her and she puts her arm around me. "Oh wait, I didn't tell you about the elevator!" I scooch back again to tell her the story.

"The elevator?"

"Yeah! So Felix and I were going to go for a walk last night, but when he got here I realized I might need a sweater, so he came with me to get one, which, like, good thing, because then it got stuck! And I almost had a panic attack, and then he opened the doors with his bare hands and got out! But then! BUT THEN! He *lifted* the elevator up because it wasn't lined up with the floor!"

"What do you mean he lifted the elevator up?"

"Like he put his hands under the top part of the doorway and just... lifted it until it was out of his reach."

"I'm sorry, what do you mean?"

"I mean he lifted the elevator, Angela!"

"How?"

"I don't know! And he wasn't even amazed at himself for it. He was all 'no big deal' and just shrugging and stuff!"

"Is he ripped?"

"I mean I haven't seen him with a shirt off or anything, but I didn't think so. He's a little skinny."

"A *little* skinny means he's probably ripped."

"Well he must be. Because he lifted a fucking elevator."

||||

I have done some research. Felix texts to me on Monday night.

Have you? What kind of research?

Hazel Grace Lancaster research.

Felix! Did you read *The Fault in Our Stars??*

Read it? No. I watched a movie?

Ah. Fair. That makes a little more sense, I guess. It takes more time to read a book than it does to watch a movie.

For sure. He types more but then stops a few times until he finally says, **I did a little crying.**

Aww. Research my other rat's name. It'll make you feel better.

Will it? Are you sure about that?

Yes. It's very excellent.

On Wednesday night, Felix texts me again. **I researched your other rat's name but there is no movie for me to watch**

What are you going to do about that? I reply

Well I did look up a bunch of spoilery reviews and I think that you might have been lying to me when you said it would make me feel better

What makes you say that? I ask. *An Absolutely Remarkable Thing* **always makes me feel better. Carl makes me feel better. Maybe I'll name my next pet Carl. Carl is good people.**

From what I've read, Carl is not people

Read the book and get back to me. And then I add a winking emoji.

I'm assuming these are favourite books of yours? he asks.

Two of many I reply. **But the characters are very human and real to me. They kind of remind me what it's like to be human sometimes. They make me feel less alone.**

And so you named your rats after them.

Yeah. It's stupid.

It's not stupid he replies. **Not stupid at all.**

Felix and I keep texting throughout the rest of the week, and I sort of hope we can hang out again on the weekend but he's probably working. I guess Carter's isn't open super late, and he could be working the lunch shift. I know I can just ask him, but I'm afraid. I don't want him to think I want to date him or something. Instead I decide to play it cool and actually go to Carter's to get a takeout pizza for myself on Friday night.

I see him taking two pizzas to a table when I walk in, and he sees me right away and gives me a little nod. I wait at the front, and in less than two minutes he meets me at the front podium.

"Did you come by yourself?" he asks.

"Yeah I just thought I'd take a pizza home."

"Oh nice. You got anything else planned?"

"No. Probably just going to watch *Twilight*."

He raises his eyebrows at me. "Really?"

"No." I laugh and he chuckles a little. "I'll definitely just be watching TV, though. You should come hang out when you're done your shift. You know, if you want." That was too forward, wasn't it? He's going to think I want to date him.

"Sure, sounds fun."

He puts my pizza order in and I wait awkwardly at the front of the little restaurant as he and the other server working tonight run around and get people their food and open new bottles of wine for them. I watch Felix as he works, and I can't help but continue to assess the way he's walking. He only does his weird fast forward thing when he's dealing with the food. If it doesn't look like he really has anything to do, he walks at a normal speed. He brings me my pizza fifteen minutes later, at a normal pace, and I run out of the restaurant a little too quickly. Except that my body definitely moves like a person trying to move faster. Felix's doesn't. It's weird.

I take the stairs up to my apartment; I've been taking them all week, and I know my pizza won't be quite as hot by the time I get up there, but I'm not taking any chances. Especially by myself. I stream a few *Corner Gas* episodes, but my mention of *Twilight* earlier is making me want to watch it. I feel embarrassed just thinking it, so instead I decide to make chocolate chip cookies.

But once they're done, I sit on the couch with a few of them and search for *Twilight* on Netflix. I can't help it. I don't care how bad it is, once someone mentions *Twilight* even semi-seriously, I have to watch it. I was obsessed with it in high school and it has a special place in my heart. It must be done.

Felix buzzes my apartment less than halfway through the movie so I let him in but tell him not to use the elevator.

"Is it broken again?" he asks.

"No but it might break on you, you never know!"

"I think I'll be okay." I can hear him laugh.

He knocks once and then comes in slowly. I say hi to him from the living room but don't get up from the couch. I'm trying to play it cool.

"So you ended up watching *Twilight*." He sits next to me on the couch but keeps a bit of a distance and I wonder if he's also trying not to make me think he wants to date me, or if he actually for sure doesn't want to date me. Do guys think this sort of thing too?

"I wasn't actually going to, but then because I mentioned it, I couldn't stop thinking about it. I haven't seen it in a really long time. But we can put something else on."

He picks up Hazel Grace from the couch next to him and cradles her in his hands. She sniffs him and crawls up his arm, her dark grey fluff disappearing into his t-shirt sleeve. "No, it's okay, I'm actually kind of interested," he says with a bit of a giggle, probably because of Hazel. "I've never really been a fan of vampire stuff, but now I'm curious."

"Okay so wait, when you say you're not a fan of vampire stuff is that because you've watched some of it before but didn't like it? Or you've never been interested and so you've never seen a vampire movie?"

"Uh, the second one. Do I smell cookies?"

"Yes, they're on the kitchen counter."

"Excellent." He gently pulls my rat out of his shirt and hands her to me, then gets up and disappears into the kitchen. I get up too, and put both Hazel and April back in their pen beside the TV.

"So you've never even seen, like, *Interview with the Vampire?*" I ask.

He comes back with two cookies, already taking a bite out of one, and shakes his head.

"*Dracula* anything?" I ask.

He shakes his head again.

"This is madness! Do you at least know like, the rules of vampires?"

He laughs. "Yes, Reese, I know the rules. I haven't really watched vampire movies, but I haven't been living under a rock."

"Do you want to watch a better vampire movie?" I ask as we both sit back down.

"No, it's okay. Just catch me up on what's happening in this one."

"No, I think I'll start it from the beginning. Also just, please, be nice. I was a sixteen-year-old girl when I saw this for the first time, so it hit different for me than it will for you."

It takes us forever to watch *Twilight* because Felix keeps asking questions or making comments and we have to keep pausing it. He says he's interested in this take on vampires and doesn't want to miss any of it while we talk, but he can't not ask questions.

"Okay but I like the idea that vampires *can* go out in the sun, like they're doing, but what if they could go in the sun but just don't like it?" Felix says. "Like they get really bad sunburns, and it's too bright for their eyes and makes them nauseated? Are there any vampire stories like that?"

"Hmm, I don't think so. In *Vampire Diaries*, they have magic rings that make them not allergic to the sunlight."

"I like this sparkling business. I don't like that vampires are supposed to just completely burn up or catch on fire in the sun. That doesn't make any sense. What, just because you live off blood means you can die super easily if you go out at two in the afternoon?"

"It's so hard to kill them otherwise, they need to have a weakness."

"Why?"

"I don't know," I say slowly. "Otherwise that's not realistic."

"But literally catching fire in the sun is?"

"Oh, but sparkling in the sun is okay?" I counter.

He tilts his head from side to side. "It's cool. I like that it's a new idea. Plus all the sixteen-year-old girls probably love it."

"Yeah, I can guarantee that."

"Okay, so are most vampire movies like this one, where just biting someone will turn them?"

I shake my head. "It's different in almost every story."

"Which way to turn into a vampire is your favourite?" he asks.

"Hmm. I don't know. What theories have you heard, from not living under a rock?"

"Drinking vampire blood? I don't know." He turns back to the movie, which is almost over at this point, but paused again. "This movie isn't terrible, you know. It just feels a little amateur." He grimaces a little bit but then grins. "Plus it has an excellent soundtrack."

"I'm glad you think so," I say, beaming. "But we should watch more vampire movies. It seems they give us a lot to talk about."

"I think we have a lot to talk about without them, too."

I melt a little at that comment and can't help it when the corners of my lips start to curl again.

"What about werewolves?" he asks.

"What about them?"

"Do you have any werewolf movies?"

"Oh," I say, taking a second to think about it. "Not really, actually. But there are werewolves in the rest of the *Twilight* movies."

"Oh good. I was hoping we would get more out of that wolf story."

He smiles, and I give him a bit of a side eye before pressing play.

Angela and her husband Josh are going camping for the May 2-4 weekend, and Claire and I are pretty sure Emily's going to propose to her sometime over the weekend. She has some special getaway at a bed and breakfast thing planned. So I'm at home alone all weekend. This will be fun.

That was sarcasm by the way, in case you couldn't tell.

Any plans this weekend? Felix texts me on Saturday afternoon.

Nope all my friends have left me.

We could hang out if you want. I don't have any friends.

Don't you have to work? I ask.

Tonight I do, but the restaurant is closed Sunday and Monday for the long weekend.

That's weird.

He sends a shrugging emoji. **I've found a lot of small businesses close for holidays.**

But it's a restaurant. People like to go out to eat on long weekends.

And there are plenty of chain restaurants that are open for them to go to.

Fair enough. What did you have in mind?

I feel like this is a date. He didn't say it was a date, but it feels like a date. First of all, he's picking me up at my apartment, to drive me to his apartment, so that he can drive me back to my apartment at the end of the night. So that I don't have to get out of my car alone and walk into my building alone when it's late. Which I didn't even think of whatsoever, I mean I come home late from Angela's pretty often. The parking lot is well lit, but now that I think of it, I don't unlock my car door until I'm absolutely ready to get out, and I basically sprint to the main entrance. Okay, so maybe Felix's idea is a pretty good one, and not just because he's trying to impress me. Maybe he just actually has a heart, and actually has concern for his friends.

Felix is also going to be making me dinner, and he told me to wear something pretty. Or comfortable, or both, it's really my decision. That's what he said.

He said, "Oh and wear something pretty. Or comfortable. Or both. I mean it's your decision, really."

I laughed at him. "Okay."

"Just, I'm going to wear something pretty, so I didn't want to show up to your place and have you feel underdressed."

"You're going to wear something pretty?"

"Nice. Handsome. Whatever word you want to use, I'm going to dress up a little."

"Okay." I couldn't help but smile. "Good to know."

So I'm standing in front of my mirror, wondering if what I'm wearing is okay. I definitely like to dress up for special occasions, but if we're going to be watching a movie or something after dinner, I don't want to wear a dress. I also don't want him to think that *I* think it's a date. I don't know why I'm so hung up on this dating thing. I mean I like him, so why am I making a big deal out it? Maybe I'm just still nervous about possibly starting something new with someone.

I settle on dark skinny jeans and a pretty top with a bit of a swooping neckline. It's got loose, flowy capped sleeves, so you can see my hummingbird inner-bicep tattoo in its entirety. It goes pretty close to my armpit, and I love how it looks when I wear something sleeveless, or with such tiny sleeves like this shirt. I smile at myself and put on some mascara before straightening my hair.

Felix is driving a fairly new Mazda 3 hatchback with extremely tinted windows, and he pulls up right in front of the main doors. But get this. He gets out of the car and walks around to my side to open the passenger door before I can open it myself. He's wearing sunglasses, and he's got on clean, dark blue jeans and a fitted black button up with a black tie, which looks fabulous on him. His hair is still messy. But that's okay, I like it that way, and I have a feeling he styles it like that.

"I'm glad you went for somewhat casual," I say, not sure how else to greet him. He's standing next to the car with my door open. Are we supposed to hug? We've never hugged before. I mean, if you don't count the elevator fiasco. And I'm not counting the elevator fiasco. "I wasn't sure about wearing jeans."

"It seems we both made perfect choices," he says with a warm smile.

I smile back, still not sure what to do. He smells like sunscreen. "Um, thanks," I finally say, getting in the car. He shuts the door gently and gets in the driver side almost instantly. "Whoa," I gasp. "That was fast."

"Was it?"

"Yes, it was like you just hopped over the car instead of walked around it."

"Well I did. Walk around it, I mean."

"Anyway, you look nice," I say.

He grins at me before driving out of the parking lot. "So do you. I haven't seen your hair like that before."

"Oh, yeah." I touch it and pull it over my shoulder. It comes just past my shoulders when it's straight, but it doesn't really stay in front of them easily. "It's naturally pretty wavy."

"It's beautiful both ways."

"Felix, is this a date?" Ugh, I can't believe I just blurted that out. Why can't I just let things happen without questioning them out loud?

"Not if you don't want it to be."

"But when you planned this, was it because you wanted it to be a date?"

"Not necessarily," he shrugs.

"You're not answering my question."

"I feel like you're asking this because you don't want it to be a date."

"Not necessarily."

He glances at me quickly and smirks. "We're not very good at this, are we?"

"No, I guess not," I sigh. I bite my bottom lip and look out the window for a few seconds before turning back to him. He's focused on the road but I'm pretty sure he's also watching me from the corner of his eye. "A part of me wants it to be a date," I say before I lose my nerve.

"Just a part of you?" he asks.

I just offer a shrug as an answer. I don't really want to get into why I'm hesitant to start something new with someone. I feel like it's too much for a not-even-date.

"So then it's just two friends having a nice evening together," Felix finally says. "And if both of them decide they would like it to be a date, that's what it can be. But if it isn't something they both want, it won't be a date."

"How do we know that we both want it to be a date?"

"Well, we have to start with one of the people saying they would like it to be a date. All of them has to want it too, not just part of them. And then the other person would have to agree."

"What if no one says it first?" I murmur.

"Then it doesn't turn into a date."

"Okay."

"Okay."

We pull into the parking lot for Felix's apartment building before we have a chance to add to our conversation. He's in the fancy little building near downtown, which I thought was ridiculously expensive. Maybe it is. Maybe Felix is rich. He drives into the parking garage and gets out of the car as soon as he's parked so he can open my door for me again. I try to open it before he gets there, but he beats me somehow.

"How did you do that?" I ask.

"Do what?"

"Also how can you afford to live here working at a tiny restaurant?"

"I don't have any debt, so it's easy to pay a little more for rent." He takes his sunglasses off and hangs them on his breast pocket.

"A little more? Just a little?"

He shrugs and starts walking towards the elevator. "I also save a lot on groceries."

"How?" I ask, following him.

"It's a secret."

"Of course it is."

We stop in front of the elevator and he turns towards me.

"Now Reese, are you okay taking the elevator, or would you like to take the stairs?"

"It depends. Does this elevator have a history of getting stuck or plummeting?"

"Not since I've lived here. But I've only lived here for two months, so my answer can't be fully accurate. But this is also a fairly new building, so I'm sure the elevator reports can't go back that far. But I'm also sure that since it's a new building, the elevator and its parts must also be fairly new, which gives me confidence in its ability to bring us to our desired floor without any issues."

I can feel my grin stretching across my entire face.

"Can I take that smile to mean that you're okay getting in the elevator with me?"

I hit him lightly on the shoulder and laugh. "Yes."

I give him a few quick glances as the elevator brings us to his floor, but I don't catch him looking at me.

"It smells like Wonderland in here," I say to break the silence.

"What?" He turns a bit to look at me with a crooked smile.

"All I can smell is your sunscreen, and it feels like I'm on my way to Wonderland."

"Oh."

"I'm sorry, that was a weird thing to say." I shake my head in embarrassment and the elevator doors open in front of us.

"Not weird," he replies. "Just an observation."

"An unnecessary one."

"Come on." He tilts his head towards the hallway and I follow him to his apartment. "How do you like your steak?" he asks once we step inside.

"Medium rare," I say, slipping my shoes off and immediately making my way across the living room to the huge window that takes up almost the entire wall. "Wow, this view is amazing."

"Yeah. It's nice that the building is up on a bit of a hill. It doesn't need to be a high rise be able to get the good views that yours does."

I almost choke on laughter. "My building doesn't have good views, are you kidding me? You can see the water from here."

"Yeah, it's even better when it's dark. There are lights lining the docks, and the lights from downtown glow this orangey colour."

"Sounds nice."

"It is. Come sit down."

I step into the dining area of his kitchen, where he's got a dark wooden table set up with fancy plates and silverware, crystal wine glasses, and cloth napkins.

"Wow," I say. "This is… Super nice."

"Sorry, is it too much? I just haven't used any of this dinnerware in like, thirty years and I wanted an excuse to bring it out."

"I'm sorry, thirty years?"

"I - I didn't mean to say that."

I narrow my eyes at him as I sit down and unfold my napkin. "What did you mean to say?"

"That my mom had it for thirty years and I haven't used it since she gave it to me."

"That's… very different."

He turns towards the stove and puts two steaks on a pan. "I started everything before I came to get you, so I just have to cook the steaks."

"Sounds good." I try to ignore the fact that he isn't acknowledging my reaction to his weird 'mistake'.

He plates everything else while the steaks are searing, and then he puts the wonderful chunks of bacon wrapped meat with the pile of asparagus and roasted potatoes. He puts a bowl of warm buns in the middle of the table and sits across from me.

"This all looks and smells so amazing." I cut into my steak and it's so tender it basically rips apart on its own. It's perfectly pink in the middle, with some juices still oozing out, and my mouth waters before I can take a bite.

"Oh shit, I forgot the wine. Do you like wine?"

"Sure," I say. I'm not huge on wine, but I don't want to be rude.

He gets up and goes to the counter where he uncorks a new bottle, and then pours it into my glass for me. I put my first bite of steak in my mouth while he's doing that, and I almost make a noise in delight.

"This is the most amazing thing I've ever had in my mouth," I say, immediately taking another bite.

Felix looks a little uncomfortable but laughs.

I drink all my wine while we eat dinner, and he gets up to go to the washroom before he brings out dessert. I think about texting Angela to ask her how her weekend is going, and tell her what I'm doing. I want to tell her about our not-necessarily-date conversation, and tell her that she needs to convince me to tell Felix I want tonight to be a date. I want to tell him that the part of me that wants it to be a date is bigger than the part that doesn't. I want to tell him that I like him, and I want to see more of him, but that I also want to keep taking things slowly. My heart starts to hammer just thinking about it, so in an attempt to calm myself, I get up and head to the fridge. Maybe Felix has pop or water or something that I can drink. I need something to wash down my food and nerves besides red wine. Although more wine would certainly help with the nerves. No, I need to be sober if I'm going to tell him that I like him. I open the fridge and then close it right away.

What? No.

Did I actually just see what I think I just saw? I lift my hand to the door handle and can see my fingers trembling. I can't feel them trembling though, because I can't feel anything. My brain is fuzzy and everything else about me is non-existent, it's like I'm not even in my body. It's like someone else is opening the fridge for me and I'm just watching. I wrap my fingers around the fridge handle and tug it open one more time, only to reveal the very thing I was hoping wouldn't actually be there the second time I looked.

His fridge is filled with blood bags.

Part Two

TURNING (THIRTY)

|

Everything is happening in slow motion, but somehow also too fast for me to register any of it. I stare at the blood bags that are so neatly stacked on the shelves in his fridge, illuminated by the soft Frigidaire glow, and the cheesecake sitting on a shelf of its own. I don't know how long I stare at it for, but I don't think it's longer than a second. It feels like it, though. It feels like my eyes have been glued on the blood in his fridge for hours. It feels like I haven't blinked in hours, like my eyes are drying out.

"Ah shit," I hear Felix say from the doorway of the kitchen. I turn to look at him, my left hand still holding the fridge door open, and he walks towards me with his hands out but I let go of the fridge door handle and step back. I don't know what to do. He stops walking towards me once I start to back away from him, but I'm panicked. I back into the counter and immediately reach behind me, hoping to grab something sharp to defend myself. I feel the knife block and I fumble my hand around until I find the handle of one of them, and I pull it out, pointing it at Felix.

It's a fucking knife sharpener. I stare at it with wide eyes for a second, trying to register what's happening. I think I squeal, and I step back again, hitting my hip on the edge of the counter and then backing around it. I hold the knife sharpener out at him as if it will actually do damage to him if he comes closer.

[49]

"Reese, can I please explain?" he asks gently.

I shake my head and extend my elbow, pointing the knife sharpener at him like an idiot.

"Reese, please," he begs. "Can you... Can you put the sharpener down?"

"I can ram this into your neck!" I screech. "I'm strong! And it'll hurt like a bitch because this is dull as fuck!"

It looks like Felix stifles a laugh, and I scoff. He's laughing? He's *laughing* right now? While I'm frightened for my life and he's cornering me in his kitchen?

"I can't believe you're laughing," I say, a crack in my voice.

"I'm not laughing. I wasn't. I didn't laugh. None of this is funny. I'm really sorry that I scared—that I'm scaring you. Can we please just talk?"

"Talk? About what!? About the fucking blood in your fridge?"

He nods slowly and takes one step towards me with his hands up.

I try to take another step back but I'm against the wall now.

"Reese, please. I swear, whatever you're thinking, whoever you think I am, I'm not."

"What, you're not a murderer?"

"No," he says evenly, his hands still up.

"A sociopath?"

"No."

"A liar?"

I can hear him take a breath to answer me, but then he stops.

"What have you lied to me about?" I ask carefully, the knife sharpener still extended in my arm and pointed at him.

"A few things," he says slowly.

"That's it? You're not going to tell me anything else?"

"I would love to, but you're not in a great state of mind right now, Reese."

"I'm sorry? I'm not in a great state of mind? I wonder why!?"

He takes a breath and looks away briefly. "If you... if you put the sharpener down, and we, um, if we sit?" He slowly lowers his arms, but I don't loosen my stance. "I can tell you why I have forty blood bags in my fridge. But you won't believe me."

"I won't believe you? What ever could your answer be, Felix? That you're a sick freak?" I immediately regret calling him a sick freak, for fear of him murdering me in retaliation.

But he sort of hangs his head a little like he's embarrassed and then looks up at me. "I mean... no," he says quietly.

"You're not a sick freak who keeps dozens of blood bags in your fridge?"

"I keep blood bags in my fridge, but I'm not a sick freak."

"Then what the fuck are you, Felix!?"

"I..." He tosses his arms up in the air a little and then lets them fall back to his sides as he shrugs. "You won't believe me," he says again.

"Try me."

I stare hard at him and realize that my breath has gotten quicker, my heart has started pounding. But I try my best to mask it, try my best to make him think that I'm not afraid of him.

He swallows and looks away briefly before letting his eyes land back on mine. "I'm a vampire," he finally says.

I raise my eyebrows at him and we stare at each other for probably a full minute. "Oh my god, you're a psychopath," I finally say. "See, this is why I don't like dating!"

"Reese, I'm not-" but he cuts himself off and lets out a breath. "I promise I'm not lying."

"You don't have to be lying to be a psychopath. You can totally believe that you're telling me the truth when it's actually absolutely bonkers!" Oh my god, Reese, stop insulting him, or he's going to murder you. "I want to leave."

Felix puts his hands up in surrender again and steps back, out of the kitchen doorway. I slowly walk around the counter peninsula and through his kitchen, past the fridge that holds apparently forty blood bags, and stop at the doorway. He backs up into the hallway and nods his head towards the front door.

I hesitate for some reason, and then reach for the doorknob. Why is the murderous psychopath just letting me go?

"Reese?" he asks before I'm more than two steps into the hallway.

I stop, but I don't say anything or turn around.

"Uh, can you not tell anyone about this?"

I stay still for a few seconds, and then without answering him, I wipe away a tear and head towards the elevator.

"Reese, please!" Felix calls into the hall.

I hunch my neck into my shoulders and take a quick glance back, relieved to see that he hasn't actually followed me out of his apartment. I wish I knew the right thing to say to him. Do I lie to him? Do I let him explain himself so he can believe that I believe him? Will that be safer? If I just leave, he's going to think that I'll tell everyone and he'll come after me or something, won't he? If he's a murderer, that's definitely what he'll do.

But having blood bags in his fridge doesn't mean he's a murderer. It feels like the opposite. It doesn't mean he isn't a creep, but he's probably not slicing people's throats and then collecting their blood in neat bags you would find in the hospital. That's just ridiculous. Maybe more ridiculous than having blood bags at all.

I stop and close my eyes, let the tears fall down my face, and then I take a deep breath and turn around. Felix falls into the doorframe with a sigh and half smiles. But when he gets a better look at me, his face stiffens up.

"Are you going to tell anyone?" he asks.

"I don't know," I say.

"What... what *would* you tell them? Out of curiosity?"

I shake my head. "I don't know."

"You can leave. We never have to see each other again, and I promise I won't even try to contact you or look for you. But please, *please* don't tell anyone about this."

"Why not?"

"I think the repercussions of this would be much worse than anyone could anticipate."

"Excuse me?"

"I fucked up, Reese. I haven't been doing this by myself for very long, and I just, I fucked up, and if I could go back and start the evening over, I would, but I can't, and I can't erase how I've made you feel, but if we can just pretend that this never happened, I would really appreciate it."

I start walking towards him for some reason. "I can't just forget that this happened, Felix."

"I know."

"So why would you ask that of me?"

"Because it's all I know how to do at this point. All I can do that doesn't... that isn't..."

"Spit it out," I say, suddenly feeling brave.

"I can't. Not out here."

"Fine. Let's go back into your apartment and you can spit it out there."

He raises his eyebrows at that, and he looks back into his apartment, then back at me.

"You... Do you feel safe?" he asks. "Coming back into my apartment?"

"Not really, no. But I don't feel safe going home either."

"Why not?"

I shrug. "You know where I live." I realize in this moment that I'm still holding on to the knife sharpener, and that I don't even have my shoes on. I was fully going to run home in my fucking socks. With a knife sharpener in my hand. I slowly walk down the hall towards Felix, and hand the sharpener to him as I pass him in the doorway. He takes it from me and lets out a breath as I walk to the couch in his living room.

"Okay, tell me," I say, sitting down. My tears have streaked my glasses so I take them off and wipe them with my shirt. They're cloudy when I put them back on and I sigh.

"Tell you?" he drags his feet across the hardwood and stands across from me on the other side of the coffee table.

I nod. "Tell me the thing I won't believe." I breathe on my glasses and wipe them again. I wipe them more than I need to because I'm nervous and I'm afraid to look at him. I finally put my glasses back on and this time they're much clearer. Felix has been quiet the whole time, I think waiting for me to be done before he answers. When I finally look up at him, I'm startled to see him looking at me, but not in an intense way. He looks hurt. Defeated.

"I already did," he finally says.

"That you're a vampire?"

"Yes."

"Don't make fun of me," I say, tears welling up in my eyes again.

"How is that making fun of you?"

"Because of the vampire stuff I like!"

"That's ridiculous!"

"Then show me!"

"What?"

"You heard me," I say, crossing my arms. "Prove to me that you're a vampire, or I'm telling the police that you have forty blood bags in your fridge *and* that you tried to keep me from telling them." I slide my hand into my back pocket, ready to triple press the power button on my phone if I need to. It'll send my location and the last 5 seconds of sound to Angela.

[54]

"Reese, this really isn't a good idea."

"Okay." I get up from the couch and pull my phone out of my pocket so I have it handy if I need it. "I'm going home."

"No, wait."

I stop and let him continue, but he doesn't say anything.

"Yes?" I say.

He shakes his arms out a little as if he's warming them up for a workout, and then tilts his head from side to side. Is he nervous?

"Are you going to show me?" I ask.

"Yeah," he says slowly.

"Without-" I start, "Without biting me."

He smiles just slightly, but then his face gets sad again almost right away. "I would never do that, Reese. Please know that I'm not going to hurt you, okay? I would never hurt you."

I can't seem to form any words, so I just nod.

He nods too, and lets out a deep breath as he closes his eyes. But just as he starts to open them again, his face changes. His cheeks get hollower, his jaw somehow sharper, and the circles under his eyes get darker. The darkness spreads across his cheekbones and then he opens his mouth, bares his teeth, his sharp, pointy teeth that have come down from his gums and overlap his regular human teeth. They're not just two pointer teeth, either, there's a set of them, coming from his top *and* bottom gums.

I've crumpled to the ground and scrunched myself into the side of the couch, my arms curled up into my chest. The couch is lined up with the edge of the wall, so I could back up into the hallway, but I can't do anything besides try to hide inside the couch that's beside me. I just stay like that, crouched down on bent knees, letting the tears well up in my eyes once again. Felix closes his eyes and mouth, and I watch as his face morphs back to how it was before.

"Are you okay?" he asks quietly.

I feel the tears run down my cheeks, but I still can't say anything. He slowly walks back around the coffee table and sits on top of it. I can tell he wants to lean forward and grab my hands or something; I can see it in the way he leans forward, the way his hands tremble, the way he's holding them out a little, palms up, but still resting his forearms on his knees.

"But I've seen you in the sun," I finally say, which is a silly thing to say because obviously he's not actually a vampire. What I just saw was something else. Definitely not him being a vampire. "And eat food and stuff," I add.

"I can go in the sun," he says gently. "With the proper protection."

I swallow and blink more tears out. "And the food?" I ask, feeling silly.

"I can eat food," he says with a shrug, but his tone still gentle. "It doesn't sustain me, but I can eat food. Food is delicious."

I nod again, now at a loss for words.

"I can take you home, if you want," he says.

"I think I should take a cab," I say. I wipe my face and let out a shaky breath. "Or I can walk. I think I need to walk."

"Reese, please -"

"I need to go home. Please, just- I need to leave."

He sits up straighter and puts his hands up in surrender. "I'm not holding you here. You can do whatever you want."

I nod at him and get off the floor, using the couch armrest to pull myself up. I put my shoes on and look back at him still sitting on the coffee table, looking like he's watching his world fall apart. I give him a weak smile, for what reason I don't know, and open the door.

||

Will you let me know when you get home so I know that you're safe? Felix texts to me halfway through my walk home.

Sure I reply.

It's almost dark out by this point, so I pick up my pace and try to look confident as I cross through town. I don't like walking alone at night, and I find myself looking over my shoulder so often that it's making me a little dizzy.

I'm almost home I text to him when I've probably got about fifteen minutes to go. **But I'm scared.**

Of me?

Of being alone.

I can come get you if you want

No thank you.

Can I call you?

No.

Calling someone would be a good idea. I open the contacts page on my phone and open Angela's number. Just as I'm about to dial, I realize she's still camping with Josh. Dammit. And Claire's off on her weekend with Emily, not that I would call her about this anyway. I wish I was closer to more people. I'm mostly just acquaintances with people. I look behind me to make sure that no one's following me or anything, and then I start to walk faster.

Are you okay? Felix texts me.

I don't really want to talk to the person with blood bags in his fridge, so I don't answer him.

Can we talk about this more when you're at home? he says.

No I reply.

Okay

It's still really warm out I end up typing, just trying to keep my mind from spinning.

That's good

It'll be beach weather soon.

Yup.

Do you go to the beach, Felix?

Yes, I love the beach

During the day?

Can we actually talk about this in person sometime? I'll answer any questions you have.

Probably not.

Okay.

I'm at my building now, so I tell him I'm home and pocket my phone before I step inside. I feel so weird. This is so weird. Once I'm in my apartment, I call Angela. I know she won't answer but I have to leave a message or something. I wait patiently for the beep after her greeting.

"Angela. You have to call me the minute you get home. No. Better yet. Come over. Take a shower, go get Blizzards from DQ, and come to my apartment. I need to talk to you. It's absurd. Quite possibly actually more than absurd. Whatever word describes more than absurd, it's that. Also I'll take cotton candy, but just a small."

Felix doesn't text me for the rest of the night, or the next day either. I stay in bed basically all day, and have to drag myself to the door when my buzzer goes off in the afternoon.

"I'm coming," I say, knowing the person downstairs can't hear me. "Don't go, I'm coming!" It buzzes again and I make it to the intercom by my door. "Hi, hello, I'm here," I say into it.

"I'm here with blizzards but they didn't have cotton candy so I got you Smartie."

"Acceptable." I buzz Angela in and unlock my apartment door for her.

She comes in with my Blizzard with delicious, candy coated chocolate pieces, and immediately starts eating her own, mint Oreo. We sit on the couch and face each other, our legs pulled up and crossed underneath us.

"Tell me," she says, a mouth full of green ice cream.

"I don't know where to start."

"Well, did something happen with you and Felix?"

"I mean, nothing romantic or sexual happened, but something definitely happened."

"What do you mean?"

"I don't even... He's um, mentally deranged."

"Excuse me?"

"Or he's... something. There's something wrong with him. He's not... I don't..."

She puts her Blizzard down on the coffee table, takes mine from me and puts it on the coffee table too. "Okay," she says, "why don't you just walk me through everything that happened."

So I tell her. I tell her about him picking me up and being a gentleman, and about me not sure if I wanted it to be a date, and him being perfectly reasonable about it. I tell her about some of the weird things he said, which reminds me of the weird things he's said previously. Like that he's 274 years old. She sort of squints and tilts her head at me as I talk, but she doesn't interrupt.

And then I tell her about the blood in his fridge. Her eyes bulge and she almost says something but instead she covers her mouth and lets me continue. I tell her about threatening him with a knife sharpener and how he let me leave. I tell her about how I went back into his apartment so he could show me his fangs and vampire-like features that he could just summon and then suppress within seconds. I tell her even after everything that happened that evening, I still let him text me because I was afraid of walking home alone.

"Wow," she finally says after a few minutes of silence.

"Yeah."

We sit quietly for so long that by the time I remember about our Blizzards, they're almost completely liquified. I pick my cup up and sigh at the condensation that has pooled all over my table. Angela grimaces a little and pulls the bottom of her shirt up to wipe the water away.

"Don't worry about it," I say, waving her off.

I bring my Blizzard cup close to my mouth so I can eat the melted ice cream without it dripping all over me, and we continue to sit in silence.

"Oh he also asked me not to tell anyone about this," I finally add.

"Naturally."

III

Felix doesn't text me all week and I'm not sure how I feel about it. I'm also not sure how I feel about not knowing how I feel about it. I should be glad that the psychopath isn't trying to contact me.

But what if he's not a psychopath? What if he's actually a vampire?

Hahahahaha.

Ha.

Okay, now that I've got that out of my system, why don't I go over this rationally? So. Number one, he had a lot of blood in his fridge. They were in blood bags, like the kind that get hooked up to IVs in the hospital for transfusions, and number two, they were neatly stacked and organized. I'll bet they were even organized by expiry date. I'm not sure if this makes things better or worse. Psychopaths are really neat, and keep all their murdering things organized, don't they? But he did seem upset about the whole situation, and made it very clear that I could leave at any time. He was not kidnapping me, nor did he want to hurt me.

But what if he kidnaps other people and hurts them? You know, by drinking their blood? No, Reese, that's what the blood bags were for. So he doesn't hurt people. Right? But what about all the people who need that blood to survive? He must have stolen them from a hospital or a blood bank or something, stolen them from people who would surely die without blood donations. He's gotta be taking it from them. Because he's a psychopath. Of course he is. I don't know why I've tried to stray from this conclusion.

||||

It has now been two weeks without any communication from Felix. Which should be fine. I should be fine with it. Excellent, even. We only knew each other for two weeks to begin with, and hung out like, three times. I've now not talked to him for the same length of time that I was talking to him, and so now I should get over it and move on. He was a cool guy to hang out with but then he became a scary murderous man and now he doesn't have to scare me anymore because we're not friends anymore.

Does Felix still work at Carter's? I text to Claire.

Yes why?

Just wondering.

So he hasn't left town. And clearly hasn't told anyone else about his vampirism, or else they would all be screaming about the psychopath who drinks blood and also might possibly be a real live vampire. Or. Dead vampire. Undead? I don't know.

I don't know why I'm texting you. Oh my god. I just texted Felix. Why have I done this? **Never mind I don't know why I texted you. I didn't mean to do that. Please don't reply to this message.** What the hell is wrong with me? Never reach out to the psychopath, Reese!

Okay. he replies.

No, I said don't reply.

Okay.

Felix!

Yes?

I should definitely not continue texting him. I should block him, even. **I have questions** I type.

Uh oh, then I hit send. Because believe it or not, I do actually have questions. They won't stop burning a hole in the back of my head because all of this is ridiculous, but I also know that something happened at Felix's apartment that seems unexplainable. I need him to explain it. Again. Or better, or *something.*

His reply comes almost immediately. **You can ask any questions that you want.**

I don't want to be alone with you, though. Yes, this is good, Reese. Set boundaries.

Fair.

But I don't want to text all of this either.

I could call you.

Can we meet somewhere public? During the day?

Sure.

I can't believe that Felix is going to meet me by the water downtown at two o'clock in the afternoon. If he's really a vampire, this wouldn't be happening. I know he told me that he can still go out in the sun, but come on. What vampire can go out in the sun without *something* happening to them? Also he's not a vampire. Vampires aren't real. I find an empty picnic table under one of the pavilions but just as I start to cross into the shade, I change my mind. The reason I wanted to meet him during the day was so he would have to come out in the sun. I want to have this conversation with him in the sun. Oh my god, even just thinking this is absurd. *I want to have this conversation with him in the sun.* Why is this possibility even crossing my mind? Why is sitting in the sun a requirement as if it'll mean something?

"Hey," I hear from behind me. I jump a little and turn around, to see Felix standing with me just inside the line of shade from the pavilion roof.

"Hey," I reply slowly. "I didn't mean to come over into the shade. I mean, I did, but then I didn't. I meant to get a picnic table in the sun."

He narrows his eyes at me but finally nods. I think he understands what I'm doing. "Let's get a spot in the sun, then."

Felix takes his sunglasses off from the collar of his shirt and puts them on his face. He adjusts his Blue Jays hat and curves the beak even though it's already curved, and I can't help but think he's nervous. I know he said he could go out in the sun, but does it hurt him? Make him uncomfortable? Ugh, why am I asking these questions? These are ridiculous questions! Of course the sun doesn't hurt him! Unless he legit has an allergy. No. Stop.

"After you," he says.

I lead us out into the sun and I can't help but look back at him the second we leave the shade, but he seems fine. He doesn't flinch or anything. He doesn't seem to be in any pain. I walk across the grass and to a picnic table near the docks. He sits across from me so that I'm facing the water (and him) and he's facing the parking lot (and me).

"So," he says.

I let out a deep breath. "So." We're quiet for about a minute, and I can feel my heart beating harder than it should be. "I just want to be clear that I'm not asking you here because I want to date you, or because I'm infatuated by you."

He smirks a little. "Okay."

"I mean I'm just- It's just all very- Like I saw your fridge and then you did that- I don't-"

"I get it," he says, cutting me off. "You're curious."

I let out a deep breath. "So fucking curious."

"So what are your questions?"

I bite my bottom lip. Chew on it a little as I look around at everything except for him. I just realize in this moment that I haven't really been looking at him since we sat down. Glances here and there, but I haven't held his gaze at all.

"Are you afraid to be alone with me?" he murmurs.

I think I might be. I thought meeting him in public would be okay, but now that I'm here with him, I'm not sure how I feel.

"Shit," he breathes. "I'm not here to make you feel afraid. We don't have to do this." He holds his hands up in a casual surrender and starts to swing his leg out from under the picnic table.

"I'm not- I didn't-" I stammer, because I don't want him to get upset. I still don't know what's going on and I don't know what he will do if I make him upset.

"It's okay," he says slowly, now straddling the bench. "I'm not offended. I was surprised you wanted to meet, to be honest."

"Why didn't you want to?" I ask without thinking. "I mean, why haven't you reached out to me?"

"Because I didn't want you to feel threatened."

"Oh."

He looks at me for a second, and then swings his other leg out from under the table and stands up. "Yeah."

"I'm sorry," I say.

"Me too." He gives me a weak smile and walks away.

Claire and Emily have invited me out for dinner with their friends to celebrate their engagement. I wanted to ask if that Isla girl was going, since she's best friends with Claire, but I didn't want to be rude and make them think I was only asking because I wanted to meet her famous boyfriend. Which is the only reason I wanted to ask, so I didn't, and I'm now heading over to the restaurant by myself. Angela's really only friends with Claire because I'm friends with her, and they've never done anything together besides being at the same party, so I'm probably not going to know anyone there. I mean, besides Claire and Emily, obviously.

"What's going on with Felix?" Claire asks me quietly about halfway through the night. I think she noticed that I wasn't really engaging in conversation with anyone and just felt like she needed to say something to me that I could respond to.
"Oh. Um. Nothing," I start. "We stopped hanging out."
"Why? He's asked about you a couple times, you know."
"He has?"
She nods and takes a sip of her drink.
"Like, what has he said?" I ask. "What does he ask?"

She shrugs. "Just how you're doing. But like, in a concerned way."

"In a concerned way?"

"Yeah, he doesn't say 'oh how's Reese doing?', he says, "is Reese doing okay?'"

"Really?"

"Yeah. Did something happen between you two?"

"Sort of."

"Oh no. Do I need to kick him in the shins?"

I laugh. "No, I don't think so. We're just, he's just…" I don't know how to continue without making her afraid to keep working with him. But maybe she should be afraid to keep working with him? Should I tell her that he keeps blood bags in his fridge? "He's kind of a freak," I finally say, but I regret it immediately. "That sounded bad," I add. "He's not a freak. He's just…" I take in a deep breath and lower my voice. "I'm a little worried that he's not 100% mentally stable. In a possibly dangerous way."

"What?"

I look around at the rest of the party chatting and laughing and not paying any attention to us before I continue. "He thinks that-"

"No, sorry, I couldn't hear you, you were practically whispering. What did you say about him being a freak?"

"I said that-"

But then two of her friends come around the table and start screaming as they put their arms around her. "We need to order shots! The three of us need to do a shot together!" one of them shouts.

"And Emily! Emily has to do a shot with us too!" the other friend adds.

"Ah okay! Let's go up to the bar." Claire gives me a bit of a sympathetic head tilt and mouths 'I'm sorry' at me as she slides out of her bar stool and leaves the table.

I look down at my drink and then across the table at all the other people I kind of sort of know but don't actually know. Felix has asked about me in a concerned way. He didn't seem dangerous when I met him by the water. He was even the one to end the meeting, because he sensed my discomfort. Was it all an act, because of psychopathic stuff? Or was it real? Does he actually want me to understand what's going on? And is he actually dangerous?

"Oh my god, hi," Emily says, almost crashing into me. She's very drunk.

"Hi," I laugh.

"Thanks for coming! I'm sorry we don't get to hang out much. I feel like we have different every day friends so we only see each other at big things like this."

"Yeah, you're right."

"Do you want me to introduce you to anyone?" She puts her arm around me and then puts all her weight on me, like she can't hold herself up.

"No, that's okay. But we should probably find Claire."

"I was just with Claire! But you were sitting alone and looked kind of sad, and I don't want you to be sad."

"Oh. I'm okay. I'm not sad. I'm just thinking."

"Okay as long as you're not sad."

I chuckle a little. "I'm not sad."

"Okay! Come hang out with us, then! We never get to hang out!"

Emily straightens up and tugs me off my stool, so I follow her to the bar, where we do shots with Claire and the two other girls from earlier. We all end up convincing Emily to move to water, and the bar tender gives her a shot glass with water any time we get more shots so she can still knock them back with us. I move to water fairly quickly too, and manage to stop thinking about Felix and whether or not he's dangerous.

It's Canada Day and I'm camping with Angela and Josh. I've never been camping with them before, and was both excited and nervous when they invited me. I didn't want to crowd them or make them feel like I was ruining their alone time, but they politely reminded me that they wouldn't have invited me if they didn't want me there. So I said yes. And I had to buy a tent and an air mattress and a sleeping bag and everything. And now I'm sitting in a folding camping chair with a beer in one hand and a bag of marshmallows in the other.

"Tell me again about this Felix guy," Josh says, leaning over to grab the marshmallows from me.

"He thinks he's a vampire," I say with a sigh.

"You thought he was a vampire too!" Angela says playfully.

I shake my head. "No. No, I was going to give him a chance to prove his non-sociopathic tendencies."

"And?" Josh asks.

"And nothing. I met him at the park and then I basically freaked out and left." I go to take another drink of my beer, but the can's empty. "I'm getting another beer." I get up and half stumble to the cooler.

"Well let's all go find where they're setting off the fireworks," Angela suggests.

"We'll see it from here," I say. "And then we don't have to sit with the crowds."

"All the trees will be in the way."

"Why don't you and Josh go? I'm not bothered about seeing them."

"Really?" She sounds disappointed, but then Josh snuggles into her.

"If Reese stays here, we can kiss while we watch them," he says.

"We can kiss, or we can watch them, we really can't do both at the same time."

"Angela, your husband is going to kiss you under the fireworks," I say. "That sounds lovely. Please go let him kiss you under the fireworks."

She smirks at me and stands up, grabbing the blanket from the chair arm. "Okay fine. As long as you promise that you don't actually want to go and that you'll be totally fine here on your own."

"Yes, I'll be perfect on my own. I'll just read my book."

"Okay." She leans down and kisses me on the forehead. "That was because I love you."

"Will you be offended if I don't get up to kiss your forehead?" I ask.

"Only a little."

"Okay then I won't get up."

She smiles. "Okay."

We both laugh a little, and Josh shakes his head at us. I watch them walk out to the path and make their way towards the beach, and then I sigh and stare at the fire. The fire's warm but the night air is a little damp and cool, so I get up to grab a sweater from my tent. The sound of the zipper brings back hard-core childhood memories and I have to stop and take a breath before I finish opening it. We've already been here one night, and the feeling isn't going away no matter how many times I hear a tent zipper. On mine or on Angela and Josh's tent. I swallow the weird tingle in my throat and shake my head, and then continue unzipping it enough for me to step inside. Even the sound of the tent bottom crunching under my feet is giving me flashbacks. I grab a hoodie from in my bag, but before I leave, I notice my phone blinking. It's snuggled in with my sleeping bag on the air mattress, but the green light flashing on and off is pretty noticeable in the dark. I pick it up and swipe open the screen to see that I have a text message, which is weird because I've had no signal so far throughout this trip, except by the washrooms. Maybe the text came through the last time I was there and I didn't notice. I pull down the notification bar and almost gasp when I see who the text is from.

I'm really sorry I scared you. the text from Felix starts. **Scaring you was never my intention. I get it if you think I'm insane, or a creep or a psycho or whatever, but I can tell a part of you wants to believe me. You said you had questions and I can still answer them. If you want. If you don't answer me, I promise I won't bother you again. The last thing I want to do is make you feel uncomfortable or unsafe. But I can't stop thinking about you (in a non-creepy way, I promise) and I would hate myself if...**

The text is too long so I have to open a new page to read the rest.

... this ended with you being afraid. I completely understand you not wanting this relationship or friendship or whatever it is to continue, but I don't want it to end with you fearing being in your apartment because I know where it is, or even fearing just going for pizza. I promise that I'm not the scary things you think I am, and if you are still curious, I can prove to you that I'm not.

That's all. If you don't answer this message, I promise I won't reach out or try to contact you. If we don't talk again, take care.

Hmm. I hear the first set of fireworks go off and instinctively look up, even though I'm inside a tent. A mosquito buzzes by my ear and I only just realize that I've left the tent open for far too long. I sigh and step out, taking my phone with me, and zip the tent back up, dreading sleeping in there later with all the bugs. I make my way back over to the fire and turn on a bug repellent thing that glows different colours (Angela got it from Home

Depot and was quite proud of it). I pull my hoodie over my head, sit down in my camping chair, then get up from my chair and head to the cooler to get the beer that I didn't end up grabbing. *Then* I sit down and pull out my phone to compose a reply to Felix.

I don't think you're a creep.

No, don't write that, he might be a creep.

Delete.

How does one constantly think about someone without it being creepy?

Delete.

I appreciate you not wanting me to be afraid, but it almost seems like a selfish thing? Do you not want me to be afraid because it sucks to live in fear, or do you not want me to be afraid because you're afraid of what I will make people think of you?

Ugh. Delete.

I look up and towards the direction of the lake to catch some of the fireworks that have been booming overhead, and I can see bits and pieces of the colourful sparkles in the sky. Some of them boom and then make crinkly sounds as they disperse and fall behind the trees. I sigh and look back to my phone.

I guess a part of me was waiting for you to reach out. I want to believe you, but I don't know if I can. I don't know what to think, really. I said I would meet you to ask questions because I think I just wanted a fantasy to be real. But I know that it's not. I pause and think about adding more. I don't want to sound harsh or hurt his feelings in case he does decide that he wants to murder me. I want to at least try to end this nicely so he likes me enough to want to keep me alive. **I'm really sorry.**

Send.

I watch the little circle beside my message spin for longer than a second and I throw my head back in frustration. I could go to the washrooms to send it, but it's dark and I really don't want to walk over there by myself. Maybe I will just let the signal decide. If the message doesn't go through, it's a sign that I'm not supposed to send it.

So I close my eyes and take in a deep breath and look back at my phone. Spinning circle is still going. I can't tell if I want it to go through or not, and it's giving me anxiety. And it's weird, because there's no signal, but not so little signal that there's a symbol of a circle with a line going through it where my bars should be. The bars are there, just none of them are coloured in. The circle is still spinning.

I groan and throw some sand on the fire. I turn off the bug repellent thing and head back to my tent. The fireworks are constant now, bangs from the sky and cheers from the watching crowd with no breaks in between, so they must be at the finale. I get in my tent and zip it back up as quickly as I can, and then turn on the flashlight on my phone so I can see the mosquitos flying around inside and kill as many as I can before I go to sleep.

"Reeeeese! Reeeeeeeeese! Are you sleeping!?" My tent gets unzipped and I groan.

"Come in quick and close the tent before all the mosquitos get in!" I say.

Angela zips the tent back up and curls up next to me on top of my sleeping bag. "Why are you in bed?"

I shrug. "I was bored."

"I thought you were going to read."

"Didn't feel like it."

"Are you okay? Are you bummed about getting a crush on a serial killer?"

I cover my face with my hands. "He's not a serial killer! I don't think."

"Come sit by the fire with us. We're roasting spider dogs."

I nod and sit up, but wait a minute before leaving the tent. Angela turns back to me and I tell her I'll be right there. She smiles and zips the tent up behind her. I grab my phone to see if my text went through or if it stopped trying. I unlock the screen to see a text notification and my heart leaps into my throat. In a good way or a bad way, I couldn't even tell you. I swallow and pull the notification bar down. Oh, the message didn't go through. I stare at the words on my screen, telling me to tap to retry, and I actually think about it for a second. But I don't. Instead I sigh, turn my phone screen off, and go outside to hang out with Angela and Josh.

Angela, Josh, and I go to the beach right after breakfast the next day so we can enjoy it before it starts to get busy. We bring a couple bags of chips and some water with us and sprawl out on a big blanket for an hour or so before we head into the water to cool off. We splash each other, and Angela sits on Josh's shoulders a few times and lets him flip her into the water. They laugh and dunk each other's heads under water and I watch with a smile, until I start to feel like I'm invading. I make my way back to our blanket and open a bag of dill pickle chips. Angela follows me not long after, and plops herself down beside me.

"Beach chips are the best kind of chips," she says.

A couple kids run past us, kicking up sand and flinging it all over our faces. I flinch and close my eyes.

"Ugh, that went in my mouth," Angela says.

"Yeah. I think I'm going to head back."

"What? Already?"

"It's starting to get crowded. I won't have fun here for much longer. You two can stay if you want. I think I might check out some of the hiking trails."

"Ugh, that sounds awful."

I laugh at her. "It sounds fun to me. I'll be back before we have to start packing up."

"I hope so."

I throw my towel over my shoulder and grab a handful of chips for my walk back to our campsite. Once I get back, I throw a white t-shirt over my bathing suit top and pull on a pair of denim shorts. I would love to just go on my hike in my flip flops, but know that's probably not a good idea, so I wipe my feet off and put on a pair of socks and shoes. I fill up my water bottle and grab a few granola bars and head off towards the trails.

It takes me a little bit to get out of the camping and beach area, but I finally make it past all the signs directing me where to go, and I see the first trail going into a forest and up a mountain-like terrain. I say mountain-like because there aren't actually any mountains around here. The air is getting really humid, but at least I'm not getting much sun under the cover of trees. Especially since I just realized I didn't take any sunscreen with me. I'll just be careful and try to stick to the shady areas.

I pass a few people on the way up and find it a little strange that they all seem to be on their way back. Maybe they wanted to get their hiking done before it got too hot. I liked our idea of going to the beach before it got too busy. Everyone nods at me as we pass each other, and a few people tell me the view is amazing at the top. I smile at them and tell them I'm excited to see it.

I realize after about half an hour of walking that I've been looking at my feet the whole time. I haven't wanted to trip over anything so I've been watching the ground directly in front of me instead of the world ahead of me. I try to look forward but it's hard. I laugh at myself and shake my head, really hoping the view is worth it since the only view I've gotten so far is of my dirty Asics.

I finally make it to the top of the... hill? Cliff? And continue to walk along the dirt path that's been naturally formed from years of footsteps. It takes me around a bunch of trees onto a huge rockface that overlooks the forest below. I take out my phone and snap a few pictures, and then just stand there staring at the world in front of me. It almost feels like I could leap off the edge and fly. I take a seat on the rock and cross my legs to enjoy a granola bar while I admire the view. I never realized before how many shades of green there are. I'm about to take my phone out and take another picture when a loud crack of thunder makes me hunch my neck into my shoulders. I look up at the sky and wonder where the black clouds came from all of a sudden. And then I scream, get up, and start to run for cover under the trees. Oh no, not the trees! What if one of them gets struck by lightning and I in turn get electrocuted? It starts to rain all of a sudden and it comes down in heavy sheets so hard that I can hardly open my eyes. Why did none of our weather apps tell us about this? Or did they and we just didn't check far enough ahead to see what was coming? I wipe at my face, which does nothing, and take another step only to slip on the wet rocks beneath my feet, and fall directly on my ass.

"Oh ow," I half shout as my tailbone smashes into the hard ground. My water bottle slips out of my hands and slides down the hill like a happy little kid on a water slide. I put my hands on the rocks beside me and lift my butt into the air a little, taking the pressure off it. Ow. My poor bum. I groan and then slowly lift myself, trying my hardest not to slip again. I take careful steps onto the dirt, which is now mud, and still just as slippery, and then continue onto the grass. Which, still slippery. A flash of lightning brightens up the dark clouds and then a boom of thunder follows much too close for comfort. I don't like the idea of being out in the open, but I also don't like the idea of going under the trees, so I just waddle back down the trail as quickly and carefully as I can.

Of course I slip again. I fall right onto my back this time, and slide down the muddy trail for a few feet. I dig my left heel into the ground to stop myself and almost start to cry. I'm covered in mud and now my back *and* ass hurt. My glasses are covered in rain drops and I can't see very well through them. Wiping them on my wet shirt won't do anything to fix that, so I want to at least wipe my face, but my hands are covered in mud.

"Ugh, why is Angela always right? Of course hiking sounded awful! Why did I think this would be fun!?"

"Reese?"

"Who said that?" I spin around at the sound of the man's voice, hardly noticeable over the downpour raging around me.

"It's Felix!"

"Oh my god." I squint and see him across the path, under a cover of trees.

"I'm not going to hurt you! And I swear I didn't follow you; I didn't even know you were here. I just saw the weather forecast and decided to come for a walk."

"In a thunder storm?"

"Yeah, I like the rain," he says with a shrug. "And I haven't been to this trail before, and it's close to home."

"But you could get struck by lightening!" I shout.

"So could you. Why are you out here?"

"Unlike you, I did *not* see the weather forecast. I need to get back."

"Sure. Sorry if I scared you."

I'm about to head back down the trail when a loud bang and bright light practically knocks me off my feet. The ground seems to shake around me and I stumble into the bushes on the other side of the trail behind me. I take in a few deep breaths, afraid to open my eyes. What just happened?

"What was that?" I call over to Felix. I open my eyes and gasp at a fire across the path where he had been standing. Was that lightening? Did we almost just get struck by lightening? I run over to the fire in a crouch, because for some reason I feel like if I stand up, lightning will strike me directly this time.

I find Felix lying beside the fallen tree, right by the edge of the fire.

"Felix, are you okay?"

He groans and rolls over, but then sort of shouts a little, like he's caught off guard with a shot of pain.

There's a shard of tree or something stuck in his neck! And in his leg! Oh my god, there's one in his side, too. The tree must have splintered when it got struck, and pieces flew into Felix. Jesus Christ.

"Oh my god," I say out loud.

I lean down next to him and put my hands on his shoulders. I need to pull him away from the fire. I reach under his armpits and lift him off the ground a little, making him shout out in pain.

"I'm sorry!" I drag him a little, but he's heavy, and I have to stop and take a breath. "I have to move you," I say to him. "I'm sorry."

He screams out again as I lift his shoulders off the ground and drag him farther away from the fire. Once I think we're safe from it, I drop him as gently as I can and crawl over to his side that has the branch sticking out of it.

"Can you pull them out?" he asks, his voice hoarse.

"No, I can't fucking pull them out, are you kidding me!? That's the one thing I know about this stuff. If there's something inside of you that shouldn't be, never remove it! It's usually stopping you from bleeding out!"

"I won't bleed out," he says.

"The fuck you won't. I have to call for help."

"No, don't. Please. I just. I can't- I can't do it myself. This hurts so fucking much, I'm shaking."

I look down at his hands that are wrapped around the branch in his side. He's holding it kind of tightly but I can still see his fingers tremble around it.

"I can't do it myself," he cries.

"Okay, okay, hang on, let me look at it."

He lets out a deep whimper and then shouts a little in pain, and I can't help but feel bad for him. I grab at the hem of his t-shirt and rip it apart so that it splits up his side and I can see the branch that's been lodged into him. It already looks infected, which is impossible, right? This literally just happened.

I gently grab his hands and move them away from the tree shard so I can see better, and he lets out another cry.

"Sorry," I say. "This looks really bad."

I force myself not to gag as I lean in closer to get a better look. It's literally festering. There's white bubbly pus coming out of his wound, and it smells like rotting meat. The rain is still coming down pretty hard and I try to wipe it out of my face with the back of my arm after putting my glasses on top of my head. I shake my head a little and put my hands around the branch.

"If I take this out, you're going to start bleeding," I say.

"No I won't. I promise."

I look him in the eyes and we just stare at each other for about a minute, and I wonder how such a weird psychopath can seem so scared. His face is tight in pain but his eyes are focused on mine. He lets out a breath and lets his head fall to the side a little, not looking at me anymore. He closes his eyes tight and takes a few deep breaths, but I can hear how shaky they are. As if this guy can seem this soft and also have a fridge full of blood bags. I shake the thought away and look back to the wound in his side. Which somehow looks worse than it did the first time I looked at it. It looks almost rotten now. I'm not even sure what rotten flesh looks like, but the bubbly white stuff has stopped bubbling, and now it's this weird foam stuff, but the skin around the wound is almost black.

"What is in this tree?" I ask.

"Nothing; I'm allergic to wood," he says, raising his head off the ground a little to look at me.

"You're allergic to wood? What kind of a person is allergic to-" I cut myself off and catch him noticing my realization. His face changes from the soft boy who was unsure and in pain, to the man who might finally be understood. It's a little heart breaking.

"Maybe take the one out of my leg first," he suggests. "Then you'll see what I'm talking about."

"Um. Okay." I turn a little to get the branch sticking out of his calf, and this one looks the same as the wound in his side. It's like his flesh is rotting. I wrap my fingers around the branch and put my other hand on his leg to keep it still, and pull it straight out. I immediately gag at the feel of it sliding out of his muscle, and his scream when I free it from his leg is just as unsettling. I drop the branch and turn away from him, dry heaving into the wet leaves around us.

"Are you okay?" he asks me.

"I should be asking you that," I say, taking a deep breath.

"I will be as soon as you get the rest of these out. Now look at my leg."

"What?"

"Look at my leg."

The rain pours over his calf and into his clean wound. Wait, *clean* wound? Where did all the festering pus and rotting black stuff go? It looks like he was sliced with a sharp knife instead of impaled by a dirty piece of tree, and as I keep looking at it, I see the wound close up completely. The skin pulls together on its own, leaving only the faintest of scars.

I look back to Felix, who's looking at me with a curious expression.

"What just happened?" I ask, looking back to his leg. The white scar is gone now, too. As if nothing even happened.

"Do you believe me now?" Felix says. "Help me get this one out of my side."

"I…" I try to answer him but I'm speechless. In disbelief. Maybe it wasn't actually infected and the rain pouring down around us coupled with my panic for the situation clouded my vision. I crawl around him and sit on his other side so that I don't have to lean over him to get the tree piece out.

"It's okay," he says, nodding at me. "It'll feel better once it's out."

"Felix, this is absurd," I say.

"I know it seems like it is, but it really isn't. Can you please help me?" His voice is so strained, so full of pain. It's breaking my heart and making me angry at the same time. He shouldn't be breaking my heart. He's a murderous psychopath! And he has tree shards stuck in him, of course he's in pain! Any normal person, psychopath or not, would be in pain. Stop trying to see the good in him, Reese!

"I'm not... I don't... You're going to bleed to death!" I cry.

He lets his head drop onto the ground beneath him and he lets out a big breath. "I can't do it myself, Reese; it's too much."

I don't know when it stopped raining, but I only just now realize that I haven't had to wipe at my face for a little while, and I look up at the tree tops above us to see only a few leftover raindrops rolling off their leaves. The fire a few feet away has gone out, and I wonder if I even needed to move him.

"Please, Reese," he says quietly. "You have no idea how much this hurts."

"Okay," I finally say, closing my eyes for a second. I wrap both hands around the piece of tree and hesitate. "Are you ready?" I ask.

"Yes. Yes, please, just do it."

I nod once and then yank it out of him. We both scream, and I watch for a second to make sure blood doesn't immediately start pouring out of him. When it doesn't, I crawl around him so I can get a good grip on the one in his neck. It's kind of in his shoulder, poking out at a weird angle. I pull that one out too and we both scream again.

I let myself sit on my butt and I cross my legs, taking a breath. I can't believe I just pulled three shards of tree out of him.

"Thanks," Felix says, startling me.

"Um. You're welcome," I say, looking back at him. I put my glasses back on my face and the drying raindrops luckily aren't very noticeable through the lenses. "I guess you need a new shirt."

"I guess so." He smiles a little and sits up, holding himself up with his arm out beside him like a kickstand.

"We should get you to a hospital," I say quietly, starting to get to my feet.

"It's okay, it's already healing, look."

I lean over him and pull his ripped shirt aside so I can see his wound heal just like the one in is his leg did. The rotten fleshy area is already more red and pink than black, and the bubbly, oozey stuff is going away.

I lean in closer and watch the skin fade from pink to the pale white of his normal skin tone and I almost touch him, almost put my hands on his stomach as I continue to watch as it seems to heal in time lapse. But I don't touch him. I can't take my eyes off it, though. Felix wipes the pus away with his other hand, and I can see his gash closing up, the skin around it looking healthier and healthier with the second.

"How did you do that?" I manage.

He only sighs as a response.

"Felix, how are you doing that?"

"I thought we went over this," he whispers.

"What, that you're a vampire?" I chuckle and snort a little. "Yes."

I don't know what to say to him anymore. I don't know what to think, either. Am I foolish if I believe him?

"Hey, you're hurt too," Felix says suddenly, sitting up.

"What?"

"You're bleeding."

"No I'm not. Where?"

He reaches out and gently grabs my shirt and lifts it up in the back a little. "Your back is all scraped up. We need to clean it out."

"How did you know I was bleeding under my shirt?" I stand up and straighten my shirt out. "Also why do we need to clean my scrape but not your festering wound from being impaled by a tree?"

"What festering wound?" he asks innocently, standing up and showing me the unbroken skin on his side and on his shoulder.

This time I can't help but touch it. I step into him and carefully put my hands on his shoulder, on either side of where his wound was. "That was so gross two seconds ago."

"Why aren't you getting this, Reese?"

I've still got my hands lightly placed on his shoulder and neck, and I slowly look up at him. He's got the slightest smirk, it's like he's amused but doesn't want me to know that he is. I rub my thumb along his muscle, where a tree branch poked through not ten minutes ago, where his skin was black and rotting, but is now milky white and pristine.

"Reese," Felix says quietly.

I jump a little and step back, snapping my hands to my sides.

"I know you're probably not going to want to, but if you have a drop of my blood, we won't need to clean your scrape up."

"Excuse me?"

"It'll heal it. Take the pain away too."

"It doesn't hurt."

"Well you've got mud and shit in it, so it might get infected."

"I'm not drinking your blood, Felix."

"You don't have to drink it; you literally just need a few drops."

"Is that so?" I find myself saying, but not without a sarcastic tone.

He pauses a little and licks his lips as if he's unsure. "Yeah," he says quietly.

"So if just a few drops of your blood heals people, why aren't you healing people at the hospital?"

"It's only for flesh wounds."

"It's only for *flesh wounds?* What the fuck does that mean?"

"Exactly what I said. It only heals a mortal's flesh wound. Like a cut or something. Or if you got stabbed or shot but it didn't hit any vital organs."

"Why does it only heal *flesh wounds?*" I can't help but ask these questions as if I'm irritated with him. I'm not irritated with him, but it's the only way I can ask without feeling like I'm losing my mind. And for some reason, like, I'm not expecting him to answer me?

He shrugs. "Why does Polysporine only help with minor cuts and not say, a gaping stab wound? It's the same principle. And vampire blood wasn't designed for mortal consumption per se…" He trails off a little and I feel my eyes widen and I take another step back.

"Okay, I see that I've gone too far," he continues. "You weren't asking me seriously, were you? No, you know what? Forget we talked about my blood at all."

Instead of answering him, I turn back towards the campsite and to try and leave Felix behind, but he catches up with me in less than a second. I almost break into a run but I don't want it to look like I'm running away from him. Even though that's exactly what I'm doing.

"Reese!" he calls.

I look behind me to see him standing in the middle of the muddy path with his hands by his sides. Well he's not chasing me, so that's good. I turn back around and continue down the path without him. I look behind me every now and then to see that he's still following me, but he isn't *following* me. Like, he has to get back too, and this is the way you have to go, but he's keeping his distance, which I appreciate. The sun starts to come out and it warms me immediately. I close my eyes and tilt my head back so I can feel it on my face. This is lovely. Maybe my clothes will be somewhat dry by the time I get back.

But then I hear a groan behind me, and I turn my head around a little to see Felix covering his face with his arms. He runs into the tree line and I stand and watch him as he takes his arms away from his face and then inspects himself.

"Are you okay?" I call over to him.

His attention snaps over to me, like he's startled to hear me talking to him, and he sort of shrugs.

"Is it the sun?" I feel stupid as soon as I ask, but it just comes out.

My phone chimes and I pull it from my pocket, wipe it off as best as I can, and check to see who it is.

Where are you?

Are you okay?

Did you get struck by lightning? It's Angela, and turns out she's texted me a bunch of times, I just didn't notice until now. Her newest text says **Seriously are you okay? Hopefully you're okay and you just don't have service.**

I have full service up here but I didn't hear my phone. I reply. **I ran into Felix and we actually did almost get struck by lightening. Felix got hurt and I had to help him** I say. **When do we need to leave?**

Wait are you serious? What happened? I've literally been standing by the washrooms with my arm in the air to get any bars because I'm worried about you and you're with the murderer?

I promise I'm fine. I'll tell you about it later. I'm on my way back to the campsite.

Okay.

You don't have to stay by the washrooms. I'm coming right now.

I pocket my phone and look over at Felix, still sitting under the shade of the trees off the path. He looks at me with a sad expression and I slowly make my way over to him.

"Is everything okay?" I ask.

"The weather forecast wasn't totally right," he half whispers.

"What do you mean?"

"It was supposed to be drizzly for the rest of the afternoon, and I don't know what happened to my sunscreen. It's not in my pocket anymore."

His nervous stammer makes me feel bad for him and I have to remind myself that this is probably a tactic of his. Serial killers make themselves seem weak, right? So girls will feel bad and help them and get all close to them, making it easier to murder them. Right?

"I should go," I say.

His eyes widen as soon as I say it and he opens his mouth to say something, but then closes it almost immediately. Was he going to object? Was he going to ask me not to leave?

"Will you be okay? If I leave?" I ask, taking half a step back.

"I'll be fine. I'll just hang out until the sun goes down."

"Okay." I take another step back, but don't turn around just yet.

"Thanks for helping me earlier."

"You're welcome." I turn around this time and head back out onto the path, where the sun is hot and bright.

"Reese!"

I stop and turn back to him.

"I'm sorry again, for scaring you. For making you think...
For..." he sighs and looks down at the ground, and it's only at
that moment that I notice his arms. They're brighter than a freshly
cooked lobster.

"Whoa, you're really burned," I say, sort of cutting him off.
He was trailing off anyway, so I didn't really interrupt him, but *his
arms.*

He looks down at them and then back up at me. "Oh. yeah.
This is nothing."

"But you were in the sun for all of ten seconds."

He shrugs. "Yeah. If it helps you understand more, I
could... I mean, I could show you what it *can* look like."

I scrunch my eyebrows at him. "What do you mean?"

He stands up and lets out a deep breath. Then he closes his
eyes and steps out of the shade and into the sun. He covers his
face with his arms again, and I can see his arms getting redder
almost immediately. I see little blisters start to form along his
forearms, and I watch in horror as he just stands there and lets
them grow. In a matter of minutes, they're like little floppy, yellow
water balloons hanging off his skin.

I'm about to tell him to stop, to come back into the shade,
but he lets out a groan and walks towards me on his own.

"Oh my god, your arms," I say.

"Yeah," he says quietly. "Back of my neck, too."

"You have to go to the hospital!"

"A hospital isn't going to be able to help me. It'll go away
on its own; it just takes a while."

He sits back down under a tree so I sit down next to him
and put my hands over his arms, not touching him, but in a way
that sort of shows that I wish I could make it better. After I realize
I probably look like an idiot, I take my hands back and look at his
face. He's looking at me, probably has been this whole time, and
I let out a breath.

"That only took like five minutes," I say, looking back at his arms.

"Yeah, it happens pretty fast."

"Does it hurt?"

"Of course it hurts."

"But you've been in the sun before. I don't understand."

"When we met by the water, I was wearing a UV shirt, a hat and sunglasses, and SPF 100. And the sunglasses don't even really help that much; it's still bright as fuck with them on."

I smirk a little but don't know what to say. We're quiet for a minute or two, and I find myself looking into his eyes.

"So you're allergic to wood and the sun," I finally say.

"That I am."

"What about garlic?" I ask.

He chuckles. "I can eat garlic."

"What if I rubbed it all over your skin?"

"I don't think anything would happen, except I might smell like garlic."

"If you were out in the sun for longer, would you catch on fire?"

"No." He laughs nervously and looks away from me for a second. But once his eyes find mine again, he continues. "But sometimes it's so bright that it's blinding. And disorienting. Makes me feel sick. And the blisters will cover me completely if I let it. Sometimes it takes a while for them to go away. Sun damage takes the longest to recover from."

"So if you were out in the sun for too long, and you didn't have any protection, would you die?"

"Probably."

I swallow, thinking about all the other questions that were racing through my head when I allowed myself to believe he was telling the truth for that short time. What other things did I want to know? Is it silly for me to ask them now?

"So…" I start, and his eyes change again, from sad to hopeful. "You can run really fast, then?"

"Yes," he says with a bit of a laugh.

"And it's natural for you? Like, to move really quickly?"

"Sometimes it's hard to walk at a normal pace, to be honest."

"So that's why you're such a good server."

"What?"

"Oh you just- I just- I just noticed…" Now it's my turn to have a nervous stammer. "Uhh." I laugh and try again to get my words out. "I just noticed you when we were at Carter's. You're just, uh, really good at your job. You were moving so quickly but so smoothly at the same time. It was mesmerizing."

"You thought I was mesmerizing?"

"To watch you juggle plates and tables so quickly and effortlessly, Felix, don't get full of yourself just yet."

He grins. "Okay. Sorry."

"So… It's true then," I say with a bit of a gulp. "You're a," but then I look around to make sure we're still alone, "a vampire?" It feels weird saying it.

"Yes."

"This whole time. You were trying to tell me you're a vampire, and it's true."

"Yes."

I look at him for a few seconds, and his expression is tight, his eyebrows pointed down a little. "Is it hard for you not to bite people?" I ask quietly.

"Not at all."

I nod. "What about me? Is it hard not to bite me?"

He shakes his head.

"Why not?" I ask.

"Because I don't want to hurt you. Or anyone. Remember when I said that to you? I wasn't lying just to try and make you feel safer."

"Oh. It's just, in the movies and everything, they always make it seem like it's the hardest thing in the world to control."

"In the beginning it's harder, for sure. Plus your mind is different in the beginning. It doesn't rationalize the same way. But after a while it gets easier."

"So before... Before you knew what you were doing, did you kill people?"

He shakes his head. "The person who turned me was there for me the whole time. She helped me through it."

I don't know why, but I'm suddenly jealous. A girl turned him into a vampire? Were they in love? Is that why she turned him? Where is she now?

"And now..." I start again. "Now, it's easy because you know that if you bite people, it'll hurt them? But don't you still get urges?"

"Think of it this way. If butter tarts were actually people, you wouldn't eat them anymore, right? It would be nice if you could, but you wouldn't dream of killing anyone just so you can eat a butter tart, right?"

"I suppose," I say with a smile.

He smiles back. "I think that's the best analogy I can come up with."

"Okay but what about your blood bags? Sure, no one got hurt for you to get those, but they're not *for* you. They're for people who are dying, people who would die without it."

"People like me? I would also die without it."

"You know what I mean."

"What would you rather I do?" he asks.

"I don't know. What did you do before blood bags were a thing?"

"Sometimes we took it from animals, but it's not the same. It doesn't sustain us in the same way."

"Like *Twilight*?" I dare to ask.

"Worse," he laughs.

"So what did you do then?"

"Well just biting someone and drinking their blood won't turn them into a vampire, so we could feed off people without killing them. We knew some people who wanted to donate to us. It was a different time, then. Information obviously didn't spread as easily, so it was easy to keep it a secret."

"Wait, so people *let* you bite them?"

He nods without saying anything.

"Didn't it hurt them?" I ask.

He shrugs. "In a good way, I think. When we bite people-"

My phone chimes again and cuts him off. I look down at it to see my message.

Where are you? I'm back at the washrooms cuz youre taking so long. Are you close? Did he murder you? We only have our camping spot until 3.

"Shoot," I say, looking back up at Felix. "I have to get back."

"Yeah, okay."

"What are you going to do?"

"Wait here until dark, I guess."

"It's not going to be dark until like, 10pm."

He shrugs and I notice that his arms are starting to heal. The blisters are much smaller and don't look as painful.

"Did you walk here?" I ask. "Like, with your superspeed?"

He shakes his head and smiles as he answers. "People would have seen me and freaked out. I drove. I'm parked nearby."

"Can you run to your car? Maybe no one will see you. Or if they do, they won't know it's you because you'll be gone so fast."

"I can't risk something like that, but thanks. It'll be fine once the sun starts to go down; it doesn't need to be *dark* dark."

"We're not far from the campsite," I say. "After we pack up, I'll bring you some sunscreen and a sweater."

"You don't have to do that."

"I know I don't *have* to."

"Okay."

"Okay." I stand up and look down at him. "I'll be back later."

"I'll be here."

PART THREE

|

"Oh my god, Reese, I'm so glad you're okay!" Angela practically squeals when I get to our campsite.

"I told you I was okay," I reply.

"I know, but after the storm, and you said you almost got hit by lightning, and you said you were with Felix, and then you didn't reply again! I thought he kidnapped you or murdered you or something!"

"He did no such thing. I really don't think he's a murderer."

She puts her hands on her hips. "What makes you say that?"

"I think if he was, he would have killed me by now."

"That's what he wants you to think."

"None of it adds up," I say. "You weren't there. Like, the day with the blood bags."

I notice Josh's head tilt a little from where he's packing up outside of their tent and know he's listening.

"Reese, you didn't just say that. I'm actually worried now. He had *blood bags in his fridge!* Who does that?"

I want to make her believe me. I want to tell her about pulling the branches out of Felix, about the oozing pus coming out of his wounds, and about it healing in minutes as if nothing had even happened. I want to tell her about the sun, and his blisters, and those healing too, but I know she's just going to think

I'm stupid and irrational. She'll forbid me from seeing him because she obviously cares about my safety and I'll feel silly going to see him anyway. There's no way she'll believe this unless she sees it all for herself.

So I close my eyes and let out a deep breath. "You're right," I say. "I don't know what got into me. I guess I'm just attracted to pieces of shit, and I've been single for so long that even this walking red flag seemed good to me."

"Oh my god, girl, no. I can set you up with someone if you want. I just thought you didn't want that."

"I don't want that. Things with Felix were moving at a nice, slow, and comfortable pace and I liked him. We were friends and I wasn't against the idea of it becoming more than that at some point. I guess I just wanted to believe that there's nothing wrong with him because other than the murderous stuff, he seemed great." Oh my god, even just saying the words makes me want to gag. Other than the murderous stuff, he seemed great? Who even thinks like that?

"I feel like I need to move. He was in my house, Reese. A murderer was in my house! And he works with Claire! Oh my god, what if he murders Claire?"

"He's not going to murder Claire. Plus he's not a murderer."

"Right. He just likes to pretend he's a vampire and drink from blood bags that he steals from the hospital."

"Still not murder."

"Whatever."

Packing up the campsite is a little tense, and Josh just keeps looking at me and then at Angela as if he wants to say something but is afraid of offending us or something. Finally, once we're all packed up, I grab one of my hoodies and my sunscreen that I purposely left at the top of my bag, and announce that I'm going to the washroom before we hit the road.

I turn and run towards the trail that I took earlier, trying my best to hide the sunscreen and not make it look weird that I also have a hoodie with me. I'm out of breath by the time I make it to Felix, and I practically throw the stuff at him and turn back around in one motion.

"Thanks," he says.

"No problem. Sorry I can't stay."

I run back down the trail and slow my pace once I'm closer to the campsite so I don't seem so suspiciously out of breath.

Most of the ride back to my place is quiet, and I can't tell if Angela is mad at me or not. I don't know why she would be mad, but I feel like she's something. Like she thinks I'm stupid and I'm going to get myself killed. Which is fair, I guess. But as soon as I get my stuff inside and my tent and air mattress into my storage locker in the basement of the building, I text Felix.

I still have questions. I type to him.

Do you want to come over?

Maybe.

Why don't I go over to your place? Then I can leave if you feel uncomfortable and you don't have to worry about getting yourself home.

It's probably a bad thing that I'm nervous. I shouldn't be nervous about a guy coming over. Well no, that's not true. It's totally normal to be nervous about a guy coming over. But I'm nervous about him coming over because a part of me is still afraid that he's going to kill me. Which is so much better, right? Oh my god.

Except I still don't think he's a murderer. I think he's a vampire. And I'm afraid he won't be able to control himself and he'll bite my neck and rip out my carotid and lick all my blood off the floor after he drains it from my body. But these are ridiculous thoughts, right? Because if vampires aren't real, then he definitely won't do that, and if vampires are real, he probably still won't do that because he's already not done that. Right?

My intercom buzzing scares the shit out of me and I practically jump off my couch and run to the door.

"Come up," I say into it, and then press the unlock button so he can let himself in.

I open the door and wait for him so I can see him coming down the hall. I'm not sure why, but it makes me less nervous than going back and sitting on the couch and waiting for him to knock. He comes out of the elevator and waves as soon as he sees me so I wave back.

"Hey," he says as he gets closer.

"Hi."

"How was the rest of your afternoon?" he asks.

We both go into my apartment and I shut the door behind us. "Um, weird."

"Weird?"

"Well I told Angela that you were on the hiking trail, and she thought you were stalking me, and I had to lie to her and tell her she was right, that you're a creep and I don't want to get to know you. But now she's worried because she thinks you're a murderer and she's afraid you're going to murder Claire."

"Why would I murder Claire?"

"I don't know, because you work with her?"

He sighs and looks around my apartment before landing his gaze back on me. "If you're really worried about it, I can like, um, make her not care about it."

"What do you mean you can make her not care about it?"

"I don't like doing it, and I haven't done it in a really long time, but I can sort of ease people's worries. Like if someone is scared, I can calm it, or make them not bothered about something that's eating at them."

"Have you done that to me?" I ask.

"No, of course not. I just said that I don't like doing it. And I won't do it to Angela if you don't want, but if you're worried that she's going to make this spiral into something that it isn't, then I can help."

"How do I know you haven't done it to me?"

"Because if I did it to you, I would have done it the night you found the blood. Most vampires would have, but I don't think that's fair. Do you want me to do it to you right now so you can know what it feels like?"

My heart stops. I swear, it stops and my blood goes cold and I don't even know how to think anymore. What if I say yes and he does it but then he can't stop? What if he makes me not care about something that I should be caring about?

"I-I- I don't know," I stammer.

"I don't have to do it. To anybody. We can think of an explanation for Angela."

"I don't know if we can."

"Okay, well you just let me know."

"Okay." I bite my bottom lip and sit on the couch, trying to decide if that's a good idea or not. It's pretty violating to do that to someone. Unless someone asked for it, I don't like the idea of just changing the way someone feels about something.

"Did you have other questions?" he asks, sitting beside me on the couch.

"Did you do the mind thing on people you drank blood from?"

"I did it to the people who were scared."

"People were scared?"

"Before we found the group who let us feed off them. We had to eat; there was no other choice." He shrugs. "It made it less scary for them. But when we bite people, it gives the person a bit of a euphoria anyway. So even if we didn't ease their fears, once you start feeding, that fear sort of goes away anyway."

"What do you mean? Does something come out of your fangs when you bite?"

"No, nothing comes out of our fangs. It might be our saliva mixing in their bloodstream, but I'm not sure."

"Has anyone else believed you? That you're a vampire, I mean?"

"Throughout a lot of the 1800's people believed. That's when we fed directly off people, who knew what we were. There were secret societies of people who believed in it. I think the people who let us use them to feed hoped we would turn them one day as a thank you."

I don't say anything to him; I don't know what to say. This is all so unreal.

"But as time went on, I dunno, things changed and people grew out of the societies and nobody new joined," he continues. "We had to be more careful, and once blood donations started being a more regular thing for the public, we started stealing those, but we couldn't stay in the same place for too long because they would figure out who was stealing it all. We tried living off animals for a while but it didn't make us strong enough. It was enough to keep us going, but we were hungry all the time, no matter how much we drank. It made us irritable and-" he cuts himself off and takes a deep breath. "I haven't told anyone new about me since the early 1900s."

"What?"

"Yeah." I think at first that he's going to elaborate on that, but instead he asks, "What other questions do you have?"

"Okay, so you said that it's easy to not eat people, or bite them or whatever. But what if you were starving? Like what if you were going to die if you didn't get some blood in you?"

"I still wouldn't."

"Really?"

He just nods as a reply.

"Do people smell good?" I ask. "Like if people were butter tarts and I couldn't eat them, I would still like to smell them, I think."

"Yeah, people smell good." His lips curl into a grin.

"Do I smell good?"

"Yes," he says easily.

"Okay so you won't bite me because you don't want to hurt me, but have you..." I pause for a few seconds. "Have you thought about biting me? Like, have you fantasized about it?"

His jaw clenches and he looks away. I shift a little closer to him on the couch and put my hand out, wanting to put it on his knee or something, but I change my mind and take it back, put it in my own lap.

"Felix?" I whisper. "Have you?"

He turns his head back towards me and stares for another few seconds before nodding his head once.

"Oof. Okay," is all I say, and I'm not sure if it's a good response or not.

"I said I would tell you the truth," he says, his voice cracking.

"I know," I reply. "I appreciate it."

"I never would, though."

"I know," I say again.

We're quiet for a bit, and all I can hear are Hazel and April running on their wheels. I still feel strange believing him. Even though I've believed him since seeing his burns, it feels wrong. Supernatural things don't exist. Paranormal things aren't real. They're all just made up stories. But now all of a sudden it isn't. And even though there has been so much evidence that I feel no one would be able to doubt, I feel wrong admitting that I believe him. Asking all these questions doesn't feel real. It feels like I'm playing along in some game, and if I tell myself that I'm not playing, I'll feel like I'm losing my sanity.

He just told me that he's fantasized about biting me and drinking my blood for Christ's sake, and I said 'oof!' I said 'oof!' What the fuck is that? I feel like the only way I'll be able to believe him without feeling strange or wrong about it, is if I'm able to experience something myself. It has to be something more than just seeing.

"Do the thing," I blurt out, before I tell myself that I'd actually decided.

"What?" he asks.

"Make me less worried about something."

"Reese, are you sure?"

I nod my head slowly. "I feel like it's the only other thing that's going to make me absolutely believe you."

"You're positive?"

I nod my head and move closer to him. He readjusts himself on the couch and pulls one of his legs up under him so that he's facing me more directly, so I do the same.

"Okay," he whispers, leaning in closer to me. "Okay," he says again, and I feel like he's nervous. "Um, is it okay if I touch you?"

"Yes," I murmur.

He brings his hand up next to my face and tucks a curl behind my ear. He traces my cheekbone down to my jaw with his fingertips and closes his eyes, and all of a sudden I feel tipsy. I'm warm inside like I just had a glass of champagne and I'm so content with everything. I feel like I've just had an excellent time at a party and I'm coming home halfway to sobering up and I'm excited to curl up in bed. And without even thinking, I lean in to kiss Felix. But as soon as my lips come within a few centimetres of his, he pulls away and I sort of fall into him a little bit.

"Sorry," he says quickly.

I pull back and look at him, confused. "Why are you sorry?"

"I didn't know what you were worried about, I didn't mean to make you do that."

"What?" I still feel warm inside.

"I just completely took away all your inhibitions, I didn't mean to do it that hard, I'm sorry. I need to put it back."

"What?" I bring my face in closer to his again, and again he pulls away.

"Stop," he says. "You don't actually want to kiss me."

"Yes I do. I've just been afraid of it until now." Afraid doesn't feel like the right word, but it's all I can think of in the moment. I guess it's close enough.

"Right. Okay, same thing. Let me fix this."

"Or you could kiss me."

"Reese," he says slowly.

"Yes?"

He puts his fingertips back on the side of my face, and I look into his eyes. They're beautiful. *He's* beautiful. I realize that I've never thought that about him before, but here we are.

"Are you going to kiss me?" I ask.

"No," he says quietly as he traces my jawline again. He moves in closer to me and I lean in and close my eyes, ready to press my lips against his. "Just stay still for a second," he whispers.

"Okay," I whisper back, my eyes still closed.

His thumbs sweep gently across my eyelids, and I shiver. He does it again, slower this time, and I melt into his touch. But when he takes his hands away, I open my eyes and I feel different already.

"Better?" he asks.

I shift back on the couch so that I'm farther away from him and bring my hands up to my mouth. The warm feeling from inside of me is gone and now I feel like I've been invaded. Violated, even. But what's worse, is I feel like I violated Felix. I tried to kiss him, and after he pulled away, I tried to kiss him again! It's like he took away all my sense to care about anything, including other people!

"No," I whisper, embarrassed. "I'm sorry I did that."

"It's not your fault. I literally took all your cares away."

"Don't do that to Angela," I say.

"I won't."

We don't say anything for a few minutes and I finally take my hands away from my mouth.

"Why didn't you do that to me before? When I found your blood?" I ask, my hands still up at my mouth.

"It didn't feel right," he says quietly. "I wanted you to understand me on your own. Plus it's really invasive, isn't it? I can't just control people's emotions like that without their permission. Even if it would help me get out of trouble."

I nod, but I don't know what to say. I want to say thanks, but that's weird, saying thanks to someone for not violating you.

"Should I go?" Felix asks.

"No."

"Are you okay?"

"I don't know."

"Is it okay if I move closer to you?"

I nod my head and he starts to scoot towards me on the couch but then stops. He runs his hand through his hair and then continues moving closer. He lifts his arm that's closest to me and without even thinking, I tuck myself under it and snuggle into him. He smooths the hair out on the top of my head and presses his cheek onto it a little.

"Felix," I say.

"Yes?"

"Thanks for not letting me kiss you."

"Of course."

"Felix?"

"Yes?"

"I think I really like you."
"I really like you too."
"It's weird that you're a vampire."
He laughs, and it makes me smile.

‖

I end up falling asleep cuddled up with Felix, which should be weird, right? I've just been convinced that he's a vampire and now I'm all of a sudden comfortable enough with him to fall asleep wrapped up in his arms? Excuse me? How did I get here? When I wake up and these thoughts go through my head, I scoot away from him a little, which wakes him up.

"Oh man," he says, yawning. "Guess we fell asleep."

"Yeah."

"Is everything okay?"

"Am I stupid? Is Angela right to be worried about me?"

"You're not stupid. And she's worried about you because she thinks I'm delusional."

"What if we're both delusional?"

"You were there when I changed your mood, right? You remember watching me heal in a matter of minutes, don't you? The sun blisters?"

"I know, I know," I say. "It just sort of all feels like a dream. This is weird."

"I know it's weird. It's weird for me too."

"Okay. So what do we tell Angela?"

I text Angela and tell her to come over so I can try to explain. I can picture her huffing before grabbing her keys and heading over. She steps into my apartment with a box of Timbits and I take them from her while she takes her shoes off.

"Okay. Explain," she says, sitting down on the couch.

"So Felix's friend is a nurse, and was supposed to be helping out at a blood drive. But the location was double booked and the other event was already there set up when everyone got there with their stuff. People with appointments to donate blood were showing up too, and everyone was sort of panicking, so Felix offered up his apartment. Not everyone went, but a lot of people did, and they did the blood drive in his living room. But the transport team got the wrong address and didn't show up until two days later to pick up the blood. So Felix was keeping it in his fridge."

Angela narrows her eyes at me. "But instead of telling you that the first time, he told you that he's a vampire?"

"He thought he was being funny."

"Yeah, I don't like this guy."

"I was also freaked out from seeing all the blood, so I wasn't thinking properly. He told me that he tried to explain it to me after he realized that I thought he was being serious, but I wouldn't listen. Which makes sense. He tried to explain it to me again when we met up a few weeks ago, but I got freaked out again and left before he had a chance."

"I'm looking this up."

"What?"

"If a blood drive got moved to someone's apartment, there's got to be a story about it somewhere. There's no way something like that goes unnoticed. Felix should be named a local hero for doing something like that."

She pulls out her phone and starts typing stuff into Google, but of course nothing comes up. She goes to Facebook and searches for things, but of course, nothing comes up. Then she goes to Instagram, and after a few searches, she sees a picture of someone at a blood drive with a caption that says "Blood drives aren't as fun when they're set up at the rec centre. I say we do it at that guy's apartment again." I almost breathe a sigh of relief.

Felix and I had made a fake Instagram account, but were nervous about it, because all the posts we added to it to make it look real were obviously all posted on the same day. We just hoped that Angela wouldn't look that far into it.

Angela looks at the comments section of his picture to see a couple people saying they were at that last blood drive and they were surprised at how well they organized the new, last minute location, and were even more surprised to find out it was just a regular guy. All fake accounts, of course.

"Hmm," she says. "This seems weird."

"I thought it was a little weird, too, but it seems like he's telling the truth."

"Have you been to his apartment since then?" she asks.

"No."

"Good. I still don't think you should see this guy. But it's good to know that he's probably not a psychopath."

"He's not a psychopath."

"Reese, I'm worried about you. This guy is just a walking red flag."

"How?"

"Well he- he thinks he's a vampire!"

"No he doesn't! He was trying to joke with me."

"What about all that weird stuff that you told me? About him lifting the elevator and stuff?"

"Angela, do *you* think he's a vampire?"

"No, of course not. But what about his fangs? Didn't you say he had fangs? You said he showed you fangs!"

Did I? Did I tell her about that part? Oh no. How am I supposed to get past this one?

"No," I say slowly.

"Excuse me?"

"I don't remember telling you that."

"Reese, you *told* me that he showed you retractable fangs! We were sitting right here with our Blizzards melting all over your coffee table! I remember!"

"No, no, I never said he showed them to me. He just told me he had them. When he was trying to joke." I can't believe I'm lying to her about this. This is horrible. Making up the blood bank story is one thing, but trying to make her believe I said something completely different to her is not okay. I can't just make her think that her mind is playing tricks on her. Felix really does have retractable fangs! And I did tell her about it! "Why would you think he's a psychopath if he actually had retractable fangs?"

"I don't know, maybe he had them installed! Because he's a psychopath!"

I let out a deep breath and close my eyes. What will Angela say if I tell her he's a vampire? "He was joking when he said that, I swear," I whisper instead. "I was just freaked out, so none of it was coming across to me the way he intended. I was practically hysterical."

"As any normal person would be. He had fucking blood bags in his fridge."

"Right. And he was nervous and he thought saying he was a vampire would be funny. He was planning on telling me what actually happened once I laughed at his joke, but then I wasn't laughing, and he realized he had just made everything worse. He knows now that it wasn't a good joke."

"Why didn't he try to explain it to you sooner?"

"Because I wouldn't listen to him. Remember when I tried to talk to him down by the water? He hardly got a word in before I left."

Angela nods. "Right."

"I'm really sorry I made you worry about me. And I swear I wasn't going to pursue him or try to date him when I thought he was a murderer. I was very actively trying to stay away from him. But then he got stuck by lightening and-"

"Wait, what? He got stuck by lightening?"

"Yeah, I told you that."

"No, you said you *almost* got struck by lightening."

"Right. Well, I guess that's true. He didn't actually get struck by lightening, but the tree next to him did, and shards of it flew off when the tree snapped, and he got pieces of it stuck in him."

"That's wild! Oh my god!"

I tell her about finding him on my hike and about the lightening and thunder knocking me to my feet, about not knowing what had happened until I saw Felix and the little fire the lightening had created. I tell her about pulling the branches out of him and about his festering wounds, but I leave out the part where I watched them heal in minutes. I tell her that while we were under the trees waiting for it to stop raining, he explained everything to me, about his terrible joke and how he did it because he was nervous. I say that as Felix was telling me he was a vampire, his brain was telling him to stop, but he couldn't. He knew he was blowing it but his mouth wouldn't shut up. He was embarrassed. I tell her that I was embarrassed for freaking out so hard and I tell her that he assured me I didn't overreact. I don't tell her about the sun incident and bringing him sunscreen, so instead I say that when I went to the washroom before we left, I actually went back to find him and make sure he wasn't dying, and make sure someone was coming to help him. I tell her that he went to the hospital and got antibiotics for his infections and got his wounds dressed.

Felix and I hadn't even made up this part of the story together; I didn't even know I was going to tell it like this. I had forgotten that I told her about his fangs, and this was the only explanation that seemed to make the most sense to me. I would be worried about my friend dating a possible murderer too if I was in Angela's shoes, so I really hope my story is convincing enough to not make me seem like a girl just asking to be killed. I don't want her to think I don't have any respect for myself.

"Wait, he told you all this today, before we left the campground?" Angela asks.

"Yes," I say.

"So Felix told you about the blood bank and everything today, before you and I spent half an hour in the car together. After I asked you about it."

"To be fair, you didn't ask me about it," I try. "You just kept calling him a murderer."

"You could have told me that he's not a murderer!"

"I did! I said that multiple times!"

"Yes but you didn't back it up with 'he's not a murderer or a psychopath because he's actually a town treasure who holds emergency blood banks in his apartment!'"

"I didn't think you would listen to me! You were calling him a murderer!"

Angela is about to say something else but she stops herself. She lets out a deep breath and closes her eyes. "Okay," she says. "This Felix guy isn't a murderer or a psychopath, he just has a millionaire complex."

"What's a millionaire complex?"

"I don't know, someone who wants to live like a millionaire? I just made it up. It sounded cool."

"Do millionaires hold blood banks in their houses?" I ask.

"I don't know, probably."

|||

Felix and I have been texting all week and I keep checking my phone while I'm at my desk at work. It's easier for us to text than actually talk on the phone because we basically have opposite schedules. I check my phone during any down time at work and so does he. Although he has less down time than I do, which makes sense. Even when I don't have down time, I act as if I do, and just do less work. I should be paying more attention to what I'm doing, but I can't help it. I keep looking at my phone and smiling every time I see that I have a new message from him.

We should have a vampire movie marathon he texts to me on Friday.

Why, so you can judge everything they do and tell me all that's wrong with the movies? I text back.

Yes.

Ha. Yeah, okay, sounds fun.

He responds with a sly face emoji and I'm not sure what he means by it exactly. I never know how to interpret a lot of emojis that guys send. Especially because guys seem to use them a lot less than I do, so when they do it feels like it's some big gesture of some kind and I have to figure out the meaning behind it. Is he flirting with me or is he just using this emoji to be funny? I don't know. I don't know anything.

When do you want to do it? I ask.

When do I want to do it? Whenever you feel comfortable with it I'm good to go, to be honest. And there's a winky emoji. Okay, so he's definitely flirting. I don't know what to say. What do I say!? I don't want to do it with him. I mean, maybe I will want to later. Yes, probably I will want to later. But I don't know! I need to be super close with someone before I want to do that. Sex, I mean. Sex related things. I know he's just playing, but I also know that he's probably partly serious. Or fully serious. Oh my god.

I meant when do you want to have the movie marathon I reply. I add in a smiley face with the tongue sticking out to keep it light. Ah. I'm not good at this.

Ah yes that makes more sense given the context of our conversation.

Yeah lol.

He doesn't text back so I get back to work and imagine a world where I'm better at flirting. I want to say something else to him but I don't want to text him again before he messages me. I know that's stupid. It's stupid, right? But I don't want to anyway. So I don't. I have a lot to do today anyway, spending time texting a vampire is probably not the best idea. I need to finish designing a logo for the new bookstore downtown and I still haven't made up an invoice for my last client, which has a lot of stuff on it, and I have about 17 emails I still need to reply to.

Felix still hasn't texted me by the time I get home and I know he's probably working now, so I flop down on the couch and stare at my phone. I open our text conversation and stare at his name at the top of the screen. I reread our last few messages and finally decide to start typing to him.

You never answered my question, Snappy Jack I say.

What question? he texts almost immediately.

When do you want to have this movie marathon?

Tonight? I should be home around 10
Oh so we're making it a late night, alright I say.
It's almost always going to be a late night with me. And
he puts another winky face!

Oh is it now? I type. But then I erase it instead of hitting
send. If I was comfortable being physical with him, then I would
be more comfortable with this kind of flirting, but since I'm not,
I feel weird flirting back. Him flirting with me doesn't make me
uncomfortable, but being the one to continue it does. Am I
weird? Ugh. Dating is stupid. **Makes sense** I say instead. **I forgot**
about the vampire thing.

It's about twenty minutes before he replies and I've had my
phone in my hand the whole time like a loser, just waiting for it
to go off. **Yes that is a thing people tend to forget** his text says.

Totally get it.

He sends me a crying-laughing emoji about ten minutes after
that, and I decide not to reply anymore. I'll wait until he tells me
that he's home. He's working, and I know he doesn't have to
respond while he's there, but I don't want to make him feel
obligated to. He should be paying attention to his customers.

Also I don't want to seem clingy.

But mostly it's the first thing.

Felix sends me a voice message at 9:40 which says, "Heeeey
I'm just leaving work now. Want me to swing by your place and
pick you up? Also I have some pizzas with me so I hope you're
hungry! Also I hope you still want to hang out because there's no
way I can eat all this pizza by myself. I'll be eating it for three days
if you don't help me and then all my blood will go bad. Oh my
god, you're alone, right? Nobody else heard that, right? Fuck.
Anyway, I'm sure you're alone. It's okay though, I can put it in
the freezer."

I laugh out loud for more than three minutes before I'm able to collect myself and answer him. I actually haven't replied to him with a voice memo yet, and I sort of feel bad that I haven't. He never told me that he wants me to, but I feel like if he's sending them to me, he would like it if I sent them to him. Voice memos don't make me nervous, per se, for some reason I just feel like they need to be snappy or punchy. Like you have to hit a perfect punch line or something. And besides flirting before I feel more comfortable with someone, I feel like it's one of the only things I'm not good at. I'm probably overthinking it, so I just shut my brain off for half a second and press the little microphone icon at the bottom of the screen.

"You're ridiculous," I start. "I just laughed for over three minutes, so thank you for that. Yeah, you can come get me as long as you don't mind driving me home. And pizza sounds great. I don't want you to have to put your blood in the freezer to give you time to finish it all on your own." I feel super weird joking back about the blood thing, because who jokes about putting blood bags in the freezer? Me and Felix apparently. It feels weird in my mouth when I say it and I get this weird little heeby jeeby feeling in the back of my neck like I just stepped in something gross or thought I felt a spider crawl on me. I want to be able to joke with him about it, and I'm sure that over time it will get easier and not feel weird, just like I'm sure over time I'll be comfortable flirting and probably doing sexual things with him, but right now… Right now it's still weird.

"Oh no, I wouldn't be putting the blood in the freezer, that's way more delicious than pizza. The pizza can get freezer burn and be there for a day when I need something for guests. Like you!"

I press record so he can hear me laughing again but I only send about a second and a half of it. It's a real laugh, but it's a little less fun sounding than my last one. He didn't hear my last laugh, so he doesn't have anything to compare, but now I'm suddenly worried that it came across as an awkward laugh that I only sent because I didn't know what else to say.

Stop being bad at this, Reese! You know you can be good at this! At some point. At some point in this relationship, you will be good at it.

I'm about to send him another message, one with actual words this time, but my phone starts ringing. Oh good, this is much better. One might think that talking on the phone is worse than voice memos, because at least with a voice memo, you can discard a message and start again if one feels the need to, but you can't do that in a phone conversation. But phone conversations are more natural. There's no turn taking, there's no back and forth, and there's no pressure to sound concise or cute or cool in every clip. You can interrupt each other, or agree, or laugh at the same time. Yes, this is much better.

I smile and accept his call.

"Hey cutie," he says before I even have a chance to say hi. "I'm almost at your place but I thought calling you would be safer than continuing to record voice memos while I'm driving."

I'm glad he added another thing I can easily respond to because I don't know how to deal with him calling me cutie. "You were sending those while you were driving!?" I scold.

"Yeah but I stopped because I realized it wasn't safe."

"You should have realized that before you even did it! You're not the only one in danger when you do stuff like that, you know."

"I'm not in danger at all, Reese. But I could be putting other people on the road in danger. That's why I stopped. I'm sorry."

I let out a deep breath and close my eyes for a second. "Okay."

"Alright. So before I get there, I have a question for you."

"Shoot."

"That laugh you sent me. Was that a nervous laugh or a genuine laugh because you think I'm hilarious?"

"That was a real laugh. I mean I guess your vampire comments make me a little nervous, but only because it's so new to me."

"Right. Okay. Noted. No more vampire jokes."

"You don't have to-"

But he cuts me off and says, "Meet me outside? I'll be there in about thirty seconds."

"Yeah okay, see you soon."

I grab my purse and head down to the lobby. His car is already out front when I get there, so I wave as I walk towards the doors and he waves back.

"Hey," he says as I get in the car.

"Hey. How was work?"

"It was great. How was your evening?"

"It was okay."

"Did you bake anything?"

"No, not tonight. I just watched a bunch of episodes of *Neighbourly*."

"Oh cool. I haven't seen that show."

"It's pretty funny. The guy who plays the main character, his girlfriend is best friends with Claire!"

"What!? No way!"

"Yes way! But I have a very important question to ask you, Felix."

"Okay." I can hear the nerves in his response and it makes me smile a little.

"What kind of pizza did you get?"

He laughs for a few seconds, and it's one of those deep belly laughs. Like a real, genuine, can't-help-yourself laugh. "I'm glad this is what you find important. I got goat cheese and prosciutto, plain cheese, and garlic bacon.

"Oh my goodness I'm going to die of deliciousness."

"Excellent. If you're going to die, that's definitely the best way to do it."

I try to grab the pizza boxes out of the back seat but Felix gets there before me with his superhuman speed, and winks at me from across the top of the car. I huff but smile, shut the door I opened for no reason, and follow him to the elevator.

Felix grabs us plates while I get comfortable on his couch and wrap myself in a blanket.

"You're really getting under a blanket?" he asks as he comes into the living room. "It's July."

"So? It's cold in here."

He smirks at me and sits down, handing me a plate.

"I've never had this goat cheese one before," I say, taking a slice of it.

"Oh man, it's so good." He takes a slice of the same pizza, along with a slice of plain cheese.

I take a bite of mine and nod my head, eyes wide in silent agreement. "Amazing," I say once I swallow.

"I gotta say, I've never had such fancy pizza before working at Carter's."

"What? Nonsense."

"It's true," he chuckles. "I mean I've had authentic pizza from Italy, which is just," he pinches his fingers to his thumb with his free hand and kisses them before dramatically throwing his hand away from his mouth. "This stuff, though, is way better than classic fast food pizza. Even the plain cheese is superior."

"Of course it is. Tom Carter is a genius."

"That he is."

We start with *From Dusk till Dawn*, and I'm super interested in Felix's take on it.

He laughs throughout most of it.

Then we watch *Blade*, and he laughs throughout most of that as well.

Watching the movies with him is fun and cozy though, because we're cuddled together on the couch with the blanket over both of us, and every time he laughs it bounces my head a little.

"Are you up for another one, or did you want me to drive you home?" Felix asks as I fight to keep my eyes open.

"I would love to watch another one but I don't know if I can stay up."

"Amateur," he laughs.

"It won't be over until after four," I whine, sitting up and moving away from him a little so I can look at him easier.

"You're telling me you never stayed up that late partying in high school? Or in college?"

"Yeah but I'm thirty now. Recovery is not the same."

"We're not even drinking! Also you were up pretty late on your birthday there, missy."

"That's different! It was my birthday! I only turn thirty once, you know."

"Unless I turn you into a vampire, then you can do it every year if you want."

I stop. Like everything inside of me just stops. I swear my heart stops. I stop breathing. I don't blink. Everything inside of me has turned to ice.

"Whoa, I'm sorry, that was too soon," he says pretty quickly. "I'm sorry, I was just joking. I wasn't being serious."

He reaches a hand out to me and gently touches my wrist. When I don't flinch or back away, he lifts it off my lap and puts my hand in his.

"It's okay," I finally say. "I uh, it just… It just caught me off guard."

"I'm sorry. I haven't done this in a while. Interacted closely with humans, I mean. I'm not always good at it."

"What do you mean you haven't interacted with humans?"

"I've been living exclusively with vampires since the 1920's. I only interacted with humans when I needed to, so it was easy to pretend. I haven't had a mortal friend in a very long time."

"Oh wow."

"Yeah. My friends and I joked about regular vampire stuff all the time because it was normal everyday stuff for us. Sometimes I forget that it's not normal for you. Vampire talk is so natural for me."

"Is that why you told me you were 255 years old?" I ask.

"274. And no. I was trying to be funny. Sometimes I say something that I think will be funny and then it's very not funny."

"I mean I did laugh," I say.

"That's true, you did. I just, I knew you weren't going to think I was telling the truth, but the fact that I knew it was the truth was a little hilarious to me."

"But when you told me you hadn't used your dinnerware for thirty years, that was a mistake?"

He sighs. "Yes. And lifting the elevator, and talking about your heart rate, and letting you come over when I knew I had a fridge and freezer full of blood bags. I didn't have to think about these things until now. And also, I really didn't think you were just going to get up and help yourself to something in my fridge. Is that normal?"

"Yes. I'd say it's very normal, especially if you're comfortable with the person."

"Oh." He looks a little surprised, and then smiles.

"Were you ever going to tell me?" I ask. "About being a vampire, I mean?"

"I didn't plan on it," he says quietly. "I mean, realistically I didn't see it going well."

I laugh a little. "Right, understandable."

"Not that I specifically planned on lying to you, either. I mean, I like you, and I liked you from the first night I met you, but I don't want to make it a habit to tell every cute girl I meet that I'm a vampire."

"You plan on meeting other cute girls?"

"Well I am going to live forever unless someone shoves a wooden stake into my heart, so."

"So what were you going to do? Date me for a year and then ghost me?"

He takes in a deep breath and lets it out really slowly. "I don't know. I'm sorry. I have no idea what I would have done. I haven't done this before."

"But if you didn't know what you were going to do, you at least knew there was a huge chance that you would break my heart."

He grimaces a little. "I'm not that full of myself. I wasn't sure if you liked me, or how much you liked me. Can I be honest?"

"Yes, of course," I say.

"I wasn't planning on finding a girlfriend or anything. I was just trying to start a new life, blend in, and make new friends. And when I met you, I thought you were cool. I thought that I would really like to be your friend. You made me laugh. And not only that, you made it feel so easy. It was like everything about interacting with you was happening by accident. Like all my responses to you were falling out on their own. And for a little while, I forgot that there was a big secret I wasn't supposed to tell you. I forgot that I was different, or that you were different from me, I don't know. And then I just," he pauses for a few seconds, and then continues. "Then I just didn't want to stop getting to know you."

I realize that my smile has been growing as he talks, but all I can think to say in response is, "Okay, so then what do you plan on doing now that I do know about you?"

"Taking it one day at a time?"

"That sounds okay to me."

"Yeah?"

"Yeah."

"Okay. One day at a time, then." His smile is so infectious and it warms my chest. Figuratively, not literally like when he did the mood control thing on me.

"I have another question," I whisper.

"Shoot."

"You've called me cute twice now."

"That's not a question."

I realize in this moment that he's still holding onto my hand, and I look down at our fingers cradled against each other, and then back up at him. "You're right, it's not a question."

"So what's your question then?"

"Well it sounds stupid now," I say with a bit of a giggle.

"I'll bet you it isn't stupid. Ask your question."

"Okay. Um, you think I'm cute?"

He grins and I can tell he wants to tell me that I was right, that it was a stupid question. But instead he leans in a little closer to me and says, "Of course I think you're cute."

"Okay I have another question."

He doesn't answer me, he just looks at me with hope in his eyes.

"If we kissed right now, would it be dangerous?" I ask.

"I think kissing is a very low risk activity, Reese."

"Even for vampires? You won't suddenly want to like, bite my lip off or something?"

"You wanna risk it?"

I back up a little. "*Is* there a risk?"

"No," he chuckles. "I promise I won't hurt you. Lips only. Maybe some tongue."

I lean forward again, and suddenly his hands are on either side of my face, his fingers in my hair.

"I just want to say something before we do this," I whisper.

Again he doesn't say anything, he just waits for me to continue.

"I'm a big fan of moving slowly."

"Like, literally?" he asks. "You like to kiss slowly, or you like moving slowly towards each step in a sexual or romantic relationship?"

"The second one. But kissing slowly sounds nice, too."

"Alright. Moving slowly it is, then."

He closes the gap between us and presses his lips to mine. His lips are so soft, and when he opens his mouth, I almost gasp. His tongue sweeps against mine and I pull him closer to me, pressing myself against him as much as I can. He lies me back on the couch and puts a little bit of weight on me, which is nice, and continues to slowly move his mouth around mine. I match his movements, his speed, and sigh into his mouth a couple times because let me tell you, I've never been kissed like this before. I never thought a slow, gentle kiss could have so much feeling and passion behind it. I've heard of passionate kisses being described as 'hungry' before, but this is like we're eating a decadent piece of cake that we're trying so hard to savour. That if we eat it too quickly we'll miss it. Like it's a piece of cake we only get to enjoy once in a blue moon and we want it to last as long as possible.

"How 'ya doing?" he asks softly, hardly taking his mouth off mine.

"Oh, just lovely. You?"

"Same." He smiles against my mouth and I kiss him again, starting this savouring all over again.

||||

I can't believe I just made out with a vampire for half an hour. I. Made out. With. A vampire. Like what? No. But yes. It's true. He's a vampire and we kissed. For half an hour. A vampire's tongue was in my mouth. *My* tongue was in a vampire's mouth! Oh I wish I could tell Angela about this. I mean, I can tell her that Felix and I kissed, but I have to leave out the fact that he's an undead supernatural creature. Maybe one day I'll be able to tell her. Or maybe one day Felix will move on to be a vampire somewhere else and I'll be the only one who knows the truth.

I imagine being 70 years old and sitting on the porch with Angela and her husband (I'm alone because of course I am), and they have a sweet old dog who loves them (and who loves me too, because of course), and he sleeps by their feet and we all have blankets over our laps as we sit in our separate rockers. We watch the kids play in the street in the distance and listen to them laugh. And then I turn to them and say, "Remember that Felix guy I dated for a little while?"

Angela will turn and squint at me (old age, you know, the eyes just aren't the same anymore, even with glasses), and she'll just make this small grunting noise as acknowledgement instead of using words.

"He actually was a vampire, you know," I'll say to her.

I picture Angela smiling. "Are you shitting me?"

I'll laugh. The same kind of full, belly laugh that Felix did when I asked him my very important pizza topping question. And in that moment, I'll remember it. I'll remember him, and how hard he tried to get me to believe him, and how happy he seemed once I did. I'll remember our slow, gentle, but oh-so-amazing kiss that lasted thirty minutes. And I'm sure there will be more amazing things we'll do that I'll remember in that moment. But I'll remember all the special parts about him and when I've finished laughing, I'll lean forward in my rocker, look Angela dead in the eye and say, "I swear on your dog's life that I am not shitting you."

"Whatcha thinking about?" Felix asks, startling me.

"What? Oh. Nothing. Me and Angela being old." We've shifted on the couch and I'm now lying on top of him. I've had my eyes closed with my head on his chest for a few minutes.

He smiles at me. "That's nice."

"I guess." I lift my head up and rest my chin on top of my hands, on Felix's chest.

"Do you still want to watch another movie or should I take you home?" he asks.

I bite my bottom lip in contemplation, because really all I want to do is kiss him again. I would like to kiss him until the end of time, actually, if that's at all possible.

He narrows his eyes at me. "Your heart is suddenly racing."

"What?" I'm taken aback, because I totally believe him, it makes sense, because I was trying to form the words "Kiss me more instead", but was too nervous to actually say it for some reason, and now he knows that I'm nervous about something. Oh my god. Is he always going to know when I'm nervous?

"Are you afraid of me?" He sits up a little, forcing me to back off of him.

"No, of course not."

"Shit. I'm sorry."

"Felix, I said I wasn't."

"Oh. Then what's going on?"

"Well... Was my heart racing earlier too? When we- I mean, before we kissed?"

The corner of his mouth curls into a crooked grin. "You mean when you asked me if we could kiss?"

"Yeah."

He moves in closer to me again. "Yes, your heart was racing then. I didn't comment on it though, because you were talking to me so I knew that's what it was about. Plus I didn't want to make you more nervous."

"Okay," I say.

"So what are you wanting to say to me then, Reese?"

"Nothing really."

"Oh come on, don't do this to me."

"Well I'm clearly nervous about it, and you're dragging it out on purpose."

"What are you nervous about? Are you nervous about me hurting you?"

I scoff and roll my eyes. "No. We just made out for forever and I'm unharmed, so that's clearly not what's making me anxious."

"What is it, then?"

I stare at him, wanting him to get it.

"Are you..." he starts, "Are you nervous to tell me that you want to keep kissing?"

I nod my head slightly and he laughs.

"You're ridiculous," he says. "Why? Are you afraid of me rejecting you?"

"Obviously."

"I think it's pretty clear that I very much enjoy kissing you. And I'm used to staying up late. I'll kiss you until the sun comes up if that's what you want."

This is when I melt into his couch, never to return to human form. But even though I've melted and feel like I have no bones in my body, I swing my left leg over his lap and place my knees on either side of him. He shifts so that his knees can bend off the edge of the couch and it's easier for me to straddle him. I lean into his mouth and he sighs before I have a chance to kiss him.

"You were nervous to ask me to keep kissing you but you weren't nervous to do this?" he asks.

"It's not the kissing that makes me nervous, Felix. I feel so safe and comfortable with you. It was solely the fear of rejection. I promise."

"So now that you know I want you, you're going to do more of this, correct?"

I grin. "You want me?"

"Yes," he sighs. "Of course I do."

"Well don't get too excited," I say. "Our clothes are probably going to be staying on for a while."

"That's okay. Clothes are great. I love clothes. Clothes are the best."

I laugh and kiss him on the mouth. I can feel him sigh underneath me and it almost takes my breath away.

We don't kiss until the sun comes up, because I fall asleep. We change positions on the couch a few times, and we stop between breaths to talk a little, and one of the times that I'm on top of him, I just can't keep my eyes open anymore. We're talking about our favourite kind of muffins, and I just pass out. Gone.

I wake up in a bed, in a completely dark room. My eyes can't even try to adjust to anything because there's absolutely no light coming in anywhere. Not even from the moon, or street lights outside, so I'm a little confused. I prop myself up on one hand and feel around the bed with the other hand, and I hold my breath for a second when it touches somebody else's bare flesh.

Felix groans, and I silently laugh at myself for being concerned about finding someone else in this bed with me. Of course it's Felix.

"Sorry," I whisper.

I hear him move under the sheets and then his hand is on mine, so I lie back down and let my head sink into the fluffy pillow.

"I hope it's okay that I brought you to my bed," he says. "I loved you sleeping on my chest on the couch, it was great, but this is just a little more comfortable. I thought you might be more comfortable too."

"How did I not wake up?" I ask. "Did you carry me?"

"I did." I can hear the smile in his voice. "But you were very sleepy. You talked a little, though, when I brought you to bed."

"I did?"

"You did. You said, 'did my legs stop working?' and I laughed at you, and you told me to stop being mean."

"Oh my god," I groan.

"It was cute. Are you still tired? Or did you want to get up?"

"What time is it? We can't have been asleep for that long; it's so dark still."

"No, that's just my amazing window cover. It's almost noon."

"Oh."

"We could go for brunch."

"Oh my god, I would love that."

"What?" Felix asks.

"Wha- Huh?" I blink a couple times and shake my head.

"You're staring at me."

He's got this adorable smirk on his face, with a chunk of pancake in his mouth, making a bulge in his left cheek.

"No I'm not," I say defensively.

He finishes chewing and swallows. "Are too."

"I'm sorry," I say quietly. "But I'm so fascinated."

"By pancakes?"

"I was just thinking. I haven't seen you drink… You know, yet."

"That's more of a third date thing."

"I feel like this is our third date."

He narrows his eyes at me. "I don't think we've had any dates."

I tilt my head to the side. "Oh really?"

"Really. Plus I feel like a lot of people today are sort of past the dating thing."

"Past the dating thing?"

He shrugs. "It seems people just *hang out*. There aren't really any official dates, you know? And then these hang outs happen for weeks at a time and both people in the non-relationship are like 'ahh, what are we doing I'm too afraid to ask' and it goes on for much too long."

"What are you saying, Felix?"

"I'm not saying anything." He takes a sip of his coffee, and I can't help but notice that he picks the mug up by gently gripping the rim instead of using the handle.

"Well I like where this is going," I say. "I have enjoyed the slow kissing. And the not-so-slow kissing that we did later. And the waking up in your bed."

"Is that all?"

"Is it stupid to say that I kind of want you to be my boyfriend?"

"No, it's not stupid." But then he lets out a long breath and looks at me with a bit of a sad expression. "I don't really see how it would work out in the long run, though. And that's not really as big a deal for me because I literally have all the time in the world and you don't. If we become a thing, I'd be holding you back."

"Holding me back from what?"

"From finding the person you're going to spend the rest of your life with."

"Right."

"But I do like you. A lot. And I would love it if you were my girlfriend. It's just probably not a good idea."

"Right," I say again, tears stinging my eyes. I force them back and take a few deep breaths, looking away from Felix so he can't see how red they probably are. He just told me last night that he had no idea what he planned on doing when we started hanging out, so I should have expected this kind of answer.

We end up finishing our meals in awkward silence. I look down at my plate, at the maple syrup covering the crumbs left over, and I swirl my fork around in it.

"Are you okay?" he finally asks.

"It's just."

He takes in a bit of a sharp breath and I stop. I lick the syrup off my fork, put it back down onto the plate to get sticky again.

"It's just what?" he tries.

"What happened to one day at a time?" I force myself to ask.

He reaches across the table and takes my hand, rubs my knuckles with his thumb, but doesn't say anything.

"Maybe we should talk about this somewhere else," I finally say.

He nods his head and we wait quietly for our server to bring us our bill. He pays for our meals and together we walk back to his car, but once we get out of the shade of the awning, Felix sprints across the parking lot. I get in the passenger seat and look at his already burned arms. They're bright red like they would be after an entire day at the beach without sunscreen. All his windows are pretty tinted, for that purpose, so I'm sure he feels a lot better now that we're in the car.

"You okay?" I ask.

He nods. "Fine. It'll be calmed down by the time we get back to my place." He starts the car and we drive in silence back to his apartment. I want to say something on the way, continue our conversation from brunch, but I feel weird about doing it in the car; I'm not sure why. He looks over at me a couple times and I give him awkward smiles. I want to say something every time he looks at me but I just don't know what to say.

We're quiet as we walk through the parking garage, and we're quiet stepping into the elevator. Although there seems to be some new tension that has just come up as soon as the elevator doors shut and it feels like I can't breathe for half a second. I look over at him and I can see him eyeing me over his sunglasses that are pushed down on his nose and without even thinking, I wrap my arms around him and kiss him. His hands are in my hair and then they're going down my back to my waist, and I'm pushing myself into him like I can't get enough and he's pushing me into the wall behind me, and then the elevator dings and we separate before the doors are fully opened.

I let out a deep breath and comb my fingers through my hair.

"Let's go get this talking thing out of the way," Felix says, already ahead of me down the hall.

"Oh." I follow him to his apartment and I'm surprised when he sits at his kitchen table instead of on the couch in his living room. I sit at the table across from him so we can look at each other easily.

"This feels oddly formal," I say.

"Yeah. I thought it would be easier to talk this way."

I scrunch my eyebrows at him. "Okay." I let out a slow breath to collect myself. "You never answered my question."

He raises his eyebrows in a look of surprise, and takes a second to answer. "What happened to one day at a time, you mean?"

I nod. "Like, before, like I mean, before I knew you were a vampire, you seemed very interested in me. And you wanted me to believe you. And last night, literally last night before you kissed me all slowly and sensually for thirty minutes straight and then made out with me later and then carried me to your bed, you said you wanted to take it one day at a time. And now you're telling me that it's not a good idea for me to be your girlfriend."

He covers his face with his hands, and then rubs his eyes a little before looking at me again. "I'm really sorry. I don't mean that I don't want you to be my girlfriend. And I do still want to take it one day at a time. I just think that maybe we should just take the relationship portion of this a bit slower? Like yesterday was the first day that we kissed and the first time that you got over your fear of my rejection, and being an official couple the very next day seems like it's skipping a bunch of these days that we should be taking one at a time, you know?"

I sigh. "Okay. Yeah. Sorry. You boosted my confidence too high, there, Snappy Jack."

"I love that your confidence boosted enough for you to share that feeling, Reese. I never want to take that away from you. And I hope me not jumping on it hasn't diminished it at all."

"I guess it hasn't," I say.

"You guess?"

I shrug and give him a smile.

"I want to keep doing this if you want to," Felix says. "But can we go a little slower? Figure it out as we go? I haven't done this before. Dated a mortal, I mean."

"Can I ask you a question?"

"Of course."

"You said someone turned you, and she was there for you the whole time so you wouldn't kill anyone."

"Yes."

"So like, was she your girlfriend? Is that why she turned you?"

"Yes," he says slowly. "I don't really want to talk about it, though. Not now at least."

"Okay." I pause for a minute to think about what else I want to say. "So you would like to potentially be my boyfriend, but you think we should take that part slower. In case it gets to a point where we realize this won't work?"

"Yeah, I guess. Not that I want that to happen. But it's bound to happen. I mean. I'm not going to get older."

"So you would rather play this out, fall in love with me, and then realize we can't be together because you're a vampire and I'm not, and then have both of our hearts be broken?"

"Well it sounds terrible when you say it like that, Reese." He laughs a little but I can tell it's forced.

"So should I go home, then?" I ask reluctantly. "I mean what were you expecting to happen when you decided to live amongst the humans, Felix?"

He laughs again but this time it sounds genuine, which makes me feel slightly better. "I don't know. I thought I would make new friends. Which I have. And I'm really glad that you and I are friends. I didn't imagine falling for someone though, and definitely not this quickly." He gasps and his eyes widen. "I'm not- I'm not in love with you."

"Okay," I say, but I can't help but smile.

"I'm not. I'm not in love with you."

"Okay," I say again.

"Stop smiling, then."

"Sorry." I put my lips in a tight, straight line.

"Like I said before, I wasn't planning on telling you about me, but then everything happened, and I didn't want you to go off telling people that I'm this psycho who keeps blood in his fridge, and a part of me wanted you to believe me because I didn't want what we had started to end so soon. Even if it was just going to be friendship. I'm sorry I made this into such a mess. I wish I knew what I was doing."

"I don't think anyone knows what they're doing."

"But it's even harder for me because I have supernatural things to worry about."

"Yeah," I agree.

"So what have we decided then?"

"That you're falling in love with me."

He opens his mouth to object but then he just ends up smiling at me with a tilt of his head.

"I don't know what to do," I finally say. "I've never been in this situation before. And I guess it's true what you said, that if we're here doing this, pretending that we can be together officially with no issues, then I'm going to be essentially wasting my time when I could be meeting the person I'm going to marry. Not that I think knowing you is a waste of time but-"

"I know what you mean. I said it first, so I'm not offended or anything."

"But…" I add.

"But?"

"But I like you too. And I have enjoyed the kissing and the cuddling and the sleeping next to you. And watching vampire movies. I don't want to stop doing any of that any time soon."

"Neither do I."

"So we'll keep going slowly, then. And if I happen to meet someone else, we'll go our separate ways. Or we'll just be friends."

"Okay," he says quietly. "That sounds okay."

"But we're not boyfriend/girlfriend."

"No, I don't think we should put a label on it like that. It would make it too hard to walk away when the time comes."

"I think continuing this is going to make it hard to walk away whether or not we put a label on it."

"I think you're right."

"So are we being stupid, then?"

"No, I don't think so," he says. "I think we're being human."

I don't know what to say, so I just give him a nod.

"Okay so why don't we just stop talking about it since we know nothing good will come from that. Let's just pretend for a little while that everything will work out."

"Yeah," I say quietly. "Pretending is nice sometimes."

"Sometimes I literally can't get through a day unless I pretend something about it is different," he admits.

"So we'll pretend," I say. "For a little while. We'll pretend that there's no end to this."

"And when we can't pretend anymore, we'll deal with reality."

"But for now…" I stand up from the table and he stands up too.

"For now we pretend," he says again.

We stare at each other from across the table and neither of us moves for almost a full minute. And then without even thinking I walk around the table and meet him halfway, because he has also started walking around the table, and my mouth is on his, and his hands are in my hair and then I don't even know how it happens, but my legs are now wrapped around his waist and he's carrying me down the hall. He plops me on his bed and we keep kissing, and in this moment I'm afraid that I'm going to fall in love with him, and that I'm never going to be able to get over it.

‖‖|

"Maybe I should go," I whisper into Felix's mouth.

"Why?"

"What do you mean why?" I kiss him again, long and deep, before slowly pulling away. "Because we've been kissing for a while and the fact that you haven't even tried to take my shirt off is -"

"Oh my god, Reese, I'm sorry, I wasn't- I mean, I didn't not do that because I didn't want to, but you said that you wanted to move slowly with the sexual stuff and I didn't want to make you uncomfortable."

I can't help but laugh. "I know. You didn't let me finish. I was trying to say that you're amazing. You're making me swoon too much."

"Did you just use the word swoon?"

"Yeah, I did." I kiss him again.

"I thought you were leaving."

I sigh. "I should."

"But why? What are you going to do once you get home? Oh wait. Oh shit, what time is it?"

"I don't know, 4:00?" I say, reaching for my phone.

"I have to go to work!"

"Oh no! Are you late?"

"I start at 4:30, but I need to shower, I need to-" he stops himself and sort of clears his throat. "Eat," he finishes.

"Okay. I'll definitely go home, then. I don't want you to get in trouble."

"But I picked you up. I don't think I have time to drive you home."

"Felix, it's fine. I can walk."

"Are you sure?"

"Yes. Get ready for work. I'll talk to you later."

Can I come over when I'm done my shift? Felix texts to me at about 9pm.

Hell yeah you can. When are you done?

11ish?

Sure but I don't know how much fun I'll be.

Too late? he asks.

Not too late.

My buzzer goes off at about 10:45 and I get up right away from the couch so I can let him in. As soon as I buzz him in, I walk down the hall towards the elevator, but then he's coming out of the stairwell and I'm actually startled.

"Whoa," I say. "How did you do that so fast?"

"I took the stairs."

"Yes, because that makes sense."

He smirks at me. "It does when you're a vampire."

"Ha, ha," I mock.

But then we start to walk back towards my apartment together and he grabs my hand and links his fingers through mine. And that right there, just him taking my hand to walk down the hallway, almost makes my knees give out. I lean into him as we walk to my apartment and he presses right back against me.

"How was work?" I ask once we get inside.

"It was great. I can't believe I was almost late, though. I completely lost track of time."

"Me too. It didn't even occur to me that you would have to work. Angela and I both work Monday to Friday and she's basically my only friend so I didn't even think of it. Even though I know you work weekends, I just completely gapped it."

"Is Claire not your friend?"

"Oh, yeah, Claire's my friend. We're just not as close. We usually talk at parties and stuff, or hang out in groups, but I don't think we've actually hung out just us two."

He nods once. "Is it too late for a vampire movie?"

"It might be. I know it's Saturday but I'm such a grandma."

"Okay. What do you want to do, then?"

I just smirk at him, and that's all it takes.

The next time that Felix and I hang out, we make butter tarts together. He says he's never really baked before, and that baking with me would be fun. So I show him how to mix the butter in so that the pastry comes out perfectly, and we take turns adding our own extras to each butter tart. One with pecans, one with raisins, one with chocolate chips, one with peanut butter and jam, one with Reese's Pieces. Of course we have to have one with Reese's Pieces. I make him pour the filling into all of them after, and then we put them in the oven.

Felix slowly and gently pushes me against the counter behind me, and I respond by tugging on his hips. He kisses my neck, just under my ear, and I shiver. He pulls back and smiles, and then I press my mouth against his so we can kiss while we wait for the butter tarts to bake.

By the time they're done, I'm sitting on the counter with my legs wrapped loosely around his thighs, but all our clothes are still on without even any attempt or questions from either of us to take anything off. When the oven timer goes off, I startle a little and pull back from him, and we both laugh. I lean my head into his chest and I feel him tighten for a second, and then feel all of him relax again, as if me pressing back into him was unexpected but desired.

"I love kissing you," I whisper, trying my hardest not to think about the fact that I won't get to kiss him forever.

"Oh good, I was worried for a minute there that you didn't like me at all," he chuckles.

I grin at him but hop off the counter so I can take the butter tarts out of the oven.

"We need to let them cool," I say. "You have to show me how to do one of your things now."

"One of my things?"

"Yeah. What do you like to do besides bring people pizza really quickly and critique vampire movies?"

"I like to run. And climb trees."

"You like to run and climb trees?"

"Yeah. Like, really fast. Inhumanly fast."

"Okay. Let's go, then. Let's go for a run."

"Did you not hear me when I said I liked to go inhumanly fast?"

"You don't like doing it if it's at a regular human speed? Even if it's with me?"

"Oh, if it's with you then I guess going at a regular human speed wouldn't be so bad."

I get changed into something more comfortable for running, and then we drive to Felix's, so that he can get changed into running gear as well.

"Do you sweat?" I ask him as he puts his shoes on at his apartment door.

"No. But it looks weird to other people if they see me running in a pair of jeans, you know? Plus it's still more comfortable even if I don't sweat."

"Alright. Makes sense. Let's go."

We start by running around the outdoor parking lot of his building, the bright white lights casting our shadows across the dark pavement. We head onto the street, avoiding the sidewalk, and I twist my head in a bit of confusion.

"Why are we on the road?" I ask. "Shouldn't we go on the sidewalk?"

He shakes his head. "No, the road is softer."

"What? That's ridiculous. Plus the road is dangerous."

"The road is dangerous? The quiet, empty road that we're currently on?"

"Yes," I say slowly, and he grins at me.

"Okay, get on the sidewalk then," he says. "And tell me the road isn't softer."

"Okay, okay," I say with a sigh. "I'll try it."

I hop over the curb and start to run on the sidewalk, and he's right! Every footfall feels more intense, as if my shoes are stopping abruptly and smacking into the ground instead of just simply landing. When I move back onto the road, I can almost feel the pavement curving around the soles of my shoes and bouncing them back with every step. That's obviously exaggerated, but a good comparison, I think.

Oh no. I'm already out of breath.

"You're not saying anything," he says.

"Because I'm running."

"The road is softer, isn't it?"

"No. It's dangerous."

"Then get back on the sidewalk."

I smile over at him, but I stay on the road.

"That's what I thought," he says with a smirk.

We're right next to the curb anyway, and going against the traffic, so if and when a car does come by, we'll know it's coming.

"You doing okay?" Felix asks, slowing down and keeping pace with me.

"I don't run. I walk a lot. Like, I like to go for walks or hikes, but running is hard."

"If you keep doing it, you'll get stronger and it won't seem so hard anymore."

I look up at him and smile, but my legs are burning and my lungs feel like they can't process the air I'm breathing. I shake my head and stop, leaning forward to put my hands on my thighs. I'm under a flickering streetlight so I force myself to walk until I'm under a light that isn't threatening to burn out.

"That's all you got, Snappy Jack?" Felix calls, still running but looking back at me.

"You go," I say, "You keep going, I just need a break."

He runs back towards me and then stops next to me, taking the same stance as me.

"That was like five minutes," he says.

"I tried, okay?"

"I know! Five minutes is awesome!"

I stand up and put my hands on my hips. "What?"

"You did a really good job."

"I did?"

"Yes! Of course you did! I'm really proud of you!"

"You are?"

"Yes!"

"Oh. Cool." I can't help but smile. I'm still out of breath, but my smile is genuine.

"Let's go eat those butter tarts, now. I think you deserve it."

"So do you, actually," I say. "You did a good job with the pastry."

"Why thank you."

The next time we hang out, Felix isn't working so he comes over to my place almost as soon as I'm done work.

"I have a surprise," he says, holding his hands behind his back.

"Do I have to guess what it is?"

"Yes but I'll give you a hint. Someone named Hank is involved."

"Someone named Hank?" I ask, confused. "I don't know anyone named Hank."

"No, you don't know this person."

"But we know that his name is Hank?"

"Yes."

I start to reach behind his back, but he moves away so that I can't see what he's hiding. "Should I know what you're talking about?" I laugh.

"I thought you should! But I guess I was wrong! Maybe I should have said Carl."

"Oh my god! Did you buy me a giant Carl statue?"

"What? No." He laughs a little and shakes his head, and then takes from behind his back, the actual hardcover of *An Absolutely Remarkable Thing* by Hank Green. "I thought we could read it together. Like, take turns reading out loud."

"Oh my god, no way! Are you serious? You want to read a book out loud with me? Even though you've read spoilery reviews of it?"

"Yeah. I mean, if you want to."

"Of course I want to! Did you bring PJs? We need to get cozy and cuddle up under the covers!" I start running to my room to find anything of mine that might fit him. "This is a cozy clothes emergency!"

Felix ends up just taking his jeans off and gets under my covers in his boxers, but he does put on one of my hoodies, which actually fits him pretty well. It's a little tight in his shoulders and kind of short on his arms, but he smiles and says it's the perfect amount of cozy.

"You're lying," I say. "But thanks."

We hang out a bunch more times over the next few weeks, mostly when he gets off work between 10 and 11pm, and before I absolutely need to be asleep by 1am. If it isn't too late or I'm not too tired, we run together in the humid night air, just until I'm too out of breath to continue. We make it a little further each time we go, but we definitely increase our time by very small increments. Because our runs are still so short, we sometimes watch vampire movies when we get back, after I've showered my sweat off, and Felix has just simply showered. But mostly we take turns reading together until I fall asleep, or until we start kissing instead. We keep moving really slowly, sexual-wise, because I'm not completely comfortable with moving forward, and also because I don't want to do stuff with him and then have it all be over. I know we're supposed to be pretending that that's not going to happen, but it's hard. I pretend by not talking about it, but I surely can't not think about it. All the time I'm thinking about it. All the time I'm thinking about how I'm falling in love with this man and I want more than anything for this to be real and not pretend.

I decide to pretend a little bit in the moment, and take my shirt off. That, I'm comfortable with. He smiles at me before kissing me again and then taking his own shirt off. I press against his bare chest and pretend that we're going to do this every day until I die. I pretend that he's not a vampire, that I was never afraid of him potentially being a murderer, and that as I reach behind my back to unhook my bra, he's probably not fantasizing about drinking my blood.

We finally have a reading night that I'm not too tired for us to read more than a chapter each, and we end up staying up until three in the morning finishing *An Absolutely Remarkable Thing*.

"Is there a 24-hour bookstore in this town?" Felix asks, getting out of bed. "I need the second one right now."

I laugh at him. "You're acting like you didn't already know how it ended."

"Yeah but just someone telling you how it ended in a heated review isn't the same as experiencing it all yourself. Like, it was interesting to read these reviews and see what people thought, but just because I knew what was going to happen, doesn't mean I knew *how* it was going to happen, or how it was going to make me feel. And it made me feel so much more than I thought a book could make me feel. This book was *incredible* and I *know* there's a second book that's already out, that we can start reading immediately."

I'm laughing so hard I can barely breathe.

"Why are you laughing at me?" he whines.

I try to answer him, but I can't catch a breath. I fall back into my pillows and alternate wheezing and laughing for probably another minute before I'm able to calm down.

"Are you done?" he asks.

I giggle a little bit. "You're so fucking adorable," I say with a grin. I climb out of bed and head into my living room. I can feel Felix following me, but I don't say anything or even look back at him. I just make way across the floor in my bare feet until I make it to my bookcase against the far wall. I pull the orange hardcover off its shelf and turn to Felix.

"Oh my god!" He takes it from me and jumps up and down. "Can we start it right now?"

"We might as well."

We read half the book together before I fall asleep against his shoulder.

Felix doesn't work on Monday and comes over as soon as I'm done work. He wants to read before we do anything else, but I laugh and tell him that I need to eat something first.

"Oh shit, my bad," he says. "I guess that's why I brought us taco salads from that new place by the mall."

"Oh yum!"

"I can read first, so you can eat while you listen."

"You're so thoughtful," I say.

"I know." He smiles and we head to the couch to unpack our meals and start reading.

Once we're both done our salads, we read a couple more chapters together, but I can't stop spacing out and just staring at Felix. Admiring him, is more like it. The way he smiles, the way he talks faster when something exciting is happening in the story, the way his fingers flip the pages. Just his face, in general. He's never looked so gorgeous before. He stops any time he notices the way I'm looking at him and asks what's going on, but I just shrug and tell him to keep reading. Finally, the fourth time he notices, he closes the book.

"Are you even listening?" he asks.

"I'm in love with you." It just slips out. Not that it isn't true, but I absolutely didn't mean to say that.

"W- What?" he stammers.

"I'm in love with you. And I'm not pretending, Felix. I've never been pretending."

He licks his lips and swallows, and for a split second I wish I didn't say anything. But then I realize that telling him I love him will change nothing. Whether he feels the same way or not, it's not going to change the way I feel, and it's not going to change what we've experienced together so far. It doesn't matter what he says in return.

"I've been in love with you since I told you I wasn't in love with you," he says. "I mean, at the time, I wasn't really admitting it to myself, but I was 100 percent in love with you."

I can feel my grin stretching across my entire face, and without even thinking, I crawl towards him on the couch and pull myself into his lap.

"I guess you're better at this pretending thing than I am," I say.

He shakes his head. "No. I'm not very good at it either."

I gently twist my fingers through his hair and kiss him, let him pull me closer. I press myself into him and get lost in his touch. His touch that goes farther than it has before. He stops every time we're about to do something new, asking me if I'm sure, or if I'm okay, and every time, I smile into his mouth and say, "Yes. I promise I want this. I want you."

We don't do anything with more than just our hands, with bare chests and unbuttoned pants, but it's so much to me. It means so much, and it feels like so much, in a good way, in the best way possible, and when I wake up in the morning with him still sleeping next to me, I can't bring myself to get out of bed to get ready for work.

"I called in sick," I whisper to him when he wakes up.

"You did? Are you okay?"

I smile and nod. "I want to stay in bed with you all day."

He raises his eyebrows at me. "Is that so?"

"Yes, it's so."

"What are we going to do all day in your bed?"

"I can think of a few things."

He kisses me, long, slow, and deep, and when he finally pulls away, he asks, "Like what?"

"Well for starters, we can finish reading our book."

He laughs so hard that he throws his head back. "Okay, yeah, you got me there."

"You could also make me breakfast in bed."

"Breakfast in bed? For what!?"

"For being in love with me."

"You make a good point, Snappy Jack." He kisses me again, but then ends it much too soon and gets out of bed. "You have to stay here, or breakfast in bed won't work."

"Fair," I sigh.

Felix makes me French Toast with maple syrup and icing sugar, and he smiles as he watches me eat. I give him a few bites of mine but he assures me that he doesn't need more than that. We finish reading *A Beautifully Foolish Endeavor,* and we talk about our favourite parts. And by noon, we've tangled ourselves in the sheets. I don't even give it a second thought when I start to shimmy out of my pyjama pants.

"Wait," he says, out of breath.

"Wait?" I ask, stopping.

"Are you sure you want to keep doing this? Keep moving further, I mean?" he whispers, sitting up.

"Do you want to?"

"Yeah, of course I want to."

"I want to, too."

"I just don't want- I mean I don't think-" he stops and closes his eyes for a second, lets out a slow breath. "I don't want you to get hurt because of it."

"I thought we were pretending, Felix," I say, continuing to take my pants off.

"I know," he says, still seeming like he needs to catch his breath. "But I still don't want any of this to hurt you down the road. I mean, knowing that… I mean-"

"I'm not good at pretending," I say, throwing my pants on the floor and then crawling on top of him. "I haven't been pretending this whole time. I've been thinking about how this is going to come to an end at some point, probably sooner rather than later, but it's tearing me up, Felix. It's tearing me up to know that we have no future. That I have no future with the man I feel the most comfortable with, out of any person I've ever been close to. You're literally the best person I've ever known and I sort of wish that I could crawl inside your chest and stay there forever. I haven't been good at pretending, but right now, I need us to pretend. I need us to pretend that this is going to last until we both die."

"Okay," he says quietly.

"Okay?"

"Yes. I want to pretend with you that this will never end."

I smile against his mouth. "Okay."

He pushes me back into the bed and his tongue sweeps against mine, but then he pulls his mouth away from my lips and kisses my jaw, my neck, my collar bone. His hands wander lower and he starts to pull my underwear down, but this is when I stop him.

"Do we need a condom?" I ask.

"Um, I mean, no?"

"Why did you answer that like a question?"

"Because," he says, kissing my mouth again. "I literally can't have any diseases, and as far as I know, I can't get you pregnant."

"As far as you know?" I say in between kisses.

"Just in case, we can use a condom. Except I don't have any."

"It's okay, I do." I slide out from under him and run to the bathroom, but he gets up and follows me. "As long as they aren't expired." I grab the box out of the cupboard and turn around to see him in just his boxers. "That was fast," I say.

"I thought you would be more comfortable if we were both wearing the same thing."

"You're cute." I lean in and kiss him again, and then I pull his boxers down. "The condoms are good."

"So how's the psycho?" Angela asks one weekend. I'm at her house with her and her husband, and we're making tacos.

"He's not a psycho," I say, rolling my eyes.

"Right. So how is he?"

"He's good." I can't help but smile.

"Reese! Did you guys finally have sex?"

"I'm not… Telling."

"Oh my god, shut up. When?"

"Um, like a week ago?"

She hits me in the shoulder. "Reese! How have you gone an entire week without telling me!? How was it? Have you done it again?"

"It's amazing, and we can't stop doing it."

Josh shakes his head and Angela shoos him away with a rubber spatula. "I'm happy for you," she says. She pours the ground beef into a bowl and I take the shredded cheese over to the table.

"Thanks, I'm happy for me too."

"I can't believe you didn't tell me!"

"I'm sorry," I say. "I just felt weird about it, because of the whole vampire thing."

"Oh my god, can we please stop talking about that? I feel so stupid that I even entertained the idea that he thought he was a vampire, and that you might have believed him. That's ridiculous. Please stop, and instead tell me about his penis."

Josh spits his beer out and it just about flies across the kitchen.

Felix and I are baking brownies together and watching the first few episodes of *The Vampire Diaries,* which Felix says is the best representation so far. He wishes someone could make him a magic sun ring, but is at least glad that he won't immediately burn up in the sun and catch on fire without one.

"Also I don't think sunscreen helps them at all," I add, taking a bite of my third brownie.

"Yes, true, at least I can use sunscreen. Even if I have to reapply it all the time."

We actually end up watching quite a few episodes, and before we know it, it's pushing midnight.

"You can stay the night," I say.

"I would love to, but I actually need, uh, some blood."

"That's okay. I'll come with you to your apartment and I'll watch you drink it."

"How about I just go home and have some, and then come back?"

I sigh. "Fine."

He chuckles and gets up from the couch.

The buzzer wakes me up and scares the shit out of me. I basically fall off the couch. I shake my shoulders out and make my way to the door as quickly as I can.

"Who is it?" I say into the mic.

"Felix."

"Okay I'm letting you in."

I buzz him in and head back to the couch, trying my hardest not to fall asleep in the three minutes it takes him to - Oh, he's opening the door. I forgot how fast he was.

"You look like you're ready to pass out," he says as he comes inside my apartment. He carries me to my room, which is so relaxing I think I might just pass out right this second.

"How was your blood?" I murmur.

He puts me in bed and pulls the covers over me. "It was okay. I just drank it cold."

"Do you... Do you usually heat it up or something?"

He gets under the covers and snuggles up to me. "Yeah," he sighs.

"That's weird."

"It's not, if you think about it. It's warm when you drink it right out of a person, so it makes sense that it would be the most enjoyable that way."

"I guess." I laugh a little but I can't even keep my eyes open at this point.

He kisses me softly on the spot between my eyebrows. "Go to sleep," he whispers.

I wake up in the morning to hear the shower going and instead of getting up and making us both breakfast or something, I take my pyjamas off and climb into the steamy shower with him.

"Good morning, beautiful," he says.

"Good morning, handsome."

I kiss him, but before long he turns me around and starts to wash my hair for me. His hands massaging my scalp is relaxing and comforting, and I lean my head back a little as he lets the water rinse the shampoo away. I turn back around to face him and we kiss slowly under the hot water. Nothing else, just washing each other and kissing.

I come to the kitchen table after getting dressed and toweling my hair off, and Felix is sitting down with two slices of toast cut into four diagonal pieces, and a glass of blood. I feel my heartbeat quicken and can't help but smirk as I sit across from him.

"Hi," I say.

He reaches for the glass, puts his fingers on it, but doesn't pick it up. "Hi."

"Is that toast for me?" I ask, trying to play everything cool.

"Yeah, I thought we could share it. It just has butter and honey on it."

"Delicious." I grab a slice and take a bite.

He picks the glass up and swirls the blood around in it slowly, the dark red liquid staining the sides.

"I brought this from my apartment last night, I hope that's okay," he says.

"Yes, of course it's okay."

He looks away quickly and then takes a little sip. I watch him out of the corner of my eye, but when he sees me, he puts the glass down. I immediately look up at the ceiling and then out the window, as if I've just been caught admiring a crush from across the room. I slowly start to turn back towards him, and watch him put the glass to his lips again. I keep my head slightly turned away, but I watch him completely. I don't know why, but I'm fascinated. I take another bite of my toast and he takes another sip of his blood. I eat, he drinks.

He ends up looking at me every time he takes a sip, and I make sure to take a bite of toast every time to match him. He smirks at me, and I smile back, and at one point he gives a nervous chuckle. I make this weird, snorting type laugh and then he laughs at my snorting, and then I snort again and then a chunk of toast flies out of my nose.

"Eww oh my god, I'm so sorry!" I cry, still laughing. "Is it on you? Did I get it on you?"

He laughs and wipes his cheek, where a nice little soggy piece landed. "You did."

"I'm so sorry."

He shakes his head. "It's quite alright."

"There's so much snot coming out of my nose now," I say, getting up from the table, and laughing so hard at this point I can barely breathe. I get a tissue from the living room and blow my nose a couple times. "Don't keep drinking!" I yell when I realize Felix is probably finishing his glass of blood without me.

"What? Why not?"

"I want to keep watching!" I throw my tissue in the compost and give my hands a quick wash before sitting back down at the table.

"You're weird," Felix says with a smile.

"I'm not the one drinking glass from a blood."

"Glass from a blood?" he raises an eyebrow at me and I start laughing again. "I think this is making you nervous," he says quietly.

"What! No! I'm not nervous, why would I be nervous? You always overthink this stuff too much, Felix. Everything's just really funny."

"Are you sure? I don't want to make you uncomfortable. You're sure you're not overcompensating for the whole… uncomfortableness of watching your boyfriend drink a glass of blood?"

"You're my boyfriend?"

"Oh. Well I mean… I'm not- I mean I didn't-"

I smile at him and he stops. "I just thought we weren't going to label this."

"Did we decide on that? Or was it just brought up?"

"I don't know. Either way, you've never called yourself my boyfriend before."

"Did you like it?"

"Yes I did, as a matter of fact."

"Okay so can I keep calling myself your boyfriend? Can I call you my girlfriend?"

"Yes."

"Are we still pretending?"

"At this point, I can't really do anything else," I admit.

"Me neither."

I nod, and he raises his glass, tips it towards me in a little cheers, and then knocks the rest back in one gulp.

"We have an emergency," I announce the second Felix enters my apartment two nights later.

"What kind of emergency?"

"An Angela-can't-find-out-that-you're-a-vampire-but-also-has-to-think-you're-a-cool-and-supportive-boyfriend kind of emergency."

"Uh oh."

"Yeah. She invited us to go camping with her and Josh."

"Oh no."

"Yeah."

卌III

"Can I just not go?" Felix asks. "I usually work weekends so it wouldn't seem weird that I can't go. Also she didn't exactly give us enough notice for me to book it off."

"You *could* not go. It's true, that's a thing that you could do. It's just that..." I trail off, afraid to continue and seem unreasonable.

"It's just that what? I'm sure they would understand."

"Ugghh," I groan, tilting my head back. "My last boyfriend never used to go with me to things. And I always said it was fine. Angela and Josh used to rent a cottage every summer and they always invited us to go with them, and he never would. Even just dinners with friends, or parties, he would make me go without him. He always said he needed alone time and I agreed that it was easy and made sense for him to do that when I was doing things with Angela and Josh. I always thought I was being chill and understanding and I never questioned it."

He raises his eyebrows but lets me continue.

"He was cheating on me," I finish.

"What?" Felix half shouts.

"Yeah," I say shortly. "Every damn time. Every time Angela and Josh invited us to do something just the four of us, or even invited us to a group event, he never came because he wanted to have sex with someone who wasn't me."

"Oh my god what a shithead."

"Yeah," I sigh. "So you have to come. If you weren't a vampire, this would be a red flag for me. And for Angela. She watches out for me."

"Even if I really can't get the time off work? Like it's less than two weeks away, the schedule's already out."

"Oh shit, you're right. Are you working?"

He sighs and looks at his phone. "I'm working dinner on Friday and Sunday, but I'm off Saturday."

"You know what isn't a red flag for this situation? Just going for part of the trip, or asking if we can schedule it for a better time. We could still go Saturday. Or go closer to the middle of September."

"I can't go Saturday. I can't go camping at all, Reese, I'll fry."

"Even with lots of sunscreen?"

He sighs. "I'll literally go through a bottle a day."

"So what if we don't show up until the evening on Saturday? We can tell them you're working lunch on Saturday and you can't get out of it. We'll get there around supper, and we'll be in the shade of the trees for eating, and by the time we're done, the sun will be going down kind of soon, we can hang out by the fire all night, stay up as late as possible, and *accidently*," I say, making air quotes with my fingers, "sleep in too late on Sunday."

"Hmm." He narrows his eyes at me.

"Minimal sun exposure, and you don't look like a scrotum who might be cheating on me. And bonus, I don't look like a stupid girl who keeps accepting guys who never want to do anything with me and my friends."

"It could work," Felix says.

"Yeah?"

He smiles at me and nods. "Yeah, I think you're a genius."

"Of course I'm a genius. I've always been a genius."

"Oh, have you?"

"Yes, as a matter of fact, I have."

"I can't believe you're not coming until after five on *Saturday!*" Angela whines. "We planned it to be the week before Labour Day on purpose, so that he *could* get the weekend off and come with us!"

"Well you didn't plan it far enough in advance," I say. "You forget that he actually has to book time off."

"Yeah, sorry about that," she says. "But what are Josh and I going to do all day without you?"

"Go canoeing? Swim? Hike? Read a book? Have sex?"

Angela fake gasps and puts her hand over her mouth. Then she shrugs and laughs a little. "Actually yeah, those all sound like great ideas. But I wanted to finally have a foursome weekend, you know? Fuckface always ruined that for us and now you finally have a boyfriend who isn't a piece of shit, no offence, and we still can't have the whole weekend! It isn't going to be as fun!"

"We can still make smores, and roast hot dogs or sausages, and play cards, and drink, and do all the fun camping things!"

"But it won't be for as long! Why don't you come with us Friday night and Felix can join us when he's done work on Saturday?"

I just give Angela a head tilt. I don't need to say anything for her to know why I'm not going alone on Friday night.

"You don't think he's making an excuse, do you?" she asks quietly.

"Do you?"

"No."

"I don't either. But I would still rather go with him. Plus he invited me to sleep over on Friday night since we won't be camping with you guys. He said we're going to make our own camp in his living room so I don't feel like I've missed out on too much of it."

"Are you serious?"

I grin and nod my head.

"Oh my god, Reese, this man is amazing. I can't believe we thought he was a murderer."

Turns out Felix wasn't just making up a cover story when he said we would make a campsite in his living room. When he opens the door to his apartment, I gasp. Like I literally gasp. Because this guy has put a tent in his living room. The opening is unzipped to show white glowing twinkle lights surrounding an air mattress with pillows and a big floofy comforter spilling over its edges. Just outside of the tent sits a plastic bonfire made from Fisher Price or something, and a giant bag of marshmallows.

"Felix, you did all this?" I ask.

"No, everything was like this when I got home from work. I thought it seemed weird."

I laugh and shove my shoulder into him. "You're amazing."

"I know."

We crawl into the tent and immediately start kissing, but after about ten minutes, Felix pulls back and says that we're supposed to play Go Fish and Madlibs.

"Why?" I ask.

"Because that's what you do when you go camping. We also have to sit by the plastic fire." He gets out of the tent and I follow him. "It lights up and makes crackling noises!" Felix turns on a switch under one of the plastic logs and the whole things glows in pulses of red. "We can't make smores because the fire isn't real, but we can still eat marshmallows."

We sit cross legged in front of the pretend fire, eating raw marshmallows but pretending to toast them first, while we pretend that our relationship isn't doomed.

I guess I am getting pretty good at this pretending thing.

"Okay wait, hang on, hang on," Felix says, a sharp panic in his tone.

I stop with my hand on the doorhandle of his car and turn to look at him. "I swear we didn't miss any spots," I say.

"Yeah but I need my hat and my sunglasses."

"You're wearing them."

"Right."

"Felix. It's going to be fine. We're in the forest anyway, we're covered in shade."

He sighs and nods his head once. "You're right."

"I know I'm right. They're going to be wondering what we're doing."

A knock on the window makes me jump. "What are you doing!?" Angela calls through the glass.

"We're just talking!" I shout back to her.

"Well talk out here! We've been waiting for you since yesterday evening! Get your butts out here!"

Felix and I nod at each other and get out of the car.

"Hi Felix!"

"Hi Angela." I can hear the smile in his voice and it makes me happy.

"This is my husband, Josh."

Josh immediately shakes his hand, and I watch his expression for any signs of suspicion. Does he notice the strangeness of his temperature? Is he looking in his eyes for signs of murderous thoughts? It seems like he doesn't notice anything, because once they're done shaking hands, which is about half a second later, Josh waves us over to the middle of the campsite. The sun comes through in random patches between leaves, but Felix notices them and avoids them without even making it look like he tried.

"We should go swimming before it gets dark," Angela suggests.

"Why don't you two go, and I'll set up our tent," Felix replies.

"Okay!" I grab my towel from the car, give him a kiss on the cheek and practically drag Angela to the beach.

"But why isn't Felix coming?" Angela asks.

"He just said he's setting up our tent. If he comes with us, we'll be setting it up in the dark. Plus he can bond with Josh."

"Ugh. Fine. I just wanted to get to know him better. See how he interacts with you."

"Why?"

"I worry about you. I just want to make sure you're not dating another douchebag."

"I'll leave him at the first sign of douchebaggery, I promise."

"Okay."

We make it to the beach and lay our towels out in the sand. Luckily there aren't too many people here; just a few families set up with umbrellas and mini barbeques so they can have supper on the lake.

"You know he set up a campsite in his living room last night," I say as I take my top off to reveal my blue bikini.

"What?"

"Yeah. He set up a tent and had this toy bonfire that lit up and made noises. It was adorable."

"Plus he reads your favourite books with you. I think Josh is pretty perfect but even he doesn't do that."

"Maybe Felix will teach him a thing or two while they're together."

"Hmm yes, this could be a good thing."

I smile and take my shorts off so I can follow her into the water. We go until the water is up to our shoulders and we just float and bob around while we talk mostly about Felix. We talk about him until we're both shivering and the sun is starting to set.

We walk back to our campsite with our towels over our shoulders and our clothes in our hands. The boys are starting a fire when we arrive, and I smile at our tent that's been set up.

"Did you ladies have fun?" Josh asks.

"Of course we did," Angela replies.

"I'm going to get changed in the tent," I announce. Felix follows me almost immediately, and I think something's wrong. "Are you okay?" I ask.

"Yeah, I just didn't want to be alone with the two of them," he whispers.

"Really? Why not?"

"Josh was grilling me the whole time that you guys were gone, and I feel like they're going to gang up on me if you're not there."

"Oh my god, Felix, I'm so sorry."

He shrugs. "It's fine, they're just looking out for you. And also they thought I was a murderer before, so I guess it's okay. I just didn't want to give them an opportunity."

"Okay."

I get changed into a pair of shorts and a hoodie and we go back to the bonfire together, where Josh and Angela are roasting hotdogs on sticks. We break into the cooler of beer before our helping of seconds, and start playing Never Have I Ever without even really deciding to. I'm not sure how it starts, really, but I know that I'm fairly drunk and Felix has to help me put my condiments on my hotdog because I keep laughing at everything and I can't spread the mayo good enough.

"Seriously though, why wouldn't you just get squirty mayo if you knew we were having hotdogs?" I say, licking a glob of it off my finger. "It's so much easier, especially when alcohol is involved."

"We're not children, Reese. We can scoop the mayo with a spoon like normal human beings," Angela says with a smile.

"Never have I ever used a *spoon* to spread mayo," I laugh.

"What! It's way easier than using a knife!" Josh steps in.

"But not easier than squirty mayo!"

"Never have I ever bought squirty mayo," Angela giggles.

Felix smirks and takes a drink of his beer, and then he eyes me and raises his eyebrows. "Why aren't you drinking?" he asks. "You just admitted to everyone that you like squirty mayo. Are you saying you've never purchased it yourself?"

"What?" I laugh and Felix puts his fingers under my beer bottle, guiding it to my mouth. "What's happening?" I laugh, but take a drink.

"We're playing Never Have I Ever," Josh says.

"Never have I ever had sex on a rollercoaster!" I half shout.

"Okay that's ridiculous, no one has done that," Angela says. "Never have I ever had a blood drive in my house." And then she looks very seriously and conspicuously at Felix.

He shrugs and takes a drink.

"Good," Angela says with a smile.

"Never have I ever," Felix starts, "Uhh, been to Wonderland."

"What!" the other three of us shout simultaneously.

"With an answer like that, why are none of you drinking?" he questions.

We all shrug and drink.

"Never have I ever been to Disney," I say, and Josh and Angela both drink.

"Never have I ever murdered someone," Josh says.

Angela hits Josh in the shoulder. "That was too obvious," she says.

"I haven't seen him refuse to drink yet," he says not so under his breath.

"You haven't seen him *refuse*?" I ask, instantly mad at them. "How long do we have to drink in this game if we've done the thing in question? Is there a time limit? Also what kind of a question is that!?"

"An important one, I think!" Josh shoots back.

"Yeah but you can't just ask someone if they're a murderer," Angela says.

"Guys, this is ridiculous," I say. "Plus he's not drinking!" I don't know why, but I feel like adding that part is important.

"I didn't!" Josh continues, not hearing me. "I stated that I have never murdered someone, in a game of Never Have I Ever, it's very different."

"Guys!" I shout again.

They both stop and look at me, and then at Felix who has now put his drink on the ground next to him.

"Sorry," they both say.

But then Josh turns to Angela and says, "That doesn't even mean anything! As if a murderer would just admit to the people he's sharing a campsite with that he's a murderer."

"Maybe we should stop talking so loudly about people being murderers," Felix suggests. "There are other people at this campground. And uh, families?"

"You're right," Angela says. "We're being completely unreasonable and inappropriate."

"Are we though?" Josh adds.

"Are you guys serious?" I ask.

Angela shakes her head at the same time that Josh says "Yes."

"Why would you invite us to camp with you if you still thought he was a murderer?"

"We don't think he's a murderer," Angela says.

Josh raises his eyebrows at her.

"Okay, I don't think he's a murderer," Angela corrects. "Josh isn't so sure."

"What!?" I screech.

"No offense, Reese, but your last two boyfriends were awful people. You don't really seem to pick good ones, and since bad things come in threes, I just…" he sighs and gives Felix a sympathetic look. "I'm sure you're not actually a murderer, but I'm not so sure you're right for her."

"Okay." Felix nods and gets up from his chair.

"Where are you going?"

"I'm going to bed. They're clearly not comfortable with me being here, so I'll leave in the morning. You can stay here with them for the rest of the weekend if you want."

"This is ridiculous," I say, turning back to Angela and Josh. "He's not a murderer. He's literally amazing. He's the best guy I've ever met. He's even better than you, Josh. And you were pretty high up there on that list, buddy."

"But I'm not anymore?"

"No, because you won't believe me that my boyfriend's not a murderer."

"I think we've used the word murderer too much," Angela half whispers.

"Just because he saved a blood drive and tried to make a joke out of it, you guys all think he's this psychopath, but he's just an awkward guy who did something good! But this man is literally the best. He's so thoughtful, and caring, and funny, he makes me feel so calm and safe. I've never felt so safe with someone before. He gives me, like, the opposite of butterflies."

Angela scrunches her nose at me in a sort of question.

"Instead of erupting something inside me, he settles everything. There's no questions, there's nothing to worry about. He's just him, and when I'm with him, I'm just me. I'm so unapologetically me, without even having to think about it. I've never felt this way with anyone before. I mean, yeah, I was nervous with him a little bit at first, but that's because I didn't know him. I didn't know where this was going. And I guess I still don't really know where it's going, but I don't even care at this point. I'm just enjoying spending my time with him so much that it doesn't even matter if we won't last forever. Because he will always be this warm thing in my chest, this comforting thought, and if it comes down to it, a cherished memory."

"Josh," Angela whispers, "look at the way Felix is looking at our friend. Look at his face. At his eyes. Can you see the way he's looking at her? He's so in love with her it's not even funny."

And I know she told Josh to look at Felix, but I turn and look at him too. And it's true. His smile is soft and quiet, and his eyes are filled with longing. They're almost wet with tears, and without taking his eyes off me, he says to Josh and Angela, "I don't care what you two think of me. Not when my girlfriend feels that way about me." He takes a step towards me and grabs onto my hand. Then he glances at them as he says, "I promise we'll be quiet." And he leads me back to the tent.

"Wait, wait," Felix whispers before we get completely naked.
"What?"

"I just remembered that you're way more drunk than I am."
"So?"

"So I'd be taking advantage."

"But you're drunk too. Who says I'm not taking advantage of you?"

"Me. I say that. I'm hardly even buzzed."

"But I'm not that drunk," I whine, kissing him under his ear.

"You're pretty drunk, actually," he says with a soft laugh.

"But they think we're doing it in here."

"So? We don't have to update them on our progress."

"But I want to do it," I whine again.

"We can do it later, when you're sober," he whispers.

"Can we keep kissing at least?" I ask.

"Maybe we should talk."

"About what?"

"About what you said out there."

"I don't know what there is to say about it." I lean in to kiss him but he pulls back a little.

"I feel the same way about you," he starts, "except for the last part. About you being okay with this not lasting."

"What do you mean?"

"I don't want this to end. I don't even want to pretend anymore that it isn't going to end, I mean I actually don't want it to. I don't want to hear about your death 60 years from now, I don't want to exist in this world if you don't."

"That's a little intense," I say slowly.

"Sorry. You're right. That's way too intense. We don't have to talk about this."

"Well like, wait, hold on," I backtrack.

Felix chuckles and tucks a chunk of hair behind my hair. "Okay," he says. "I'm holding on."

"Does this mean you want to turn me into a vampire?" I whisper.

All he does in response is shrug.

"Mmm, no, you're right, I don't want to talk about this right now," I say.

"Okay."

"Can we keep kissing, though?"

"Yes, we can keep kissing," he says with a smile. "No touching, though."

"Uggghhh fine."

Felix shakes me awake and I groan.

"You need to drink water," he whispers. "Or you'll be really hungover."

"I think it's too late," I say, half sitting up. He's turned on a little camping lantern in the corner of the tent so I can see, but it's making my head pound. The tent walls spin around me as I take the water bottle from him.

"I should have made sure you had some before you fell asleep, I'm sorry."

"The severity of my hangover isn't your responsibility," I say.

"Still."

I drink almost the entire bottle in one breath and then groan again. "What time is it?" I ask.

"2am."

"Okay so there's still lots of time for me to recover from this." I lean into him and press my head into his neck.

"Absolutely," he replies.

"I don't know if I want to be a vampire," I say quietly.

I can feel him nod, and then he says, "I'm sorry I brought that up. You don't even have to think about that being a possibility. This isn't something I would ever expect you do to."

"You want me to, though."

"Hmm?"

I pull back a little and look up him. "Expecting something from someone and wanting something from someone are two completely different things."

"It doesn't matter what I want."

"Why aren't you with the girl who turned you? She turned you because you were in love, right? So where is she now?"

He sighs and lies back down on the air mattress, bringing me with him. I nuzzle up under his arm and rest my head in the space between his shoulder and his chest.

"She cheated on me," he finally says.

"Are you serious?"

"Yeah," he says with a bit of a laugh.

"So we've both been cheated on."

"Yeah," he says again.

"Did she cheat on you with another vampire?"

"With several other vampires."

"For real?" I sit up again, and lean on my elbow.

He nods. "She actually did it a long time ago too, but she convinced me that it was normal for vampires to be like that. To be restless and to feel like nothing is ever enough. That it wasn't anything against me and there was nothing I could do to make her not want others as well as me. And I was stupid. I mean hell, I let her turn me into a vampire, so of course I believed her. Of course I accepted it and tried not to be hurt over it. And to be honest, I'm not sure if she stopped, or if she just got better at hiding it, or if I got better at pretending it wasn't happening, but for a long time I thought everything was perfect between us. That we were perfect for each other. That letting her turn me into an immortal creature was a good idea." He laughs but I'm not sure what to say. "Anyway, she did it again a few years ago and she tried to make me feel like it was my fault for being upset, that I knew what I was getting into when I let her turn me, and when I decided to stay with her."

"Whoa. Talk about toxic."

"Yeah."

"What was it like?" I ask. "When she... when she turned you?"

"Weird," he replies. "At first I felt really good, like I was high on some kind of uppers. And then I crashed. And I couldn't breathe, and my whole body shook, and I was sweating, and then I just... Died? I don't know. When I woke up, everything was super loud and super bright and just, super everything, really. All my senses were so heightened, and it took a while to get used to it."

"Did you want to eat people?"

"At first I did, yeah. But only because at first, everything is so new and overwhelming and this instinct sort of takes over. This instinct that tells you blood will quiet everything down. And at first it's all you can think about. I guess the same way a drug addict will do anything to get another hit. I feel weird saying it because of how terrible she ended up being, but she calmed me down so well every time. She taught me how to control myself and how to drink blood without gorging myself on it."

"Well that's good."

"Yeah."

It's quiet for a few minutes, so I grab the water bottle and finish it off. Felix gets up and opens his bag, pulls out another bottle for me. I take it and drink most of it right away.

"Would you do that for me? I mean- if- *if* you turned me?"

"Of course I would. But look, we haven't been together for very long, and that was such a spur of the moment thought that came out. You don't have to even think about it. We can stay together for as long as you're comfortable with, and then we can part ways and you can remember me with fondness."

I look into his eyes for a good fifteen seconds before I nod and quietly say, "Okay."

"Okay."

"I need to pee."

Felix chuckles and nods. "I'll come with you. So you don't get attacked slash eaten by a bear."

"Good call."

We unzip the tent as quietly as we can and crawl out into the dark campground. I turn back to grab the lantern or a flashlight, but Felix shakes his head at me.

"It's fine, I can see," he says.

"You can see out there? It's so dark."

"Vampire, remember? Any small light source even from far away is enough for me to see."

"Okay, sure, but I can't see."

The corner of his mouth curls as he says, "I can guide you."

I roll my eyes and smile at him, and together we get up and start to make our way to the washrooms. I link our arms together and press the side of my body into his so that I don't trip on anything I can't see. He laughs a little at me and I look up at him, even though I can barely make out more than his face shape.

"Why are you laughing?" I say playfully. "I literally can't see."

"It's just cute. You're cute."

"I know."

There are lights on the washroom building, so once we get a bit closer, I can start to make out shapes and things around us. Felix follows me into the women's side and leans against the sinks while I head into a stall.

"How do you pee and stuff when you're dead?" I ask once I start peeing.

"What do you mean?"

"If you're dead, how does your body digest things?"

"I don't know," he says. "Plus I'm not dead. I'm undead. It's different."

"What does that even mean?"

"I don't know," he says with a chuckle. "I'm basically dead, but also I'm not."

"Oh yes, that makes complete sense, thanks for explaining," I laugh.

And then everything in my body freezes. My blood comes to a still in my veins. My heart stops beating, and I suddenly can't breathe. Because someone in another stall sneezes. There's someone else in here with us! Someone else who heard us talking about Felix being undead! Oh my god. Did we use the word vampire? No. I don't think so. How did Felix not know someone else was in here? Couldn't he smell her blood? Hear her breathing? I thought he had superhuman senses! What do I do? What do I say? How do we fix this?

"Gesundheit," Felix says without hesitating.

"Um. What?" the person in the stall replies.

"You sneezed."

"Yes?"

"It's German," I say. "It's bless you in German except it means good health. Or maybe just health."

"Yeah," Felix says, with a tone that tells me he's pleasantly surprised I knew that. "I just like that sentiment better."

"Okay." The person in the stall doesn't sound impressed and I wonder if she just thinks we're freaks and wants to leave as soon as possible.

"I'm going to wait outside, okay, Reese?" Felix says gently.

"Yeah, okay."

I hear his footsteps leave, and once the door shuts behind him, the girl in the other stall flushes. I flush too, because I'm done, but I feel weird about seeing her outside of the stalls. Is she going to tell anyone about what we were talking about? Should I wait until she leaves before I wash my hands? I listen for the water to come out of the tap, and then I hear the air dryer come on, and then she leaves. I let out a deep breath and open my stall door.

"What were you talking about?"

"Oh my god," I say, startled. My heart leaps into my throat as a woman about my age closes in on me. Did she seriously pretend to leave so that she could confront me?

"Tell me what you were talking about," she pries.

"No thanks. It was private." I try to push past her but she steps to the side to stay in my way.

"Why were you talking about it in a public washroom, then?"

"We didn't realize anyone else was in here."

"Tell me."

"Or what?" I ask.

She just stares at me, her bottom jaw set forward a bit, as if she's trying to look menacing. She doesn't look menacing though, she looks really nervous. "Or I'll- I'll hurt you," she stammers.

"You'll hurt me? With my undead boyfriend right outside the door?"

She tries to come up with a response but she stumbles over her words, just saying sounds, really.

"That's what I thought." I smile at her and push her with my shoulder. She steps back with her mouth gaping open at me. I wash my hands, and then I flick the water off them into the sink, all while staring back at her. She blinks a few times and watches as I put my hands under the air dryer, letting the powerful warm air push across my skin. "Okay goodnight," I say to her, in the most pleasant tone I can muster. And she scoffs as I smile and then head for the door.

"Everything okay?" Felix asks once I come out of the washroom.

"Why didn't you intervene?" I whisper.

"Because I knew I didn't need to." He tilts his head in the direction of our campsite. "Come on, let's get back."

I link my arm through his again and rest my head on his shoulder as we walk.

"Didn't you know she was in there?" I ask. "Couldn't you hear her breathing or something?

He shakes his head. "It's easy not to hear stuff like that when you aren't looking for it. Especially when you've been around as long as I have."

I nod and sigh, and then look behind us.

"She isn't following us, if that's what you're thinking," Felix says.

"She was so weird. Why was she so insistent in finding out what we were talking about? I would have thought that she was just going to go tell her friends that she heard two freaks talking in the bathroom."

Felix sighs. "I'm not the only one like me, you know. There are more of us. A lot of us, actually. I've encountered people like her before."

"What do you mean?" I ask.

"She's probably witnessed something she can't explain. Heard things, saw things, maybe even had contact with someone like me and something happened. Hearing us talk about what we were talking about is her link to proven sanity."

"Oh my god, do you think?"

He shrugs. "Probably. She just wants someone to tell her that she isn't imagining it."

"Should I go find her?"

"No, no."

"Well what do we do?"

"Nothing."

"Nothing?" I ask. "But she's going beat herself up over this. Mentally, it can't be-"

"We can't risk it," he interrupts. "Her sanity isn't our responsibility. Maybe hearing other people talk about it so casually was enough for her. But we can't go around telling everyone that vampires are real; everyone would freak out. The whole world would probably go into chaos."

"Not necessarily," I say.

"I don't think I want to take the chance."

We get back into our tent and snuggle up under our unzipped sleeping bag.

"Are you feeling any better?" Felix asks.

"Yeah, a little. I'll probably feel pretty decent once I've had more sleep."

"Good."

"I just can't stop thinking about that poor girl."

"She'll be fine."

I let out a deep breath and close my eyes. "Okay," I say slowly.

"Goodnight, Reese."

"Night, Snappy Jack."

卌 卌

"Why are you two still sleeping!?" Angela shouts, startling me awake.

"Jesus," I say, sitting up a little. "What time is it?"

"It's almost eleven! You're missing the whole day! Josh and I already had breakfast and went paddle boarding! What are you doing in there!?"

"I woke up sick in the middle of the night," I say through the still closed tent. "We got to sleep pretty late."

"Well get up! We want to go canoeing!"

"Is it sunny out?" I ask.

"Yes, it's gorgeous! But bring your sunscreen!"

I look at Felix with probably the most cringiest cringe that could ever exist on my face.

"What do we do?" I ask him.

He sighs and starts to get out from under the blanket. "I brought UV clothes. I'll be okay for a bit."

We get dressed and I throw my hair up in a ponytail to hide how terrible it looks, and Angela literally cheers when we emerge from the tent. The air is too humid for my liking, and I sort of feel like I'm going to barf.

"Welcome to the land of the living!" Angela says after she's jumped up and down three times. "Felix, you're going to be hot in long sleeves, you should put on a different top so you don't die out on the water."

"I'll be okay," he says with a smile.

"No seriously, it's already like 30 degrees and the sun is strong out on the lake."

"Yeah, I actually burn really easily, so this is a UV top. It's nice material though, it's meant to wear on hot days."

"Okay," she says, clearly not convinced.

"I need water and Advil before we go anywhere," I announce.

"I have Advil," Angela says, going back to her tent. I open Felix's car and grab a water bottle from the case in his backseat, and immediately drink half of it. Angela brings me some extra strength Costco brand ibuprofen and I swallow them with more water.

Felix hands me a granola bar and I thank him and force myself to eat it.

"Feeling better?" Josh asks.

I let out a deep breath and nod. "A little." It's going to take a bit for the ibuprofen to kick in, but the water and granola bar helped to ease my queasiness.

I gesture for Felix to turn around so I can put sunscreen on the back of his neck, and then he takes it from me and puts it on his ears, his face, the front of his neck, and his hands.

"Wow, that's fancy sunscreen," Angela says, eyeing Felix's SPF 100. It does look fancy. It's in a semi-translucent blue container with a white screw-on lid, and looks like he spent about 80 bucks at Sephora on it.

"Yeah, it's hard to get SPF 100," Felix says casually.

"Why is your sunscreen so strong?" she asks.

"Because my skin is really sensitive."

"He burns in about 45 seconds," I say. "To a crisp. I've seen it, it's really bad."

Angela laughs and nods, and then grabs onto Josh's shirt, pulling him along with us as we start to walk.

"Sandals?" Josh asks, looking down at Felix's hightops.

"No, I'm good."

"Those are going to get soaked."

"They're Vessis," Felix says. "They're waterproof."

"Alright whatever." Josh doesn't seem too convinced, or even thrilled that we're still on this trip with him and his wife. I think he's trying, though.

The four of us walk over to the canoe rental station in complete silence, and it's the most awkward I've felt in a long time. Even more awkward than the time Josh accused Felix of being a murderer basically to his face while we played a drinking game. Last night.

"Felix isn't a murderer," I blurt out.

"Reese," Felix says quietly, shaking his head at me with a bit of a frown. "It's fine."

"I know he isn't," Angela says. "And Josh also knows that."

"Yeah," he monotones. Angela hits him in the shoulder. "I mean, yeah," he adds more enthusiastically. "Of course he isn't a murderer. That's just silliness."

"I mean if you think about it, realistically, I would have murdered you all last night," Felix offers. "If I was a murderer, I wouldn't want talk getting out about me possibly being a murderer. You argued about whether or not you thought I was a murderer, right in front of me. If I really was a murderer, I would have taken you out then. Gotten rid of any evidence."

"Felix, stop saying murderer," I say, leaning into him a little.

"He's got a point," Angela says.

"Whatever, let's just go canoeing," Josh says quietly.

"He's normally nicer than this, I swear," I whisper.

Felix just shrugs.

We get to the canoe rental station and Felix pays for all of us. Angela tries to object, but Josh tells her to stop and let him pay. We get our life jackets on while the attendant pulls our canoes down, but Felix helps me tighten the buckles on my vest. I notice Josh watching us with judging eyes, so I make sure to stand up straight and smile at him over Felix's shoulder as he bends down a little to make sure my life jacket is on securely. Josh half smiles at me before turning to Angela, and then Felix straightens up in front of me.

"Are you ready?" he asks me.

"I think the question is, are *you* ready?"

"As ready as I can be. Wait, you brought the sunscreen, right?"

"Oh my god!" I gasp and throw my hands over my mouth. But I feel too mean already, and before he can reply, I say, "Of course I brought it."

He smiles at me. "Okay good. I brought mine too, because I can't rely on other people to keep me from literally burning up in the sun, but I'm glad you were thinking of me."

We grab our canoe and carry it to the water, just in between us, each of us taking a side. Felix nods for me to get in first so he can push the canoe and get in the back. I step across to the seat at the front and put my bag in front of my feet. Felix pushes the canoe a little and gets in before the water seeps over the tops of his shoes. Once he's seated, he pushes his paddle into the shore a little to give us an extra jolt forward, and we're off!

"How'd those sneakers work out for ya!?" Josh calls, actually sounding interested.

"Great!" he calls back, giving him a thumbs up. "My feet are bone dry!"

"For real?"

"For real!"

Josh nods a little. "Cool."

"Let's canoe to that island over there!" Angela calls from the front of their canoe.

"Yeah, let's race!" I say.

"No, I don't wanna race," Felix says. "Isn't canoeing supposed to be relaxing?"

"Sounds like loser talk to me," Josh shouts.

I look back at Felix who lowers his head a little and shakes it a few times. I can see him trying not to smile as big as he is.

"You can't make us look suspicious," I say to him.

"I won't," he grins. Then looks over at Angela and Josh. "On the count of three?"

"One," Angela starts.

"Two!" I shout.

"Three!" Josh yells as he slams the tip of his paddle into the water and starts to thrust them forward.

"You don't have to do anything, Reese, except make it look like you are, okay?" Felix laughs.

"Got it." I laugh a bit too, and start to paddle, switching sides every so often, as if I know what I'm doing.

Felix does a pretty good job of pushing us faster than Angela and Josh's canoe, but not so fast that it seems impossible. I smile as we pass them, but it just makes Josh paddle harder, and Felix lets them pass us for the briefest of moments. I think Felix is rather enjoying this, and I think he's enjoying even more the fact that Josh seems to be so angry about it all. For the twenty or so minutes that it takes us to canoe to the island, Felix lets Josh and Angela pass us five or six times, and the last time he lets them stay ahead of us for probably three minutes.

"Your arms tired back there!?" Josh calls to us.

"Of course they are!" Felix replies. "And I have calluses on my palms already!" But that's when he speeds up for the final stretch and passes the other two just before sliding up onto the shore.

[182]

Josh groans and Angela immediately drops her paddle into the canoe.

"My arms are rubber," she says.

"We went pretty hard there, didn't we?" Josh says to her. "Like we hardly even took any breaks during that. We're pretty strong."

"Yes we are."

Josh gets out of the canoe and drags it up the shore with Angela still sitting in it, and then he leans over and kisses her.

"Aw," I say out loud.

"That was really good," Felix says. "I don't think anyone else could have come all the way out here that fast. You guys are definitely strong!"

Angela blushes and smiles, and Josh just nods.

"For real," Felix adds. "I'm impressed. I'm impressed by all of us!"

"I need to eat," Angela says, pulling a towel out of her bag and laying it on the sand.

"I need to put more sunscreen on," Felix says.

Felix reapplies his SPF 100 and I help to make sure he gets it behind his ears and behind his neck where his shirt could pull down. We sit down on our towels and share strawberries and Miss Vickie's Pepper and Lime chips with Angela and Josh. Angela and Josh go in the water, but when Felix declines, I stay back with him. We lie down on the sand and after Felix covers his face with his hat, I cuddle up to him and let him put his arm around me. Normally it would be too hot to cuddle with someone like this, but Felix always stays the same temperature, so it's actually really comfortable.

"Your headache gone?" he asks.

"Yes, thankfully."

"Good. But now I feel a little sick so I need to move to the shade."

"You feel sick from the sun?" I ask, getting up and helping move our towels.

"Yeah," he sighs.

We curl up under the shade of a tree, and then Angela starts to stroll over to us from the water.

"I think I'm getting a burn. Can I borrow some sunscreen?" she asks.

"Yeah of course," I say, grabbing mine from my bag and handing it to her.

"What time do we have the camping site until, by the way?" I ask.

"Four," she says. "We still have some time."

"Oh wait, don't you have to work dinner?" I ask Felix.

"No, Claire took my shift for me."

"Really?"

"Yes, really."

"Aw. Claire's the best."

"I thought I was the best?"

"Actually, I thought I was the best," I say.

"Why would you say that Claire's the best if you thought you were the best?"

We decide to canoe back at a leisurely pace, taking breaks to place the paddles across our laps and admire the scenery around us. The water is fairly calm, but there are random little waves every now and then, making us sway and bob on top of the water.

"Reese, a loon!" I look back at him so I can see where he's pointing, and then my eyes find the black and white bird glide down towards the water. It slides across the surface on its belly before gracefully righting itself and floating like a duck.

"That was so cool!" I shout, excited. "I've never seen a loon land before!"

"Aw I'm glad you caught it, then!"

I turn back to smile at him, and he smiles too, his expression warm and calming. I suddenly want to melt into the canoe and live here forever as a puddle. A warm, gentle, comforting puddle. Felix can be a puddle with me too, if he wants.

We watch the loon bob up and down over the little waves for a while, and I casually hang my hand over the edge of the canoe, and lean over a bit so I can play with the water a little. Just when I'm about to start paddling again, Felix speaks up.

"My sunscreen isn't in my bag." The worry in his voice makes my breath catch.

"What?" I turn back to him to see him frantically pulling things out of his backpack.

"Hang on," I say, "maybe I have it. If I don't I at least have SPF 50."

"Okay, that'll do."

"Oh shit," I add, "I think Angela still has my sunscreen."

"Are you kidding me?"

I look in my bag and breathe a sigh of relief when I see Felix's fancy sunscreen sitting on top of my balled-up towel. I unscrew the top for him and reach behind me to hand it to him but as I turn around, it slips out of my wet fingers and lands in the water, sinking hard and fast.

"Oh no! No no no no!" I shout, almost jumping in after it.

"Shit," Felix breathes. "Shit shit shit shit."

"Angela! Do you still have my sunscreen!?"

"Aww no, they're so far ahead of us!" Felix shouts, as we both only now notice them in the distance.

"Felix I'm so sorry!" My eyes well with tears.

"It's okay, you didn't do it on purpose," he says quickly. "But I have to get us back right now."

"There are so many people around, Felix," I say.

"No one's paying attention, it's fine. I'll slow down once we get closer to shore."

He paddles so strongly and pushes us so fast that wind blows across my face and I'm worried that someone will see. Worried that something will happen because of it. I try to paddle too, to at least make it look like two of us are making the canoe go this fast, but for some reason I feel like I'll tip out if I do, so I keep the paddle across the edges, over my lap, and grip my fingers around it so tightly that they almost hurt.

He slows us down once we're close enough for people to notice our speed, and I look back at him. His hands are already red, and the expression on his face tells me he's trying not to barf.

"Will you bring the canoe back?" he asks, getting out while the water is still knee deep. He splashes into the lake, making the canoe wobble.

"Of course."

"Thanks. And sorry." He runs through the water and splashes onto the shore, and doesn't stop when Angela and Josh ask him what's up. I drag the canoe by the front, but Josh sees and comes over to help me.

"What's going on?" he asks.

"Oh. Um." I realize that saying he needed sunscreen is a bit of a stretch for how much he's panicking and how fast he's running back to our campsite, and stumble over my answer until I finally come up with something reasonable. "He had to poo really bad."

"Oh man, that sucks," Angela says.

"Did he shit in the canoe?" Josh asks.

"No, Josh, he did not shit in the canoe. What kind of a question is that?"

"I don't know."

We return the canoe and start to walk back to the campsite together.

"Hey, Reese," Josh says. I turn towards him and let him continue his thought. "I'm really sorry about last night."

"Oh?"

"Yeah. I was just worried about you. I still am, to be honest, but he's not," he stops, tilts his head from side to side as he thinks, "he's not as bad as I thought. As least so far. I'm still watching him, though."

I smile a little. "You should tell Felix that. He would appreciate it."

|||| |||| |

Felix is taking our tent down by the time we make it back. The trunk of his car is open but most of our stuff is sitting on the ground beside his car.

"Did you make it in time?" Josh asks him as he passes to get to his and Angela's tent.

"What?" Felix stands up a little and furrows his eyebrows at him.

"Your shitty situation."

"What?" Felix asks again.

"Did you make it to the washroom in time?"

"Oh." He looks at me and I sort of shrug. "Yeah, I did, but barely. I really thought I was going to shit my pants." He laughs it off and goes back to taking the tent apart.

"I'm sorry," I say quietly, walking up to Felix.

"Stop apologizing. None of this is your fault."

"It kind of is," I say. "I pressured you to come."

"I came because I wanted to. And some of it was fun. I've actually never done anything like this before."

"Done anything like what?"

"Camping. Canoeing. Going to the beach in the middle of the day." His lips form a tight, straight line and he shakes his head a little.

"Ever?"

"Ever. I mean before I was- I mean, *before*, you know, people didn't do that kind of stuff. Not for fun, anyway. And when things weren't awkward, and I wasn't afraid of catching on fire, I had fun."

"I thought you said you didn't catch on fire."

He smiles and gives me a quick kiss. "We don't."

"Well anyway," I giggle, "I'm glad you had fun."

I help him pack the rest of the stuff into the car and just as we're ready to leave, I see the girl from the washrooms from the night before. She definitely recognizes us as she passes by our site, but all she does is watch with a turned head as she walks. I give her a nod and a weak smile, and she smiles back.

"Hey, thanks for coming," Josh says to Felix, holding his hand out to shake.

"Uh, thanks for inviting me." Felix sounds like he's a little taken aback.

"Sorry about the whole murderer thing," Josh says. "You know how it is."

"Yeah. It's cool. I get it."

Josh nods and makes his way over to his own car, so he can help Angela pack their stuff up.

"Reese, is it okay if you drive?" Felix asks, startling me.

"What? You want me to drive your car?"

"If that's okay. Just." He steps closer to me and practically whispers in my ear. "The sun made me feel pretty sick and I've been okay here in the shade, but any time I even see some sun poking through the gaps in the trees it makes me want to barf."

"Oh. Yeah. Sure, I can drive. You should put a shirt or a hat over your eyes and just try to sleep or something."

"Thanks, Reese. You're the best."

"No, you are."

"Do you want to come over for a bit?" I ask when we start getting close to my apartment. "Until the sun's gone down and you can drive home comfortably?"

"Yes," he says easily from under the sweater that's covering his face.

I smile and drive us to my building.

Felix puts his sunglasses on and tries to carry my bag in.

"Felix," I say, putting a hand on his arm. "You need to rest."

"I'm okay, but thank you for your concern. Also literally nothing ever feels heavy to me."

I roll my eyes and smile at him, and let him carry my bag.

We say hello to Hazel and April when we get in, and Felix relaxes on the couch while I get them fresh water and top up their food. I scoop them out of their pen and put them on the floor so they can run around the apartment while Felix and I, uh, do other things. I smile at him and he grins, watching me walk towards him.

"Hi," I say quietly, climbing on his lap.

"Hi."

"I'm sorry my friends suck."

"Your friends don't suck. They're just worried about you. And Josh, um, apologized."

"Yeah," I sigh. "But they still suck."

"Maybe we don't talk about your friends," Felix suggests, his hands sliding up my back under my shirt.

"Yeah, okay, that's a good idea." I lean forward and kiss him, and he almost immediately gets up from the couch, easily taking me with him, his hands cupping my butt. I wrap my legs around his waist and let him carry me to my bedroom, where he pushes me onto the bed. All of a sudden we're both eager, more eager than we've ever been, and it feels like we aren't taking our clothes off fast enough. I grab at his shirt and pull it over his head. He lifts mine and I raise my arms over my head to help him take it off, and then both our shirts are on the floor. And then my bra is on the floor, and we undo each other's pants for each other and I grab a condom from my nightstand. But then I stop, making him ask me what's wrong.

"Felix," I whisper. "What if you bit me?"

"Reese," he says gently. "We've done this so many times already. I promise I won't ever hurt you."

"No," I try. "I mean, what if I wanted you to?"

"You- you want me to bite you?"

"It won't make you lose control or anything, will it?"

"No, no, not at all."

"Do you want to?" I ask. "Do you want to bite me?"

"I mean... Yeah. Yes, I do. But I don't want to hurt you."

"You said it would make me feel euphoric."

"Yeah, but it still- I'm still breaking your skin. It still hurts."

"That's okay."

"Okay. Um." He gulps and gestures back to the bed. "Do you want to lie down?"

"Should I?"

The corner of his mouth curls. "Yes, I think that would be best."

I lie down, first on top of the covers like we already were, but then I decide to get under them. He climbs under the blanket with me and props himself on top of me. He trails his fingers down the side of my face, over my jaw, and down my neck to my shoulder. All of our eagerness is gone now, and Felix is far from rushing.

"Now you're nervous," he says.

"I'm not nervous; I'm never nervous with you."

"Your heart is racing."

"It's just something new. I want you to do it."

"I'm not sure if it's a good idea. I don't want you to be scared of me."

"I'm not scared of you, Felix."

He gently kisses the side of my neck, lingering a little before pulling away. Then he kisses my collar bone, my shoulder. Each kiss softer and longer than the last. He kisses my collar bone again, and then the corner of my neck, where it meets my shoulder.

"Are you sure?" he asks.

"Yes," I breathe. "As long as you are."

"I'm sure about me, I'm not sure about you."

"I just assured you," I try.

"If it hurts, or it's too much, tell me to stop," he half whispers.

"Okay."

"If you can't, then squeeze me, okay? Anywhere, my arm, my shoulder, my side, whatever. Okay?"

I take in a shaky breath and nod. "Okay."

"I can't do this if you're scared, Reese," he whispers.

"I'm not scared, I just don't know what to expect."

He lets out some air through his nose and looks at me. I stare into his grey eyes and we just watch each other for about a minute. It's like we're syncing, or aligning our souls by staring into each other's irises. I feel parts of his body pressed gently against mine as he hovers over me, and I can see his lips out of the corner of my eyes. I can feel the outline of his face, of his chest, of his shoulders, as if I'm touching him along all those places, but I'm not. I let out a slow breath, my eyes still on his.

"Okay," he finally says.

"Okay."

He kisses me softly on the lips, and I open my mouth a little, letting his tongue brush against mine. We kiss slowly for a few minutes and then he moves his kisses back to my jaw. My neck. My collar bone. He moves back to my neck and whispers against my skin.

"Are you ready?" he asks.

All I can do is nod my head.

He kisses my neck again, this time opening his mouth more, and then he bites down. Sharp pain pierces through my skin, into my muscle, and I gasp, suddenly having no breath to make any noise. I grab onto his back, but then I remember what he said about getting him to stop. I don't want him to stop, so I make sure not to actually squeeze him. I hope he can tell the difference between that and me just holding onto him, but I'm afraid he'll think it's too much for me already. I don't want him to feel bad.

I feel his fangs slip out of my skin and he starts to suck gently on my neck. I feel like I can breathe again, and I let out a deep sigh, but then his teeth dig into me again. I feel like I have no voice again, and this time I'm about to squeeze him to tell him to stop, but then my head starts to swim and I feel like I'm buzzed, almost how I felt when he controlled my emotions. Only this time I still feel like I'm me. The buzz travels through my body, and it pulses in my arms, down into my fingertips and into my toes. His sharp teeth in my skin don't really hurt anymore, because they feel warm, and like they're pulsating, pushing that same warmth throughout my body. I pull him closer to me and he either bites or sucks harder on my neck, I can't tell which, making me let out a groan. I can't tell if it's from pain or pleasure. All my senses are melding together and all I know is that I don't want him to stop. It feels like he's inside of me everywhere, like he's the one in my veins making everything feel warm and fuzzy. I can feel the blood coming out of my neck, but I can also feel his mouth on me, around the wound he's made, and the warmth he's giving me in return like we're doing an exchange. Like I'm giving him my blood and he's giving me his life force in return.

He eases up on my neck and I feel his fangs slide out of my skin again, making me sigh. From pain, or relief, or disappointment, I can't even tell. Maybe it's a combination of all three. His mouth is still around the bites he made in my neck, but it doesn't feel like he's drawing the blood out anymore. He licks my neck slowly, gently, and then closes his lips around the bite again, drinking up whatever is still coming out on its own. He moans a little, and licks my neck again, and I can't help but sigh a second time. The body buzz starts to calm a little, but I still feel it coursing through most of my limbs, it's just quieter. He circles the bite marks with the tip of his tongue and kisses me where he bit me. Then he kisses my collar bone, my shoulder, and then my lips, the taste of metal seeping into my mouth.

"Are you okay?" he asks.

"Yeah," I say, the buzz wearing off a little faster now.

"Did it hurt?"

"Just at first."

"Does it still hurt now?"

"A little."

"Do you want me to get some ice for it?"

"No, I don't think so. Unless you think I need some."

"It's probably fine. Are you sure you're okay?"

"Yes, Felix, I'm fine. I'm… I'm good."

"What can I do to make it better?"

"I said I was good," I chuckle. "Are you good?"

He lets out a deep breath and looks away for a second. "I should be. I should be good. But I feel ashamed at how pleasurable that was for me."

I can't help but smile. "It was pleasurable for me too."

"Really?" He adjusts himself in bed so I can lay my head on his chest, my shoulder sort of tucked under his armpit. I sigh and close my eyes, suddenly so tired I'm not sure how much longer I can stay up.

"Really," I say, opening my eyes to look at him. "It felt really nice. Like, once that euphoric phase set in, it was a good experience. Honestly. I feel like," I pause, thinking of my answer,

"I feel like that was more intimate than having sex. Like I feel like there's no way anyone can be as close to each other as we just were."

He answers by first kissing me, and then he cups my chin in his thumb and index finger, and pulls back a little. "I feel the same." And he kisses me again.

"Did I taste good?" I whisper into his mouth.

He sighs and closes his eyes for a second. "You tasted fucking amazing," he finally says. And I can't tell you why, but that feels like such a big compliment.

"Can we do it again?" I ask.

"When your wound is healed, I would love to do it again. If you want to."

"Can't I just drink some of your blood to make it heal faster?"

"Not while your blood is in my system."

"Why not?"

"Because that's how you turn."

That catches me a little off guard. "Oh."

"We can do it again in a little while," he whispers.

"Okay. Yeah," I sigh. "I would like that."

He tucks my hair behind my ear and runs his finger tips along my jaw. He kisses me again and I get completely lost in his touch, in his tongue, and our bare chests pressed together while we lie tangled in my sheets.

"I'm really tired," I manage to say.

"That's because I just drained a nice little chunk of your blood. Actually, let me get you a cookie or something, and then you can sleep."

"I'm too tired to have a cookie." I close my eyes and snuggle deeper into him. "Just monitor my heartrate while I sleep so I don't die."

"You won't die."

But I'm too tired to answer. I drift off to sleep to the sound of Felix breathing, and the little clicks of my two rats running across my floor.

‖‖ ‖‖ ‖

"Excuse me, Reese, what is on your neck?" Angela asks, pointing her finger at me as if I have some kind of contagious disease.

"What?" I startle and throw my hand up to cover it, realizing that I had completely forgotten that it was there. The muscles around the bite hadn't hurt for a day now, and I forgot to wear something today that covered the nasty bruise.

"No, no, take your hand away, what actually is that?" She leans closer and I lean away.

"Nothing."

"What do you mean nothing?" she asks. "That's not nothing."

"It's a hickey," I lie, pulling away even more. I should have listened to Felix and had some of his blood after he assured me it was safe, so it would heal faster, but I ended up feeling too weird about it. It was a good idea in theory but once the time came for me to do it, I couldn't bring myself to even try. I guess I'm paying for it now.

"No way that's a hickey," she says. "Let me see."

"No."

She recoils a little and lowers her eyebrows at me. "Why won't you let me see? What's going on?"

It's at this point that I realize I have to tell her. I can't hide it because she's going to think that Felix beats me. First she thought he was a murderer and if I don't do or say something now, she's going to think he's an abuser. What do I do? I burry my face in my hands and shake my head.

"Reese, you can tell me. Is it Felix?"

"No!" I cry. "I mean, yes, but it's not what you think!"

"What do I think?"

"I don't know, you tell me!"

"Let me look at your neck and then I'll tell you!"

I huff and slowly pull my hands away from my face. I straighten up so that my neck is easily visible, and I let Angela lean in and pull the collar of my shirt aside. She immediately pulls back.

"What the fuck, Reese?"

"What? What do you mean 'what the fuck'? Tell me what you're thinking!"

"I don't know what I'm thinking! I'm thinking you have a big ass bruise on your neck and what looks like *bite* marks! Are you... Do you guys, like... Are you two into... I mean do you guys like it, you know, rough or whatever?"

That's when I smile. Her first thought it that we like BDSM, not that he beats me.

"Oh my god, do you?" she asks, bringing her hands up to her mouth to cover an unsure smile.

"No," I say. "But I think we should order a pizza and I'll tell you what's actually going on."

Josh comes home from work just as we're putting on our shoes, and we hardly even give him a glance as we slip out the door.

"Where are you going?" he calls.

"We're going to Reese's! Sorry, emergency girl night."

"I thought we were all going to watch the new episode of-"

"We can watch it another night, that's the beauty of streaming."

"But it's the start of the new season! The episode just came out today!"

"It'll still be there tomorrow!" I shout across the driveway.

"And don't you watch it without us!" Angela adds. "We didn't watch every episode of this together for three years just for you to cheat on us!"

"Well now you're cheating on me!"

"Not really! Just don't watch it, okay? We'll watch it together on the weekend. Or we'll do a double feature next week when the next one comes out."

"Fine," Josh huffs. "Have fun."

I smile at Josh, and then at Angela, and we both get in my car.

"Carter's?" Angela asks.

"Yeah, will you call it in while I drive?"

She nods and pulls out her phone, putting it on speaker once she dials.

It rings twice and then Felix's beautiful voice answers. "Good evening, Carter's, this is Felix."

"Whoa, you sound sexy on the phone," Angela says, but then immediately slaps her hand over her mouth. I glance at her quickly to see her eyes bulging at me.

"Excuse me?" Felix asks.

"Angela!" I shout, knowing she didn't mean to say that, but still shocked at her. "Felix, it's me! It's Reese! Angela's just being inappropriate!"

"I'm sorry!" she says quickly. "That just slipped out, I swear! Reese and I just bailed on my husband very abruptly and I know it's mean to say, and I swear I love him, but I'm having so much fun already and I'm very excited for our evening of pizza and secrets and I wasn't expecting you to sound like that even though

I know what you sound like, I already know what you sound like and I don't think you're sexy. No, that sounds bad, I think you're a regular guy who I could maybe be attracted to if I wasn't in love with my husband, but I don't want to be attracted to you because I know that-"

"Angela!" I cry, trying to cut her off.

"What's wrong with me!?" Angela almost sobs, I swear.

"Did you ladies call to order pizza?"

"Yes!" Angela shouts. "Yes, we want pizza! That's it! Just regular, wood fired pizza!"

"You don't want irregular wood fired pizza?" Felix asks. "It's better."

"Oh then, yes of course, give us the better pizza," I jump in.

"Got it. Two irregular wood fired pizzas, coming up."

"Wait, but toppings!" Angela says.

Felix chuckles a little. "I was kidding. What kind of pizza do you want?"

"Well we're here now," I say, driving past the restaurant and pulling into a parking spot on the street. "So we might as well just come inside to order."

"I can't go in," Angela says. "You go and I'll give you cash."

"You're ridiculous."

"I can't go in there after what I said to Felix! Your boyfriend! I'm such a loser sometimes!"

"Don't say that. You're a loser all the time." We both laugh and I get out of the car. "What kind do you want?"

"Garlic Bacon."

"Yum, me too."

She smiles at me and I head into the restaurant.

Felix is at the podium putting a table's order in when I enter, and he looks up and smiles at me. I give him a wave and walk towards him. I wait for him to finish punching everything in and then he gives me his full attention.

"Angela couldn't show her face, eh?" he asks.

"Definitely not."

He grins. "So what are you guys getting?"

"Two Garlic Bacon pizzas."

"Wow, you two are so adventurous. Not even going to get two different kinds to share. I wish I was that brave."

"ha, ha."

"It'll be like ten minutes."

"Okay."

"So how was your day?" But then he notices my uncovered neck and his eyes bulge a little. "Reese." He motions to his neck and I look down, then back at him.

"Oh yeah, that. I forgot about it. Sorry."

"Well people are going to think someone strangled you or something," he says quietly.

"Don't worry, the marks on my neck in no way resemble a strangling. It looks like someone bit me and then sucked out half a litre of my blood."

He either doesn't think I'm funny, or is just overlooking my hilarious way of stating the truth because he's worried, and he says seriously, "It still looks really bad. Did people at work see it?"

"I don't think so. I mean, if they did, they didn't say anything about it."

Felix groans. "Nooo, this is not good. We're not doing that again until the winter, when you can cover it up with a scarf or something."

"Too bad I don't wear scarves."

"Reese, I don't think you realize how serious this is."

"I don't think people will suspect anything as long as it doesn't persist."

"Okay, maybe you're right. I'll be right back; I'm just going to check on a table's order. Yours shouldn't be much longer."

I watch him make his way to the back of the restaurant where a cook puts two pizzas on the line. He exchanges a few words with Felix, and then Felix grabs both the pizzas and walks them to a table in front of the bar. And now all I can think about is people looking at my neck and thinking the worst. How bad is it, really? I know Angela had a freakout when she saw it, but I haven't even really looked at it in the last two days. Surely it can't look worse than it did before. Can it? I take out my phone and turn on the selfie camera so I can get a look at it. I cringe as soon as I see the purple and blue splotches on my neck that spill down onto the top of my shoulder. The edges of the bruise are yellow, but the bite marks still look dark and menacing, almost like there's a line of ink coming off them. Is that a blood infection? No. I would be dying if it was a blood infection. Like, noticeably dying, right?

"Here are your very exciting pizzas," Felix says, startling me and actually making me jump. I put my phone in my back pocket really quickly and then start to pull out my wallet.

"No, no, I got it," Felix says.

"Oh. Thanks."

"Of course."

"Will you come over when you're done work?" I ask.

"Sure, I'd love to. I miss your rats, anyway."

"Oh well they don't miss you. They told me so."

"Ah damn. I guess I can't come over, then."

"Too bad."

"Okay, spill," Angela says the second we get into my apartment.

"I think we should eat first."

"What! Can't we talk and eat at the same time?"

"Ugh fine." I grab us plates and we bring the pizza to the living room and put the boxes on the coffee table. Angela sits on the carpet next to the pizza but I get comfortable on the couch.

"Eat a whole slice first," I say.

She rolls her eyes and smiles at me before taking a big bite of pizza.

We end up each eating three slices before I say anything. And luckily Angela doesn't continue to nag me about it, but I still feel a little nervous when I finally say the words.

"Felix is a vampire."

Angela just goes, "Ha!" but I continue to stare at her. "Come on, Reese, get real. Do you pretend he's a vampire? Because of the whole blood drive situation? And you let him bite you? I mean you do you, girl, but you have to be careful."

"I thought you were excited to hear my secrets," I say.

"Yes I was, until you came out with this stupid bullshit to cover up what you're actually doing. I'm not going to judge you."

"I'm not lying," I insist. "He's actually a vampire. Everything happened because he's a vampire. He lifted the elevator because he's a vampire and he's strong as fuck, and he had blood bags in his fridge because he's a fucking vampire!"

Angela just stares at me with a slice of pizza in her hand.

"And this terrible bruise," I continue, "and these bite marks on my neck? It's because I let him bite me. He drank like two cups of my blood. And Angela, it felt incredible."

She puts her pizza slice back in her open box and shakes her head. "You're being serious right now."

"Yes."

"But vampires aren't real," she whispers.

"Except that they are."

"But last weekend. The camping. He was in the sun."

"With UV clothes, a hat, sunglasses, and SPF 100."

"And he reapplied it so many times," she adds, and I can hear the realization in her voice.

"Yeah. And when he ran away so fast after canoeing, it was because I dropped his sunscreen in the water by accident."

"And I had yours," she says, more recognition in her tone.

"Yes! He was starting to burn so fast and the sun was making him feel sick."

"Oh my god." Angela lets out a breath and leans against the side of the coffee table.

"Yeah."

"Okay so there's no way, though," she says, shaking her head and sitting up straighter.

"What do you mean?"

"There's no way he's actually a vampire, though."

"But you just... You just said that you believed me!"

"I didn't, actually. I never said I believe you."

"You don't believe me?"

"Why would I believe you?" Now she's laughing, and I think she's doing what I did. She's realized how stupid it sounds to talk about vampire stuff as if it's real. As if *she* thinks it's real. She's backtracking to feel better.

"Angela. Angela, listen to me." I get off the couch and sit cross legged on the floor in front of her. I grab onto her hands and look into her eyes. "Felix is a vampire," I say clearly. "He's 274 years old, and he needs human blood to survive. He was with the girl who turned him way back in the day, but she was cheating on him the whole time. So he left her and the other vampires they were living with, and started fresh."

"She was cheating on him for over 200 years?"

I sigh. "Yeah."

"Oh my god, and I thought your exes were bad."

"You don't have to say that you believe me. You don't even have to tell yourself that you believe me. But you can't tell Josh what I told you."

"But I tell Josh everything."

"Even about me?"

"Yes."

"Even about the time that I couldn't get my menstrual cup out and I called you crying?"

"Oh yes, I told him about that immediately."

"Angela!" I whine.

"What!? I thought you would have known! He basically heard it all anyway."

"Ugh. But if you tell him this, he's going to think that Felix has brainwashed me or something. Or that I'm just super blind to his red flags because I just want it to finally work out with someone."

"Are you sure that's not what's actually happening?"

"Angela, I'm 100 percent sure. It was weird believing it at first, and I took me a while. I had to see and experience a lot to start believing. But Angela, I watched him heal in real time. Like, I watched a festering wound just uninfect itself and close up like it was never there. The sun gives him these huge blisters in less than five minutes, I've seen it! And I've seen-"

"His fangs?"

"Yes!"

"So you did tell me about them that first time."

"Yes," I say gently. "I felt so bad making you think you were wrong about that, but I didn't know what else to do."

"Does he lose control when you guys have sex? Is that why he bit you? Does he bite you a lot?"

"No, no, he never loses control. He's so calm and quiet about it all. Like seriously, he's so gentle in everything that he does. And this was the first time he ever bit me, and it was because I asked him to."

"This is so wild."

"Yeah, it's weird," I agree.

"I can't believe you asked him to bite you. Like, that's not just a love bite or a little nip on your neck, Reese."

"I know. I guess bite isn't really the right word."

"He fed on you," she says.

"Yeah."

"And you liked it?"

"Yes. Angela, it was the most incredible thing. I've never felt so close to him. It was like we were literally pouring pieces of ourselves into each other."

"Okay, I won't tell Josh about this."

"Really?"

"Really. But you have to tell your strange little boyfriend to stop snacking on you in such visible places. Can't he get it from literally anywhere else?"

I shrug. "I guess he probably could. Maybe the neck is better because the veins are bigger. Like you know how annoying it is to drink out of skinny straws."

"Oh my god, I can't believe we're having this conversation."

卌 卌III

Angela leaves two hours later, and I can tell that she's having a hard time. I wonder if I've just ruined our friendship. If she's afraid to stay in touch with me because I believe that my boyfriend's a vampire and that we share our souls while I let him feed on me. She's probably coming up with a plan to leave town with Josh as soon as possible so I don't pull her into my web of delusion. She's probably shaking with nerves, hoping she sounded convincing enough, hoping I believed that she believed. And if she tells Josh the truth about why she wants to leave, he won't want to just up and leave, he'll want to sort things out with Felix. And of course Josh won't win, because Felix is a fucking vampire. And then my boyfriend will have killed my best friend's husband and it will be a complete mess. They'll try to charge him with murder but he'll just kill those people too, and then he'll realize he actually likes killing people to drink their blood and he'll go on a vampire rampage for the next 30 or so years. Then I'll be sixty and won't even have Angela and Josh's porch to sit on. Because her husband will be dead and she'll hate me forever.

What have I done?

I'm about to pick up my phone to text her, to tell her that I had fun pretending with her tonight, and that I'll tell her the real secret next time, but before I get a chance to, my intercom buzzes.

I just about jump out of my skin, and once I've caught my breath I walk over to it to see who it is.

"Hello?" I say into it.

"Hey it's Felix."

"Oh hey! Come up!" I buzz him in and unlock my door for him.

He comes into my apartment just as I'm getting comfortable on the couch, and he strides right over to me and sits down. I give him a quick kiss and say hello.

"Hello," he says.

"I told Angela about you," I blurt without thinking. I wasn't planning on telling him that, but the whole thirty seconds I waited for him to come up, I couldn't stop stressing over it.

"I'm sorry? You told her about me? What about me?"

I visibly cringe and tuck my neck into my shoulders.

"Reese," he says slowly. "What did you say?"

"I told her that you're a vampire." I cover my face with my hands but he gently touches them with his fingertips, making me pull my hands back down.

"Did she believe you?" he asks calmly.

"I have no idea. It sounded like she did, but I'm convinced she just played along so I wouldn't murder her."

"Why would you murder her?"

"Because you're rubbing off on me. And if a murderer's best friend doesn't believe them when they tell them something huge, they might as well not be best friends anymore, right? They might as well be dead. In the eyes of a murderer, I mean."

"I don't think she thinks you're a murderer. Maybe a little unhinged, but not a murderer."

"I'm sorry I told her. It's just that she saw my neck and I didn't know what to tell her."

He lets out a deep breath and closes his eyes briefly. "Is she going to go telling other people?"

"No, I don't think so."

"Then it's fine. As long as she doesn't go telling news stations or the police or something."

"I made her promise not to tell anyone."

"Okay." He sighs and looks around before landing his eyes back on mine. "Well I brought running stuff. Do you want to go running?"

"As long as we can read after."

"I'm glad you said that because I also brought PJs."

We head out for our run, the night air cooling a lot faster than it did over the course of the summer. We start to go towards downtown, and for a little bit I'm keeping pace with Felix. I mean, not Felix's real pace, but the pace he normally keeps when running in public. Normally I'm a few feet behind him no matter how hard I try to speed up, but this time we're side by side.

"Are you running slower?" I ask, realizing I'm not out of breath yet.

"No, I'm running the way I always do." He smiles at me and we keep going.

We make a loop and end up back at my apartment after running for about twenty minutes. It's the farthest I've made it and I feel so alive. Felix high fives me and we stare at each other in the elevator, my breaths heavy and laboured, Felix's smooth and calm.

We shower together and get into PJs so we can read our book in bed. We've been reading *The Starless Sea* by Erin Morgenstern, and sometimes I think Felix loves it more than he loves me. I laugh at him as he gushes over every new magical scene, passage, or story, but he doesn't seem to mind.

"I haven't really gotten to enjoy things quietly since before I turned," he says.

"What do you mean?"

"The vampires I lived with last were all big partiers. It was like they didn't know how to live without them. The house was filled with people all the time. Loud music, people doing drugs, people breaking things…"

"Did you feed on people?"

"No, we never did that. We would take turns stealing from blood banks. It was always other vampires at the parties. But the vampires I lived with would usually manage to invite one mortal to a party every now and then, because of the smell."

"What? Really?"

"Yeah." He shrugs. "Almost like the smell of baking cookies, you know? Smelling baking cookies doesn't make you ravenous, it's just nice."

"Of course it is, but it would be nice if I could eat them after smelling them."

"Okay, then what about a scented candle? You like the smell of those, right? You wouldn't eat a scented candle."

"That's because candles are made of wax. And just because they smell good doesn't mean they'd taste good."

"Okay, point. But smelling a chocolate scented candle, for example, doesn't immediately make you go out and buy chocolate, does it? You just light the candle because it smells good."

I grin at him. "So sometimes you had parties with humans in it so you could smell them."

"Correct."

"That's weird."

"It's not weird."

"Did you guys have orgies and stuff?"

Felix actually chokes on a laugh. "What?"

I feel my face getting hot and I shrink into my pillow. "I don't know, it just sounds like something vampires who have parties and consume drugs would do. Plus in movies and stuff they're always so sexual. And your ex-person-girl telling you about how it's normal to never be satisfied…" I let myself trail off.

His laugh this time is softer and more gentle. "Do you know me at all, Reese?"

"Yeah, I think so. I mean, I know you *now*. I don't know what you were like when you didn't pretend to be human. Except for at these parties, I guess? You had to pretend at those, since there was usually a mortal there?"

"We didn't have to pretend or not pretend to be anything at the parties. There wasn't really anything that ever brought up the question. But I never talked to them anyway; I mostly kept to myself. I would converse with the other vampires. People I knew. Because I was exactly the same as I am now. I had the same girlfriend for 240 years even though I knew she cheated on me. I mean, okay, I guess I'm not *exactly* the same. I've definitely come out of my shell more. But no, Reese, we did not have orgies." He laughs again and I groan in embarrassment.

"So you moving away from them and starting fresh on your own, that was a big thing for you, eh?"

"Huge."

"And being the only vampire that you know of in the area, and having to interact with all the delicious smelling humans and pretending that you're one of us, that was hard to do, eh?"

"Obviously," he says with a bit of a laugh under his breath. "Look at where it got us."

"I'm glad you messed up," I say.

"Yeah?"

"Yeah. Because now when we inevitably break up, I won't think it's because you're some asshole who cheated on me like everyone else in my life has. At least I'll know there are some good ones out there, and I got to have one of them for a bit."

"Too bad there aren't any good ones who are fully alive."

"Too bad."

"But Reese," he adds, making my stomach queasy. He sounds so serious and I'm afraid he's decided that now is the perfect time to end everything. And before we're done reading *The Starless Sea*? "What if we didn't break up? What if instead of breaking up, we just moved somewhere remote once you started getting old and it was obvious that I wasn't? We could be together for the rest of your life and it wouldn't be that weird. It's not like you're a teenager in all those vampire shows."

"You could just dye your hair grey and put on wrinkle prosthetics or something," I say. "It would be a bit of work every day, but we would only have to do it on days that you see people."

He smiles. "I think you're on to something."

I'm smiling too, but once I think about it for more than a few seconds, I feel my smile start to fade. "But I would still die."

"You could die in my arms," he says, and somehow it doesn't even sound sad. "I would hold you while we laid in bed together and it would be just like falling asleep."

"Unless I died of an aneurism or a stroke or during a major heart surgery or something. Plus no matter what, you would still be left behind. Can you imagine me dying in your arms and then having to live for the rest of eternity after?"

"No, not really. But I would do it for you if you wanted."

"No." I shake my head. "I don't want that for you."

"What about the other option?" he asks slowly.

"What other option?"

"The option where I make you like me."

"Oh."

"I mean we don't have to do it now, or soon, even, but if it's something you could see yourself wanting in the future, I think it helps to add it to the conversation."

"How are you talking so casually about this? It's like you're just trying to discuss whether or not we want kids."

"*Do* you want kids?"

"No." I shake my head.

"Okay. Me Neither."

"Well that's good. It's too bad we're different species otherwise we'd be so compatible."

"But we don't have to be different species, that's what I'm saying. We don't have to have an expiration date if we don't want."

"I don't know," I say slowly. "I love the idea of us not having to end, but I don't think I could do it."

"Be a vampire you mean," he clarifies.

"Yeah. I'd have to watch everyone I love die. I'd have to lie to them. I'd have to fight the urge to eat people. I don't..." I stop and close my eyes for a second, but before I can continue, Felix steps in.

"Not becoming immortal doesn't necessarily ensure that you won't watch everyone you love die."

I don't know what to say; I just widen my eyes at him.

"Sorry," he says quickly. "That's a terrible thought. But I get it. It's a lot to handle."

"It's more than just a lot to handle, Felix. It would be completely changing who I am as a person."

"It wouldn't though. You'd still be you."

"I don't know. I don't think I want that. I want to be able to grow old. I wish we could grow old together."

Felix sighs. "Me too."

"Why don't we just revisit this conversation in another year?"

"Three months," he says.

"Three months!?"

"If we decide to break up, I don't want to leave you as a single 35-year-old."

"Now I'm 35 all of a sudden?"

"You know what I mean."

"Yeah, I know what you mean. I just hate thinking about it."

"So do I."

"We're terrible at this pretending thing," I say with a laugh.

"The worst."

‖‖‖ ‖‖‖ ‖‖‖‖

"I have an amazing idea," Felix says to me on the phone.

"What's that?"

"You have to come over and I'll tell you."

"Oh I have to come over, do I?"

"Yes," he says. "You have to come over."

I grab my toothbrush, a pair of pyjama pants, and a change of clothes in case I end up sleeping over, and head over to Felix's apartment. He buzzes me in and I make my way to his floor. I can hear music coming through his door as I get further down the hall, and I walk in to see him dancing in the kitchen. The curtains are obviously shut, but the overhead lights are on, which have a warm yellow glow. He's shaking his hips to *Shut Up and Dance* and sticking his arms up in the air, index fingers pointed to the ceiling. When he turns around and sees me grinning at him from the doorway, and he just smiles and dances his way over to me.

"Dance with me, Snappy Jack," he says, putting my bag on the floor for me and grabbing my hands.

I shut the door with my foot and swing my arms back and forth, hands still in his grasp, as we shuffle our way back into the kitchen. He pulls me into him and puts his hand on my lower back, keeps his other hand in mine. My free hand finds his shoulder and I let him dip me and twirl us into the living room.

He spins me, curls our arms together to pull me back into him and spins me back out again. I dance my way back to him and put both my arms around his shoulders, pressing myself as close to him as I can. But his hands move from my hips, and his fingers find mine, gently pulling them away from his shoulders. We hold hands between our bodies and we shimmy forward and back together, so I start to do the shoulder-lean-in towards him, and he catches on pretty quickly, doing the lean-back at the same time, and we go back forth like that a few times.

The song ends and I giggle, about to give him a kiss, but then *Happy* by Pharrell Williams starts, and he lets go of my hands and crouches down a little, hitting his knees in time with the beat at the beginning of the song. I can't help but watch him and laugh, but then he stands up straighter and swings his arms in the air a little, so I do too, and then we swing our arms together again while swaying around the living room. But then the clapping starts, and Felix claps along with the song, so I do too, not able to hold in a few short laughs every now and then. Felix smiles and laughs almost every time I do and we half walk/half dance around the coffee table, clapping with the song.

Jackie Wilson Said by Van Morrison comes on next and Felix immediately starts singing and clapping along with it.

"You like songs with clapping, don't you?" I ask, clapping with him.

"Don't you?"

I smile at him. "Yeah, clapping songs are fun."

"I also like songs that sing sounds."

"Sing sounds?" I ask, both of our bodies still shimmying and swaying a little.

"Yeah like doo-doo's, and de-langs, and doop-woops."

"I don't think anyone says doop-woop in their songs, Felix."

But the song starts to sing Felix's so-called sounds, that I would not call "doop-woop", but I guess I understand where he's getting it from. We both sing along together, and I pull myself into his chest again, and we dance together with our bodies touching. One of my hands on his shoulder, one of his on my waist, and our other hands linked together as we continue to sway and dip and spin around the room until the song is over.

When the song ends, Felix turns the volume down so the music continues to play but it's quiet, and we can talk and catch our breath. Well, I need to catch my breath, Felix obviously doesn't need to catch his.

"This is my amazing idea," he says, sitting on the couch.

I sit next to him and let him hand me a piece of paper with a cartoon drawing on it. It's a cartoon Jack Daniel's bottle, but it has arms and legs a face. The face has so much expression. It's winking, with a half open grin, and a round cheek under the winking eye. The cartoon legs have big sneakers and the hands are wearing micky mouse gloves. But get this, one of them is in a finger snapping position.

"Oh my god," I say. "It's a Snappy Jack."

"Do you like it?"

"I love it. It's so weird and adorable."

"Adorable enough to have it tattooed on you?"

"What?"

"Do you want to get matching Snappy Jack tattoos?" Felix asks.

"Um. Yes!"

"Really? You're okay with getting a weird tattoo with a guy who you know you won't be with in the future?"

"Yes because nothing about the way it's going to end is going to be angering. We're going to part ways because we have to."

"Right," he says with a single nod.

"It'll help me to fondly remember you when I'm old."

"I don't know about that, it might look kind of bad when you're old."

"Nah," I smile. "It'll still look good."

He smiles back and then turns the music up again. He gets up from the couch and grabs my hands, pulling me up with him.

"But wait!" I shout over the music.

"What?" he turns the music down a bit.

"Can you even get a tattoo? Will it work?"

"Yeah of course it'll work."

"Your healing powers won't make it…" I scrunch my nose before finishing my sentence. "Not work?"

"No, it'll just heal really fast. My old friends had a lot of tattoos. They had their own tattoo machine and they tattooed each other when they were bored."

"So they didn't get tattooed by a professional?"

"Well they were good at it, but no."

"So how do we know that your healing process isn't going to be noticeable to the person who tattoos us? Unless your vampire friends are going to be the ones to do it?"

Felix shakes his head once. "No, I'm not friends with them anymore."

"You're not friends with any of them? But didn't you spend like, a hundred years with most of them?"

"Yeah," he sighs. "None of them were actually my friends. I thought they were, but…" he trails off, and I get the idea that he's embarrassed to go into detail. I wonder if they were all cheating on each other and Felix was the only one who wasn't a part of it.

"Did you really spend 200 years with people who treated you like shit?"

"I didn't know. I thought it was just…." He puts his hands in his pockets and shrugs. "Vampire life. I didn't know any better. And I definitely had a rug pulled over my eyes for a lot of it. I mean, I changed my life completely for someone who didn't really love me. I didn't want to admit that I literally ruined it. My life, I mean. And I spent time reading, and running, and exploring a lot at night time. I don't even know where those 200 years went, to be honest. Looking back on it, I almost can't remember it."

"Really?"

He nods. "A lot of it, at least. I remember flashes. Bits and pieces. But the years sort of blend together. Actually the years that I remember most are the farthest away. The years when mortals knew about us, when we fed on them, and also hid from others. When people hunted us. When we had to travel once word got to the wrong people." He raises his shoulders a little and then drops them. "Once we got more into the 1900s it was just a matter of blending in and laying low. And stealing from blood banks."

"And then there were the parties."

"Yes. And then there were the parties."

"But you kept to yourself," I say, trying to remember what he told me before.

"Yeah, mostly. And even though Elizabeth was terrible in a lot of ways, a lot of ways that I knew of and tried to ignore, and in ways that she hid from me, she was also nice to be around. She was my anchor for so long when I felt lost."

"You mean your compass."

"What?"

"An anchor stops you from floating away, it doesn't help you when you're lost."

He laughs under his breath. "I guess you're right. But anyway, I thought I needed her, but I didn't."

"But for 200 years?"

"It wasn't like that the whole time. And plus I was afraid to go out on my own. I didn't know how to do anything without everyone else's help or guidance or… company. I didn't think I would be able to do it."

"So am I the first person to show you the light? What real friendship and relationships can be like?"

"Kind of. But to be fair, it doesn't sound like you've really had a chance to see what a real relationship can be like either."

"You're right," I say. "We're our each other's first non-toxic relationship."

"Is that weird?"

"I don't know." We kind of smile at each other for a few seconds, and then I change the subject. "So what did we decide about the tattoo?"

"Oh. Um. Maybe we should test it and see how my body handles it."

I raise my eyebrows at him. "Test it?"

He grins and pulls up Amazon on his phone.

"You're not going to buy your own tattoo machine, are you?"

"Why not?"

"That can't be safe."

"Reese, I'm a vampire. As long as it's not made of wood or UV rays, I think I'll be okay."

The tattoo machine comes in the next day and I drive straight to Felix's after work. He's got it out and ready to go when I walk in, and even though I know this can't end worse than him just having a shitty tattoo, I'm suddenly worried for him. I have to swallow a lump in my throat as I sit next to him, and pretend that it isn't there.

"Are you excited for this!?" he half shouts.

"Ha. No."

"Why not?"

"I don't know, it's scary!"

"It's fun!" He plugs the tattoo machine in and hands the vibrating needle gun to me.

"What? I'm not doing it!"

"You have to! You have to see what it's doing as you tattoo my skin!"

"No, there's no way I can do that! I don't even know how to do it. You can do it. Just tattoo your thigh."

"How 'bout you tattoo my thigh?"

"But I don't know what I'm doing!"

"And you think I do? I would love to have a practice tattoo on me that was done by you."

"I wouldn't even know what to make. I can't draw, Felix."

"Write your name."

I realize he's still holding the machine out to me. I step in closer to him and let him put it in my hand. My fingers feel tingly from the vibrations already.

"Wh-where do you want me to write it?"

"Somewhere where I can see it all the time."

"Well, the thigh is a good place for that. You'll see it every time you take a shit." But before I even get a chance to giggle at my own suggestion, I scrunch my eyebrows in confusion. "Do you even do that?" I ask.

"If I eat, then yes."

"So you have a working digestion system even though you're dead?"

"See, this is why we can't tell people about us. If they don't want to kill us, they'll want to do experiments on us. Because I don't know how the hell any of it works. And people would be fascinated. They would want to know. And I don't want to know, Reese. I don't want to know how any of it works. All I know is that if I eat food, I'll shit it out. If I drink water, or alcohol, I'll pee it out. If I drink blood, it stays in my system and then I don't even know. Disappears, absorbs through my veins and into my skin, keeping it young and rejuvenated and unchanging. I don't know. I have no idea. But it hurts my brain to think about it sometimes. It shouldn't be possible. It doesn't make any sense. And why does the sun make me want to barf!? Why am I so sensitive to it just because I drink blood and died once 240 years ago? I have no idea how I'm sitting here talking to you, or how a tattoo artist is going to react when he sees what my skin does after he needles it with ink, so please write your name on my thigh so I can at least remember you. If I have questions that I don't know how to answer, or things I can't deal with, at least I'll have you, staring up at me for the rest of eternity."

I don't know what to say. I'm sitting next to him on the couch, a vibrating tattoo machine in my hand, but I can't do anything but smile. It feels like I'm falling in love with him all over again.

"Reese?"

I wish I could put my feelings into words but I'm just sitting here staring at him.

"What's going on?" he laughs. "Are you okay?"

I almost tell him that I won't be okay when we eventually break up. I almost say 'I'm not okay because when we break up I'm never going to recover. Because I'll never find anyone like you for the rest of my life.' But I don't say it because it'll just make him say 'let's not break up then,' and we'll have to have another conversation about me becoming a vampire, and I just can't handle that.

"Okay seriously, what did I say to freak you out? Am I too intense? I'm sorry I'm so intense, I don't mean to be, but I've just never felt this way about someone before and I-"

I close the space between us and kiss him, cutting his sentence off. He seems surprised at first, but relaxes into me in less than a second. His lips part against mine and I drop the tattoo machine to grab at his hair. He pulls me into his lap and starts to unhook my bra under my shirt, so I just throw my shirt off.

"So, not too intense, then?" he asks.

I grin at him and kiss him again.

"Yes too intense?" he asks, pulling back a little.

"Felix, everything you do and say is obviously perfect and sometimes I can't believe that you're real. How are you real?"

He shrugs and smiles at me. "I wish I could tell you."

I chuckle and kiss him again, but then slide off him and start to put my shirt back on.

"What are you doing?" he asks, sounding hurt.

"I'm going to tattoo my name on your thigh."

"Fuck yeah you are!" And let me tell you, the level of joy that I can hear in his response nearly kills me. This man is going to kill me solely because I literally cannot handle how much I love him.

The tattoo machine is still vibrating on his carpet and if I was about to tattoo any other person, I obviously wouldn't at this point. It's no longer sterile. But since Felix is a vampire, we don't have to worry about that, do we?

"Okay, where do you want it?" I ask, kneeling on the floor in front of the couch.

Felix adjusts himself and sits closer to the edge so that most of his thigh is off the cushion. I'm not sure if he's doing it to make it easier for me, or because he's afraid I'm going to get ink on his couch, but I don't ask. I open the bottle of black ink and pour it into a little cup, and then position myself next to him so that his thigh is horizontal in front of me, like it's a table or something. I look up at Felix, who's just smiling down at me.

"Anywhere in this general area," he says, circling his hand around in the air above his mid-thigh.

"Okay. But just to be clear, I have no idea what I'm doing and I can't guarantee this is will look even a little bit good."

"Fair."

I dip the tattoo machine into the ink and then bring it over his thigh. I'm afraid to press it into his skin. I don't know how hard to press!

"Okay," I say slowly. "I'm going to do it."

"Okay."

"Getting your first tattoo by someone who has no idea what they're doing is a strange choice, but I guess we're doing it."

"It's not a strange choice, it's the best choice."

"Oh god." I stifle a laugh and bring the needle closer to his skin. "Okay I'm doing it!"

"Okay!"

"Ready?"

"Ready!"

"Okay! Here I go!"

"Okay!"

"Any second now!"

"Reese, come on!"

Felix and I both laugh and then once we calm down, I just go for it. I press the tattoo machine into his skin and for some reason scream as I make the first line. I keep screaming as I go back to the top of the line to start doing the rest of the R, and I scream until I'm done that first letter.

"How did that feel?" I ask.

"Like nothing," he laughs. "I don't know if you did it right."

"Of course I did it right. I just wrote the letter R."

"Wipe it away, wipe it away," he says, reaching for a tissue on the side table.

I take it from him and wipe the pool of black ink to reveal something resembling the ghost of a letter R. It's like if someone wrote it with a pen that was running out of ink and was also shaking all over the place at the same time.

"Okay well you sort of did it," Felix says.

I can't hold in my laugh and I almost fall back. Felix starts to laugh too and I touch it with my finger as if that will help me to understand how to do the next letter better. I take a few deep breaths to calm myself and once we're both not rolling with laughter anymore, I get ready to continue.

"Should I go over the R or leave it the way it is?" I ask.

"You choose."

"Okay I'm going over it. And I'm starting now!"

I press the needle into his skin before he can reply and I try my best to put the needle in deeper this time. I go over the same spot as well as I can, and then without wiping it away or checking it, I go right in for the next letter. I was going to do the all the lowercase letters in cursive but I decide at the last second to just print. I'm sure if I tried to do cursive with a tattoo machine it would look infinitely worse.

"I can feel it more this time, so you must be doing something right," Felix says when I'm on my second E.

"I must be!" I chuckle but keep going.

When I'm done, there's a giant pool of black ink all over Felix's left thigh. He grabs more tissues and hands them to me and I wipe it all away.

"Oh my god, Felix, I'm so sorry," I laugh.

"Why?"

"It looks like shit."

"I like it."

"Also it's upside down. I didn't think of that, I was just doing what was easier for me at this angle."

"It's not upside down," he assures me. But he's lying, because it's absolutely upside down. "I can read it this way," he adds.

"Oh true. Well it still looks terrible."

You can see where I went over the R, there's the ghosty one and then my better one like, millimetres to the side, so it looks like a double image in the spots that the first R showed up. And the rest of my letters are wobbly, with too-big spaces in between. The lines are uneven; some are thin and some are thicker, the S even has a blob in the top curve. It looks like a toddler wrote it.

"I mean, sure, as far as tattoos go, I guess it's pretty bad," he says.

"Just pretty bad?" I narrow my eyes at him. "I can't believe you're going to have that on you until the end of time."

"I can." He smiles. "I'm excited about it. I love it."

"There's already blowout," I say, examining it further.

"What's blowout?"

"When the needle goes too deep and the ink goes into the fat layer. It spreads and looks shadowy."

"Oh."

"You should really get this covered up by a professional."

Felix leans into his leg to get a better look. "Oh I see what you mean about the shadow thing. It's not that bad, though. It just looks like a faint shadow. Like when you use word art in Microsoft Word."

"Ugh, I word-arted your leg!"

"Reese, I promise I'm super happy with it. If some professional tattooed your name on my thigh, it would have no meaning. I like it because you're the one who did it. So I love the way it looks. Because it looks that way because you're the one who did it."

"Okay fine. Does it burn or sting or anything?"

"No, it doesn't feel like anything."

I run my finger along the lines of the tattoo and I can't even feel a raise in the ink. It feels like a fully healed tattoo. And there's no glossiness to it at all, it just looks like a newly healed tattoo.

"This is actually really incredible," I say, still running my finger along the ink. "It looks like a tattoo you got six weeks ago. Like, it's fully healed, but not old and healed, you know?"

"I wonder if it'll stay looking like that."

"That would be badass," I say.

"Do you think there's anything outwardly alarming about this?" he asks. "Like do you think a tattoo artist would notice it while tattooing me?"

"If they did, I don't think it would be drastic enough for them to think they're in the Twilight Zone or anything. I don't know, they might not notice."

Felix grins. "So you wanna get a matching tattoo with me, then?"

"Fuck yeah I do."

‖‖ ‖‖ ‖‖

I get my tattoo on the inside of my right ankle and Felix almost gets his on the inside of his wrist but changes his mind at the last minute and gets his in the same spot as mine. He offers to hold my hand while I get mine done and I laugh at him and tell him to take pictures instead.

"What about you?" I ask, when Felix is getting comfortable in the chair for his turn. "Do you need me to hold your hand?"

"I don't need you to, but if you want to hold my hand, I would really like that."

"You two are sickeningly adorable," the tattoo artist says with a smirk.

I roll my eyes and smile, and slip my hand into Felix's.

"This is the smoothest tattoo I've ever done," the artist says about halfway through. The outline is done and he's getting started on the colour.

"What do you mean?" Felix asks.

"I don't know. Your skin is just so easy to work with. It stretches to exactly where I need it, it bleeds for like, point three seconds, and it's taking these colours like a dream."

"Oh. Cool."

"He has magic skin," I say.

"Yeah, I'm a vampire," Felix adds with a bit of a chuckle.

The tattoo artist laughs and keeps tattooing the Snappy Jack cartoon.

We take pictures of our matching tattoos before we get them sanitized and covered with Saniderm. Our tattoo artist tells us to come back soon, that he had a lot of fun, and he would love to do something bigger and more detailed on Felix. I grin at him and we leave the shop practically dancing with joy.

"That was so much fun!" I squeal.

"It was!"

"That worked out really well, eh?"

"It did!"

"Are you going to get another tattoo now?" I ask.

He shrugs. "I don't know. Maybe. I don't know what I would get."

"My face."

Felix laughs a little and then we drive to Angela and Josh's because they've invited us over for Thanksgiving dinner. It's Saturday, and Thanksgiving is on Monday, so we can still have it with our own families if we want, but we still think it's a little weird that they invited us to a Thanksgiving dinner. Felix is sure they're just trying to smooth things out after our camping trip.

"That was over a month ago now," I say when he brings up the thought.

"But you guys haven't hung out much since then, have you? Plus Angela's probably trying to make sure you don't think that she thinks we're murderers."

"By inviting us for Thanksgiving."

"Yes. If you thought someone was a murderer, would you invite them over for Thanksgiving?"

"If I was afraid they would murder me if I didn't, then I would."

"I don't think it's weird that they invited us," Felix says again.

We show up at Angela and Josh's house with pumpkin pie and caramelized carrots. They invite us in and show us to the living room and it's immediately awkward. Did Angela tell Josh about Felix even though she said that she wouldn't? No. If she did, then we certainly wouldn't be here. Josh wouldn't be comfortable having two people over who think that vampires are real. Would he? I try to make it more comfortable in here so I pull my pantleg up, revealing the tattoo on my ankle.

"We just got tattoos!" I say.

"What! What did you get?" Angela comes over to look, but the plasma has already started pooling under the wrap and you can't really see the details.

"It's a Snappy Jack."

"What's a Snappy Jack?" she asks.

Felix takes his Saniderm off so we can see his tattoo, and it looks incredible. The lines are so clean and the colours are so vibrant. I'm going to be so jealous if his tattoos just always look like that forever.

"That's the weirdest thing I've ever seen," Josh says, cringing a little.

"I think it's actually kind of cute," Angela admits. "The cartoon is really well done and he's got a cute expression on his face. You just don't like anthropomorphized things."

"Because it's creepy. Non human things shouldn't look like humans."

"He doesn't look like a human," I try. "He looks like a Jack Daniel's bottle with a face."

"Why is he winking, though?" Angela asks.

"What do you mean why is he winking? Why wouldn't he be winking?"

"You called it a Snappy Jack, so shouldn't he be snapping?"

"He is! He's snapping his fingers!" I point to his Mickey-Mouse-style gloved hand on Felix's ankle. "See? And the lines coming off his fingers here show that they're in motion! He's very clearly snapping his fingers."

"Okay. Then why is he also winking?"

"What do you have against winking?" I ask.

"Nothing! I was just asking, in case it was important to the design. I just wanted to know."

"He's just winking because he's cute!"

"He's being flirty," Felix adds.

"Yeah!" I agree. "Yes! He's being flirty!"

Angela smiles. "Okay. Then I love it."

"But you've only been together for three months," Josh adds a little quietly.

"We've been together for longer than that," I say in defence, but quickly realize that I think Josh is right. Has it only been three months? No. There's no way.

"No, we still thought he was a murderer when were camping on Canada Day weekend."

"Right," I say. "But we've known each other since my birthday."

"When you thought he was a murderer," Josh says.

"I'm sorry, are you still uncomfortable with him being here?" I ask.

"No. Sorry. I shouldn't have said anything."

It's quiet for a few seconds and I open my mouth to say something, but then Josh continues.

"I just- It's just that you literally just started dating. Tattoos are permanent and I'm just…" he trails off.

"Well we already have them, so whatever you think, we can't change it now," I say.

"Listen Josh," Felix starts, "I understand your concern. It does seem fast when you think about it. But for us, it feels like we've been together for so much longer. We've just sort of been through a lot with each other, and it brought us a lot closer to each other, faster than we would have otherwise."

"What did you go through?" he asks.

"Uh, that's personal," Felix sort of stammers.

"Also it's just a tattoo," I add. "It's not like we're getting married or having a kid or something. And they're not tattoos of each other's names or faces or anything. Plus we can literally cover them up later if we want and it wouldn't make a difference."

Josh sighs and nods. "You're right. I'm sorry for being overly protective of your girlfriend, Felix."

"It's not a problem. I appreciate your concern."

The rest of the evening somehow goes by really smoothly. We laugh while we eat dinner, we all help do dishes before we sit down again for dessert, and we laugh at each other for our different whipped cream preferences. It starts because Angela puts so much on her pie that you can't even see the crust. It just looks like she has a giant pile of whipped cream on her plate.

"Okay, I like pumpkin pie, honest I do, but I don't like it without whipped cream. On its own it's not that good, but together, it's amazing."

"But surely you can't even taste the pie at this point," Felix says.

"I think that's the point," Josh answers for her.

But Angela shakes her head. "No. I can taste the pie. I can just also taste a lot of whipped cream, which is delicious, and the way I like it."

Josh and Felix end up talking about a video game that Josh has started playing, so they leave the table and get comfortable on the couch to play it together. Angela and I grab the pie plates from the table and put them in the dishwasher. I'm a little annoyed that the guys didn't offer to help, but at least it gives Angela and I a chance to talk.

"So you didn't tell Josh, then?" I whisper to her.

"Tell him what?"

"About Felix."

Angela scrunches her eyebrows and tilts her head to the side as if she has no idea what I'm talking about. Does she have any idea what I'm talking about? Did I imagine telling her about everything? Was that a dream that I had?

"About…" I'm not sure how to say it without sounding ridiculous, since it seems she doesn't recall the subject matter. So I stand there like an idiot, stumbling over my words and finally ending on, "You know."

"Reese, are you okay? Like I know you're all in love and stuff, and that can sometimes make your brain go all cloudy and stuff, but really, are you okay?"

"I'm okay," I say, although I'm not sure my tone of voice is convincing. "Are you pretending that we didn't have that conversation?" I force myself to ask.

"Reese, I have no idea what you're talking about."

I feel like I should leave it. Let her pretend that I didn't tell her my boyfriend is a vampire and that I ask him to feed on me. Our friendship would probably run much smoother if I left it alone, but I just can't. The only reason she's pretending it didn't happen is because she doesn't want to feel like she's losing her sanity, or like her best friend has already lost it. But I just can't leave it be at this point. I grab onto her wrist and drag her upstairs to hers and Josh's bedroom.

"What's going on?" she asks seriously, sitting on the edge of the bed.

I sit down and close my eyes, taking a deep breath before I answer. "Why are you pretending like I didn't tell you that the big bruise on my neck was from letting my vampire boyfriend feed on me?"

She stares at me, blinks a few times, but says nothing.

"Angela, you know me."

And then she starts to cry. Tears well in her eyes so fast and they fall down her cheeks like it's raining. "I don't know if I do anymore," she chokes. "I want to be supportive of you, I really do, especially because you two seem to love each other so much, but it's too weird. Vampires aren't real, Reese. Why do you believe that they're real? If we were thirteen, I would totally believe you and be so excited for you, but we're not thirteen. And you're pretending like we live in Forks and your boyfriend is going to live forever and make you live forever too, but that's not going to happen. I'm sorry you think that it will, but it won't. I'll always be your friend, Reese, and I'll be here for you whenever you need me, but I can't play along with this."

"So when I told you about it …" I trail off, not entirely sure what the question is that I want to ask.

"When you told me about it, I didn't know what to say," she answers for me even though I never finished the question. "You were so excited to tell me and I didn't want to bring you down. But I think if you truly believe this, if you truly believe that Felix is a vampire, and you let him *feed on you*, that there's something seriously wrong and you need help. Like you're letting him drink blood from your jugular, Reese. How have you not bled to death?"

"His saliva helps coagulate the blood or something. It's not really a healing thing, but it-" I stop when I notice Angela's eyes bulging.

"See what I mean?" she says.

"What can I do to make you believe me?"

"Nothing. I know how cool it would be for this all to be real, but it's not. It's literally impossible, Reese. I'm afraid that you're going to get yourself into trouble if you keep this up."

"What kind of trouble?"

"Bleeding to death."

"I'm not-" I cut myself off and take in a deep breath. "I could get him to show you something," I say. "You can watch how fast he runs. We can stab him and watch how fast he heals."

"Reese! We are not stabbing your boyfriend! What the fuck is wrong with you?"

"Okay," I say. I want to tell her that I don't actually think he's a vampire at this point, but I know she won't believe me. "Maybe we should go," I whisper.

"Okay," she replies quietly.

"But you still didn't, um, tell Josh, did you? About all this?"

"I didn't tell Josh." She smiles at me, and I can tell that she's still wondering whether or not she should.

"I promise you that I'm safe," I say as I get off her bed.

"Okay."

"Um. Thanks for having us over."

I leave her bedroom and almost stop when she doesn't follow me. I want to turn back and make sure that she's okay, but I'm sure she stayed behind because she wants to, so I keep going down the stairs and find Felix and Josh in the living room.

"Hey," I say. "We're going to head out."

"Oh," Felix says, looking a little surprised. "Alright. Is everything okay?"

"Yeah, I'm just tired and I have to drive to my parent's tomorrow so I don't want to be up too late."

"Sure, of course." Felix reaches a hand out to Josh, and they shake quickly as Felix says, "Thanks for the fun evening."

"Of course. Thanks for coming," Josh says.

"Are you sure you're alright?" Felix asks on the way to my apartment.

"Yes," I say, but I'm already starting to cry.

"Hey," he says, looking over at me briefly. "Hey, tell me what's up. What can I do?"

"Nothing," I sniffle. "It's fine."

We're quiet the rest of the drive, and we're quiet in the elevator. He grabs onto my hand before we get to my floor and squeezes it a little. I squeeze back and lean my head on his shoulder. He doesn't say anything when the elevator doors open, and he doesn't say anything when we get into my apartment and I let the sobbing really start. He just sits next to me on the couch and wraps his arms around me, letting me cry into his shirt.

"Make me not care," I finally say through my sobs.

"What?" he pulls back a little and puts his hands on my shoulders so he can look at me. "No."

"Please."

"Why?"

"Angela doesn't believe me."

He pulls me back into his chest and shushes me a little. In a gentle, caring way, not in a way that makes me feel like I need to stop. "It's okay," he says into my hair. "She'll come around."

"She won't," I cry.

"Then she'll be there for you when we break up."

"But I don't want to break up."

"We have to at some point, Reese."

"No. We'll be together until I die."

He chuckles a little and holds me tighter. "Okay."

"Please make me not care. Just until I can fall asleep."

"I don't think I can do that. We could get high or something instead. I have edibles at my apartment."

"I don't want to get high Felix, I just want to not care about this for twenty minutes!"

"Okay," he says quietly.

"Okay?"

He nods and helps me get up. He leads me to my room, and then opens my dresser drawers. "What pyjamas do you want to wear?"

I shrug, and so he pulls out an oversized t-shirt with strawberries on it, and plaid PJ pants. "These okay?" he asks, holding them up.

"Yeah," I say, still kind of crying.

He walks over to me and gently grabs at the hem of my shirt. He starts to pull it up so I lift my arms so he can pull it over my head.

"Are you going to make me not care?" I ask.

"Give me a minute, okay, sweetie?"

I sigh and nod. He kisses my forehead and unhooks my bra, pulling that off and dropping it to the floor. He bunches up my strawberry shirt so that he can put it over my head really easily, and then he lets the fabric drop. I put my arms through the sleeves myself, and then he starts to undo my pants. I lean my forehead into his chest, relaxing into him and filling my nose with his scent, and then he pulls my pants down to my knees. He gently guides me back towards my bed and sits me down, and pulls my jeans off the rest of the way. I watch as he kneels down and starts to put on my plaid PJ pants, one leg at a time. I'm not crying anymore, but I wish I were. If I were still crying, he would be more inclined to do his vampire mind thing on me, but now he might not.

"Okay, stand up," he whispers, his hands resting gently on my hips.

I do as he asks, and he pulls my soft plaid pants up the rest of the way. He pulls the comforter on my bed back, and motions for me to get under it, so I do. Felix takes his jeans off and climbs into the other side of the bed, his t-shirt and boxers serving as his pyjamas. He scoots in real close to me and pulls some hair away from my face. He traces my jaw with his finger tips and looks into my eyes that are still a little wet and probably an angry red.

"Go to sleep," he whispers.

"Make me not care," I whisper back.

"Okay." He presses his face into mine and kisses me gently on the lips, then kisses my forehead, and wraps his arms around me.

He's not doing it. I still feel the same. Except that being wrapped in his arms and breathing in his scent is helping to calm me. I feel safe with him, and even though I still care about my best friend probably not being my friend anymore, I'm more calm lying in bed with him. I feel like I can actually take a breath.

I drive to my parents' the next morning, and listen to music for the whole three-hour drive but don't feel good enough to sing along. My mom and I make pumpkin pie and pecan butter tarts together while my dad and my brother take care of the turkey and everything else. Sometimes we bump into each other in the kitchen, but we laugh about it and generally have a good time. We watch movies together after dinner and I sleep in my childhood room that's now a guest room, with boring, granny-looking floral sheets and a tiffany lamp on the nightstand.

We have waffles for breakfast and leftover pumpkin pie. We make turkey sandwiches for lunch and eat them on the back deck because it's sunny and mostly warm. Felix texts me every few hours and I reply with heart or smiley face emojis, but don't say much to him. I want to text Angela and ask her how the rest of her long weekend has been going, but I don't.

I hug everyone at about 3pm and get ready to drive home. I stop for gas down the road and get myself a bag of ketchup chips and an orange Powerade, and about halfway through my drive I start to sing to the songs that are playing through my speakers.

It's been a week since Thanksgiving, and I haven't spoken to Angela. I'm afraid of what we'll say to each other. I'm afraid of what she thinks of me. Felix and I go for runs and read books together almost every night, and almost every day I'm half asleep going into work.

But then my phone goes off halfway through the day and I'm surprised to see that it's a text from Angela.

Friday October 28th. Halloween Party. My Place. Wear a good costume. Can bring Felix. It says.

What's your definition of a good costume? I reply.

Not something fully bought from Spirit Halloween. I don't want to see cheap fake overalls if you're being a minion. Find real overalls. No masks of real people. Preferably no masks at all. Be creative.

Got it.

I love you.

I smile and stare at my phone screen for a little while. **Love you too.**

I wake up in Felix's bed a few hours after we've gone to sleep. There's a bit of light coming down the hall and under his door frame, and he isn't beside me. I slowly climb out of bed and creep to the door.

"Felix?" I whisper.

I open the door and immediately hear 20s swing music or something, playing quietly at the end of the hall.

"Felix?" I say again, this time more at a normal volume.

I make it to the kitchen to find him with his hands in a big mixing bowl, and moving his hips around to the music.

"Sorry, did I wake you?" he asks.

"No. What are you doing?"

"Making butter tarts."

"Really?"

He shrugs. "I couldn't sleep, and I wanted to surprise you."

I grin and move a little closer to see how he's doing with the pastry. It's looking pretty good so far.

"Do you want to help?" he asks.

"No, it looks like you've got it covered."

He smiles and puts the pastry on the counter so he can roll it out. I step back and admire the way he handles the pastry while he dances to the music.

"This is interesting music," I say after he's put the tart crusts into the cupcake pan.

"What makes it interesting?" he asks.

"It's super old. No one listens to music like this."

"Well clearly you're wrong, because I'm listening to it. And I'm super old, so it makes sense."

"Oh yes, I forgot."

"People tend to forget."

"You say that as if all your other friends know how old you really are."

He smiles again and washes his hands. "Do you not like this music?"

"I do, actually. It's fun."

And without another word, he reaches a hand out to me, and I take it. We swing and spin around the kitchen together, and even though I have no idea how to dance to this kind of music, I'm not embarrassed to just follow his lead and have fun with him. The music eventually changes to something a little slower, and he turns me so that I end up with my back against his chest and our arms folded over themselves across my chest. He leans his face down beside mine and I lean my head back into his neck a little and we just sway from side to side a little.

I feel him take in a sharp breath as if he's about to say something, but then he doesn't. I want to ask him what's up, but

I have a feeling I know. Any time a moment like this happens, I think about not wanting it to end. I'm sure he has the same thought, but his would be followed by thoughts of me becoming like him. I know that's what it is, and I know that's why he doesn't end up saying anything.

So we dance slowly around the kitchen together and continue to pretend.

卌 卌 卌 |

"I'm not sure that I should come," Felix says as we're putting the finishing touches on our costumes before Angela's party.

"What!? Why not?"

He shrugs. "They don't like me. And it's a little hard watching them pretend that they do. And I think it'll be easier for you and for them to pretend if I'm not there."

"But we're a *Jurassic Park* duo. I can't be Ellie Sadler without Alan Grant!"

He laughs a little. "You can, actually."

"But no one will know who I am without you!"

"Yes they will. Your costume is spot on. You even have the same wire rimmed glasses as her."

I look down at my peach coloured shirt, tied at the waste and rolled up over my elbows. My khaki shorts are done up over my hips with a belt, and I brush my blonde wig out of my face.

"They're going to think you're an asshole if you don't go," I say.

"I honestly think it'll be better if I don't go with you. I can say I got called into work. Maybe I'll go in and see if they need help anyway."

I stop and look into his eyes, feeling my own start to well up with tears as I come to a realization. "We can't keep doing this," I say slowly.

"Doing what?"

I let out a deep breath and look away. "Pretending."

He takes in a sharp breath and looks away for a second. "I know," he says slowly. "You still don't want to be a vampire, right?"

I let my eyes find his again and I can the feel tears threatening to fall. I can't bring myself to say anything so instead I just shake my head.

"We could pretend for a little longer," he tries, his voice cracking a little. "Maybe you'll change your mind later. Maybe you'll want to later."

"I don't..." I have to swallow and take a second before I can continue. "I don't think I will ever want to, Felix. I want to be with you, and I wish we could be together forever, but I don't think I could deal with all that comes with being, um, like you."

He nods. "Okay."

"I'm sorry."

"It's okay. We said it would come to this, and now we're here. It's okay. I just thought we would be able to keep it up for a bit longer than this."

"You thought you would have more time to change my mind," I say.

"No." he shakes his head and steps into me, putting his hands on my hips. "No," he says again.

"I thought we would be able to keep it up for longer too," I say. "But I didn't realize it would be this hard."

"Neither did I."

"I wish I wanted to be like you," I cry. "I wish I wasn't afraid of it, afraid of how it would change everything. I wish there was an easier way for us to stay together, but there isn't."

"I know," he whispers, pulling me in even closer to him. "I know."

"I'm so sorry."

"Stop apologizing."

We stand there a minute or two not saying anything, his hands on my hips and mine around his lower back, and then he pulls me into a hug. He wraps his arms fully around my back and I press my face into his chest, and he rests his chin on the top of my head.

"I'm sorry," I say again.

"Reese," Felix pleads. "Stop. It's okay. We'll be okay."

We stand there hugging for a few more minutes, his steady breathing helping to calm me. And then without saying anything else, I start to unbutton his shirt, and his fingers immediately slide over mine, helping me. Then we both move to my shirt, and then our pants, and I pull him closer to me. I tug on his bare hips and press myself into him, kissing him like I'm trying to take a breath after coming out of the water. I push him into the couch and climb on top of him, leaning down so I can keep kissing him. There's hair in the way and I push it away but it keeps coming back.

"Blegh," I say, as I pull the strand out from our mouths.

Felix starts to laugh.

"What?" I ask, wondering what's so funny about hair in our mouths while we try to enjoy our last time together.

"It's your wig," he says, bursting into more laughter.

"What?" I reach my hands up to my head, and sure enough I'm still wearing the stupid blonde wig. I pull it off and toss it onto the floor, starting to laugh myself. "We're ridiculous," I say.

"Anyone who isn't ridiculous isn't doing it right," Felix whispers, finding my lips with his.

"You're right."

"I know I'm right." He sits us both up and kisses my neck.

"Will you bite me again?" I ask.

He lets out a shaky breath and nods. "I would actually love to."

"I would love it too."

He runs his fingers along the top of my shoulder, sort of where it connects to my neck, but lower, coverable by almost any shirt. I stop moving when he puts his mouth to my skin, and I hold my breath as he sinks his teeth in. I gasp and he pulls me closer, his hands a reassurance on my bare back. I fall into the euphoria really quickly, and we move together slowly as he drinks. He pulls me closer, leans me into him, and tightens his grip on me. Pulls harder on the blood coming out of my shoulder. It's like the more he drinks, the better I feel somehow, and when his fangs slip from my skin, it fades. I still feel it swimming through my body, but as if it's lingering fairy dust, floating around my veins just looking for somewhere to go. He sinks his teeth into me again and the feeling heightens, like the dust burst into more particles and they're all trying to get everywhere at once. I pull him closer to me and squeeze his back, and he pulls away.

"Do you want me to stop?" he asks.

"No," I breathe. "I wish we could do this forever."

He smiles and kisses my shoulder where he bit me, and then he covers the wound with his mouth again, taking a bit more blood. He can't go for much longer and we both know that, and I can tell that he's savouring it, drinking as slowly as possible so that he can do it for as long as he possibly can.

He wraps me in a blanket and brings me cookies when we're done. I sit on the couch, the blanket the only thing covering me, and I eat some Oreos with my head leaning on Felix's shoulder. I'm a little shaky, I think because we were at it longer than the last time we did it, and he took more blood than he should have. I drink some Powerade too, and when I start to feel stronger, I start to get up.

"I need a shower before I put my costume back on and go to the party," I say.

Felix nods. "Okay."

"Do you want to join me?"

He doesn't even say anything, he just gets up and follows me to the bathroom. He helps me step over the tub in case I'm still lightheaded, which I'm not, but still appreciate, and we wash each other's hair. We kiss, and our hands wander, and we do everything all over again. Except for the biting of course, otherwise I would probably die.

We sigh into each other's mouths as the water falls over us and our fingers follow the drops down our skin. I can't believe we're doing this for the last time.

"Wait," I say, out of breath.

"Wait?"

"Just stop for a second."

"What's wrong?"

"Nothing's wrong. Can we make the water a little cooler?"

"Sure." Felix leans over a little and turns the handle on the tap closer to cold. "Are you okay?"

"I'm really close but I don't want to stop yet."

"Ah."

"Let's just stand here for a minute not doing anything."

Felix laughs and kisses the tip of my nose. "We're going to have to stop at some point, Reese."

"I know. But we don't have to do it *yet*."

"You're going to be late for your party."

"I don't care."

"Promise me you won't be sad for long," Felix says.

"I'll try my best."

"We can still be friends."

"That'll make it harder, I think."

"Okay. Are you going to stop going to Carter's for pizza?"

"Maybe for a little while," I say.

"I don't want to take away your pizza freedom."

"You're not taking it away, I am. Plus I could go for pizza if I wanted to."

"But you won't want to."

"I don't think you understand the impact you've had on me, Felix."

"I think I do. And if you came into Carter's for pizza, it would be hard for me too. But I would do it. Um, serve you, I mean. If you were sitting at one of my tables. Seeing you any time after today is going to be hard, and it'll be sad because I know it's all over, but I won't regret any of it. I don't regret the time I spent with you, Reese."

"I don't regret it either."

"Good. Now come back over here."

I let him pull me into him. I let him let lift me up and push me into the tile behind me. I wrap my arms around his neck and my legs around his waist and he holds me under the slightly less than warm water, until we can't hold anything back any longer, and finally, sadly, bring it all to an end.

卌 卌 卌 ||

I sit on the closed toilet with a towel wrapped around me as Felix cleans the bite in my shoulder. He puts peroxide on it, wipes it away with warm water, and then applies a generous amount of Polysporin. He reaches into the cabinet over my head and pulls out a big, square band-aid and starts to rip the paper wrapper off. I watch him as he pulls the white strips away and carefully places the bandage on my shoulder. He gently smooths it out on my skin with his palm, and then he nods.

"Thanks," I say.

"Of course."

"I'm uh, I'm going to get changed."

"Okay."

I get up from the toilet and head into the living room where my costume is strewn across the floor. I pat myself dry and drop the towel, deciding to just get dressed right out in the open. The curtains are drawn so who cares. I put on my underwear first, and when I'm picking my bra off the floor I swear I hear the floor creak behind me, but I don't turn around. Felix is probably watching me, but I mean, whatever. We just had sex and I let him drink my blood, and we're never going to do that again, so if he wants to look while I get dressed, that's okay. After I put my tank top on, I turn around to see if he's still there, but he isn't. I wonder if he even watched at all.

"Okay, I'm leaving then," I say at the door.

He walks over to me and all of a sudden it's really awkward. What are we supposed to do?

"Okay," he says in almost a whisper.

"I don't really know how to do this."

"Neither do I."

"Should we hug?" I ask.

"Yeah, hugging is good."

He opens his arms first and I hesitate, but let myself press against his chest, and almost literally be consumed by him. I melt into him and immediately feel so at peace. Even though this is the end of us, and this is the last time I will hug a man who makes me feel this safe, I'm so comforted. Nothing bad can happen when I'm in his arms, and hugging him makes me feel so cozy. I bury my face into his shirt and I can hear him let out a slow breath, and feel his entire body relax.

"Have fun at the party," he whispers into my hair.

"I won't. It's going to be stupid."

"Yeah. So is the rest of my life."

I let out a bit of a laugh. "Tell me about it."

"I'll miss you."

"I'll miss you too."

He breaks us apart and I reluctantly let go and take a step back. He's got tears in his eyes.

"I love you," I dare to say.

"I love you too."

"Okay bye." I grab onto the doorknob and whip the door open, practically jumping through it and almost sprinting down the hall. I want to look back. I want to look back and see if he's watching me from the doorway. I want to see if he's crying. But I don't. I race to the elevator and almost keep going, I almost go to the stairs because I don't want to stop and wait, but the doors are just closing, so I run faster.

"Hold the elevator, please!" I shout.

A guy with a Skip The Dishes bag puts his hand in between the doors and they pop back open, giving me time to get inside.

"Thanks," I say to him, catching my breath and adjusting my wig.

"No problem. Paleontology waits for no one."

I smile a little and he winks at me.

We don't say anything else in the elevator, but as we part ways outside the building, he calls out, "Watch out for those raptors!"

I wave and head to my car, trying my hardest not to cry.

"Where's Felix?" Angela asks, shoving a drink in my hand before I'm even fully through the door.

"We broke up." I try to give her the drink back but she gasps and pulls me in for a hug. "No hugs, please, I don't want to cry," I say.

"Sorry. You need to drink, then."

I shake my head. "No way. Alcohol will make things worse. Nice Pam costume, by the way. Is Josh dressed up as Jim?" I eye her cute cardigan and curly half up-do, and then look around for Josh.

"He's Jim impersonating Dwight, but no one is catching on, they just think he's Dwight. Which makes sense. I don't know why he thought people would know."

"Well Jim is Asian, isn't he? Dwight isn't."

Angela laughs. "You have to go tell him right now, you'll make his night."

"I don't want him to think you told me, I'll just wait until the opportunity presents itself."

"Alright. But anyway, what happened? Do you want to talk about it?"

"I just..." I sigh and look around. "I just didn't like what our relationship was doing to me. And to us." I gesture between me and her so she knows who I'm talking about. "It was weird. I mean he was making me believe a lot of weird things, and it wasn't healthy."

"Well I'm glad you're okay. Or at least safe. Do you want to skip the party? We can hang out upstairs and watch movies if you want."

"No, I want to party with everyone, I just can't drink."

"What about smoke?"

I haven't had a joint since college, but I follow Angela to her back deck anyway. Josh is out there with a few of his friends and I point at him, yelling something about identity theft not being a joke, and everyone laughs.

"Angela told you, didn't she?" he asks.

"No, I knew all on my own. I think you're hilarious."

"Thanks, Reese. So do I."

"Are you getting high with us?" one of his friends asks me.

"I think so. I haven't smoked in a really long time though, so you guys can't make fun of me."

"We would never make fun."

"Hey, is Felix joining us?" Josh asks.

I notice Angela shaking her head subtly at him, but not so subtly shaking her hand across her throat.

"It's fine, Angela," I say to her, and she stops making the 'cut-it-out' motion with her hand as if she's been caught doing something wrong, or as if she actually thought I didn't see her doing it. "We broke up," I tell Josh.

"Oh my god, are you okay? When did you break up?"

"Um, about two hours ago?"

"What! Are you okay?"

I take in a deep breath and nod. "I will be."

"But you guys just got that tattoo together," he groans.

"That's okay. I think it's a funny tattoo. And if it really bothers me, I can just get it covered up. It isn't very dark."

"Yeah, except for where the black label is on the bottle."

I shrug. "It's fine. I'm not worried about it."

Someone hands me a joint and I look at it for a second before taking it and putting my lips around it. I take a few inhales from it, and it burns my lungs and I can't help but cough. And cough and cough and cough. I'm so embarrassed, but luckily no one laughs at me.

"This is good," a guy dressed as a Jedi says, "it means it worked."

I pass the joint and put my hands on my knees, still coughing. The Jedi steps over to me and puts his hand on my back.

"Try to take deep breaths," he says.

I shake my head and cough again. "It makes it worse."

"Try through your nose." He gently grabs my shoulders and straightens me up, and I watch as he takes a big breath in through his nose. "You gotta breathe with me," he says with a smile. But it reminds me of the time Felix and I got stuck in the elevator, and I feel my eyes start to well with tears. I cough a little more, shake my head, and walk past him, back into the house.

"Is she okay?" I hear someone ask, but I don't stick around to answer, or hear if anyone answers for me.

"Oh my god, Reese!" Claire practically jumps on me when I get in the house, and I give her a hug.

"Hey! I didn't know you were coming to this!"

"We just stopped by for a little bit, we're going to a party at Emily's brother's."

"Oh nice."

Claire is dressed as Anna from *Frozen*, and Emily is Kristoff.

"We just wanted to come say hi because we knew you'd be here," Emily says. "Claire proposed to me over Thanksgiving weekend!"

"Ah! No way! Congrats again!"

"For real, I never would have thought of doing it after Emily already did, so thanks for thinking of it," Claire says.

"No problem! Was it adorable and romantic?"

"Yes it was, I think my proposal won, actually."

"Excuse me," Emily scoffs, "it's not a contest."

"I think it is. And I won."

They both laugh and I watch them hold each other as they half lose their balance with giggles, and I watch them as they tell me the story of how both proposals happened. I listen very hard but all I can focus on is the sound of Claire's voice and how happy she sounds, but not about the actual words she's using. Oh, I'm not even focusing on her voice at all anymore. What were we even talking about?

"I'm sorry," I say, shaking my head. "I have no idea what you're saying."

"What?" Claire sounds disappointed and I feel bad, but Emily mimes smoking a joint and Claire smiles and nods.

"Okay well we have to go anyway, so have fun!"

"Okay," I say. "You too! You guys are adorable!"

"I know!" Claire calls back as they leave.

"It's too bad I didn't dress up as that guy from *Jurassic Park*," the Jedi from earlier says from behind me. "Or we would have matched."

"Okay, first of all, the character you're looking for is called Alan Grant, and second of all, my boyfriend was dressed as him. His costume was amazing and we looked amazing together."

"Didn't you just break up?"

"Who even are you?" I ask.

"Shawn."

"Well, *Shawn,* I don't appreciate you making these comments when you know I'm heart broken."

"Are you, though?" he narrows his eyes at me so I shove past him to get a snack from the kitchen.

"Why are you still talking?" I ask, grabbing a handful of chips from a bowl. I start to crunch on them and an explosion of flavour bursts on my tongue. "Jesus Christ, what flavour is this?"

"Um, I think they're just dill pickle."

"They're fucking *fantastic!*"

"Have you never had dill pickle chips before?"

"Yes I've had dill pickle chips before, you idiot, but I'm very high right now and they're so good I can't even handle it. Are these Lays?"

"I- I think so."

I shove more chips in my mouth. "These are the best chips I've ever had. You should have some."

"I'm good."

"My boyfriend was amazing, you know," I say.

"That's... good?"

"No! It's not good! It's incredibly sad, Shawn, because we're not together anymore and we never will be. And he'll outlive me and it will be very sad. I'll grow wrinkly and old and he'll still be here, serving pizza very quickly to unsuspecting customers. They'll think he's just very good at his job, but I'll know the truth."

"Oh yeah?"

"Yeah!" More chips.

"What's the truth?"

"Oh don't you try that on me, mister! I'm not telling anyone! I won't make that mistake again!"

"But I'm so curious now!"

"Are you high too?" I ask him.

"Yes."

"Good."

"Does that mean you'll tell me the secret of your ex-boyfriend?" he asks.

"No! Of course not!"

"Oh come on!"

I pick up the chip bowl and carry it with me to the couch. "I can only tell you one secret," I say as I sit down with the bowl in my lap.

"Okay." He sits next to me and takes a couple chips for himself.

"Okay, are you ready?" I ask him.

"Yes!"

"He's very old."

"What, like fifty?"

I shake my head, and it feels like my entire brain is moving, but also like my skull has padding inside it. "My brain has a blanket around it," I say.

"I promise you it doesn't."

"I wasn't going to say that out loud, you know. I thought it was such a cool thing to say, but then my brain was like, 'No Reese, that's very stupid, no one will care,' so I didn't say it out loud, but then I guess I did."

"Yeah that happens sometimes."

"For sure."

"You know what are really good?" Shawn asks.

"What?"

"Miss Vickie's Sea Salt and Malt Vinegar."

"Oh my god, let's walk to the variety store and get some!" I grab his arm and pull him off the couch, and drag him around the house to find Angela so we can tell her where we're going.

"No," she says immediately when we've found her outside the bathroom.

"No?" I repeat, but as a question.

"I know what Shawn is doing, and I don't approve."

"I'm not doing anything," he says, "I promise. I know she just broke up with her very old boyfriend and she doesn't want anything with anyone."

"Not even for fun," I clarify. "Because that's not fun to me."

"Right." He nods at me and then turns his attention back to Angela. "I've put this idea of Miss Vickie's chips into her head, and to be honest it's in my head too, and she's new at being high, so I should definitely go with her."

"Excuse me! I'm not new at being high! I used to get high in college! When it was illegal!"

"Right, but have you done it since then?"

I just stare at him as an answer.

"That's what I thought," he says.

"We're just going to the variety store," I assure her.

"No funny business," Shawn says to her. "I promise."

"I'm coming with you," she says.

"Yes!" I screech, jumping up and down. "Ah, this is going to be so fun!"

"But I have to pee first," Angela says to us.

I've been sober for a few hours, but I still feel more comfortable staying the night at Angela's, just in case I think I'm sober but I'm actually not. She puts a blanket on the couch for me and I get curled up right away.

"Did you have fun tonight even though you broke up with your boyfriend?" she asks.

"Yes. I'm glad I didn't drink though, we would have been crying all night in the upstairs bathroom if I was drunk."

She laughs and nods. "Yeah, it's true."

"The weed was a good idea. It just took my mind off everything and let me have fun. And eat too much."

"Always with the eating too much. Yeah, I wasn't sure if I wanted to get high, I don't like to do it that often, but it was fun."

"It was."

"Okay. Sleep tight."

"Don't let the bed bugs bite," I say, closing my eyes.

"Gross."

卌 卌 卌 |||

I drive home in the morning and let my rats out to run around, and then I cry. I want to text Felix, but I know that will make things harder, so I bake peanut butter cookies and cry some more. And then I eat my peanut butter cookies while crying. And while watching *Twilight*. Of course.

I'm halfway through *Breaking Dawn Part 1* when Angela texts me.

Blizzards? is all it says.

She's at my apartment half an hour later and we watch the rest of the movies while we eat our ice cream.

"I'm really sorry if I'm part of the reason you guys broke up," she finally says.

I put a hand up to shush her. "Stop. I'm not talking about it."

"No but I-"

"I said no."

"Okay, but I was just worried about you; we both were."

"Angela!"

"Sorry."

We get Thai food delivered for supper and start watching the new season of *Neighbourly* on Netflix.

"You know if either of us are invited to Claire and Emily's wedding, we'll probably get to meet him," I say when Logan Jackson is on the screen.

"What, why?"

"He's dating her best friend."

"Why didn't I know that?" Angela screeches.

I shrug. "They met when they were filming that movie here."

"That doesn't answer my question," she laughs.

"You must not have known because you're not as close with Claire as I am. So I'll probably be invited to her wedding and you won't. And I'll get to meet him and you won't."

"You bitch."

I shrug and take a big bite of Pad Thai. We both laugh and go back to watching the show.

I keep eyeing the book on my nightstand with a bookmark halfway through. Felix and I never got to finish reading our newest book together and I'm not sure if I want to finish it on my own. I sigh and get into bed, and then scroll through different social media apps on my phone until I fall asleep.

I wear my costume to work on Halloween and I'm happy to see that about half the staff have also dressed up. I drive past Carter's on my way home and catch Felix going inside, and he's wearing his Alan Grant costume. I hand out candy to the kids who live in the building, but they stop knocking on my door by about 8pm, so I have a shower, put on some PJs and put on my favourite Halloween movie: *Hocus Pocus*. I eat the leftover chocolates, which consist of Wunderbar, Crispy Crunch, Smarties, and Oh Henry. By the time the movie's over, there are mini chocolate bar wrappers all over my coffee table and I feel a little like barfing.

The last episode of the weekly show I've been watching with Angela and Josh is on that Friday, and turns out we didn't get a chance to watch it at all together this season, so we decide to have a late night and binge the whole season. I'm just glad that Josh and Angela didn't catch up without me. I bring chips and beer over to Angela's and we watch it together, pausing every so often to talk about our thoughts.

They don't bring up Felix, and I'm glad they don't, but for some reason, a part of me wishes they would. I don't know what it is, but I just want to talk about him. I want something that reminds me of him to be brought up so I can say, "Oh yeah, Felix would do that all the time," or something. I just wish that everything worked out differently.

"So you seemed to have fun with Shawn at our party," Josh brings up when the last episode is over.

"A little bit," I say, raising an eyebrow at him.

"He thought you were cool."

"That's good. I'm not dating your friend, Josh."

"I didn't say you had to!"

"You implied."

"Josh, stop," Angela says. "Her and Felix broke up a week ago."

"Yeah," I agree.

"It's not like they were together for that long," he says. He turns to me and says, "You guys weren't even together for that long. You're acting like you guys just ended a five-year relationship or something."

I sigh, trying to think of my response. Trying to make it make the most sense that I can. "I can't really describe what it was about him that made me feel so safe with him, but I did. He was my anchor when I felt like I was to going float away. He was so gentle, and understanding of everything. I never felt like he was judging me, and I just…" I shrug. "I felt like me with him. I never realized it was something I could even struggle to feel until I was with him. Being with him made me realize how much of myself I was holding back with the other guys I've been with. Maybe that's just a sign of how bad the other guys were, but I've never been with someone who treated me like… like, someone they actually *wanted* to be with."

"That's really nice," Angela says. "Maybe we misjudged him."

"We didn't misjudge him," Josh says. "He must not have made you feel as safe as he could have, otherwise you wouldn't have broken up with him, right?"

"Right. He made me feel safe, but he also, um, was weird."

Angela smirks at me. "He was more than weird. And he made you believe that none of it was weird."

"Let's talk about something else. And not your friend Shawn," I say before Josh gets the chance to bring him up again.

It's snowing when I leave Angela's. I drive slower than normal because I haven't had a chance to get my snow tires installed yet, and even with driving more carefully, I still skid a couple times and fishtail a bit when I make turns. I make it home in one piece and cry the whole elevator ride to my floor. There's someone else in there with me who looks like they're trying to blend into the wall, but I can't help it. I wasn't expecting someone to be in the elevator at 2:30 in the morning and I'm not prepared to hold my feelings in. I just wish that Angela believed me. Everything would be so much easier if I could just tell her the truth and have her understand.

The snow is already melting by the next afternoon, but the air is still really chilly. I don't know what else to do, so I decide that even though the thought of going alone makes me a little sad, I'm going to continue running. I never thought that I would be good at running, let alone enjoy it, so I kind of want to keep doing it. I've noticed a difference in my body since Felix and I started running, too. My legs feel stronger and it's a little more comfortable to wear midrise jeans. It's also nice not getting winded as easily if I need to climb a bunch of stairs, so I think I'll try to keep it up.

It feels good to be out and running on my own. I thought it would be strange not having Felix by my side cheering me on or telling me I can do it when I start to slow down. I thought it would be hard having to listen to my own laboured breathing instead of having Felix's calm inhales and exhales to help calm mine. But it's okay. Nice, even. The night is still fairly early but the sun's already set; and yesterday's brief snowfall makes the roads glisten under my feet. They're wet and slick but the snow is completely gone now, which I'm sure my toes appreciate.

I think I've already been running for about twenty minutes at this point and I smile when I realize I have so much more energy to keep going. I turn a corner and end up running past Felix's apartment. I can't help but look up at it, wondering if he's looking out his living room window at me going past. I try not to glance for too long, try not to make it seem like I've been *looking* for him. I face the road ahead, but still wonder if Felix happened to be at his window. Wonder if Felix misses me. If this is as hard for him as it is for me.

The roads are a bit busier over here so I move onto the sidewalk and then jog in place while I wait for the light to change so I can cross the road. I watch my breath come out in clouds in front of my face and then the bright walk symbol turns on across the street and I move forward.

But then the strangest thing happens.

I can't even explain it in ways that make sense to me. All I know is that I'm running, and then I'm not. There's a bright light, a sharp pain in my leg, my hip, my ribs, and then my head, and then I'm... spinning? Somersaulting? I'm doing something involuntary that is not running, and it hurts. Everything is loud, but not with noises that I recognize. I can't tell if it's me screaming, someone else screaming, a car horn, thunder, or music. I can't tell what it is, but it's loud and it's in my head and everything feels wrong.

And then everything is silent. Black. I am no longer experiencing the world in any way except to know that I am a thing that exists. I don't know what I exist in, I don't know what's happening around me, but I know that I'm still me, for things to happen around.

And then pain starts to radiate throughout my entire body and I wish that I didn't exist anymore. The pain is unreal. I feel like I can't breathe. I open my eyes and everything's a blur; I can make out colours and movement, but that's about it. Someone screams. The sob is so loud it's like a banshee flying around me. And then I hear it. My name. My name coming off the lips of a voice I would recognize anywhere, even when I have no idea what's happening and my brain isn't working properly.

"Reese?" Felix is close to me now, I can feel it, but I can't make out his face as he leans over me. I know it's him even though I can't recognize his face, and even though I'm scared, I feel a little calmer knowing that it's him. Knowing that he's here.

"That bastard!" I hear Felix yell. What happened? Who's a bastard? "Reese?" he says to me.

I want to answer him but I don't know if I can.

"Reese, look at me, okay?"

I didn't realize I wasn't already looking at him, but I follow his voice and let my eyes land on the blurry colours of what is probably his face.

"That's it, good job," he says to me.

This must be really bad if he's praising my ability to look at him. What am I saying, of course it's bad. It's so bad that I have no idea what the fuck happened and I'm in so much pain that I don't even know how to process it. At least I'm not alone. At least Felix is here.

I want to say his name but it's hard to breathe, and I can't seem to even form the word.

"No, no, no, Reese, keep looking at me."

Did I stop looking at him? When did I do that? I never want to stop looking at him. I blink and find his blurry face again.

"There we go. You have to stay awake, okay? Can you do that for me?"

"Felix," I finally manage.

"It's okay, I'm right here. I'm right here."

"I don't want to die." And all of a sudden I can see everything around me. The pain coursing through my body feels more real, something I can pinpoint rather than just something that was seeming to take over completely. Felix's face isn't quite so blurry over mine, and I can hear someone sobbing. Is that me? Am I sobbing?

"I know, sweetie," he says. "I'm calling an ambulance. An ambulance is coming, okay? And I'll ride with you to the hospital and they'll make sure you're okay."

"I don't -" I try to repeat myself, because for some reason that's the only thing I can think of to say, but I can't breathe and my airway feels wet and heavy. I can taste blood at the back of my throat. "Felix," I sputter, coughing up a wet, thick, metallic substance. Oh my god. Am I coughing up blood? People always die in the movies after they cough up blood. I was okay before, Felix being here with me was okay, it was enough, but now that everything is more clear, it's not enough. I can't die. I don't want to die, I'm not ready.

"Oh my god," Felix cries. "They're not going to get here in time."

Felix's arms wrap around me and I feel myself let out a scream as he brings my body close to his.

"I'm sorry," he cries. "But I have to get you to the hospital. Where are your shoes? Where are her fucking shoes!? For fuck's sakes!"

I can't do anything except weep and say Felix's name. He carries me to his car and lays me across the back seat, I think without my shoes. I watch through the gap between the front seats as he gets in the driver side.

"I can't believe someone just fucking hit you and drove away!" Felix yells before I hear his door slam shut.

I listen to the car go up to speed and I close my eyes.

"No no, keep your eyes open," Felix says. He must be looking at me in the rear view mirror.

"I can't," I half whisper.

"Talk to me, then! Talk to me Reese. How long were you running for before this happened? How far did you go?"

"I don't..." I can't get the rest of my words out and breathing is getting even harder than it was before. "I can't..." It's like someone is sitting on my chest. I try to take in a breath but it's like there's something physically stopping me. I want him next to me. He's too far away.

"No, Reese, come on, you can do this! Stay awake for me, please!"

I manage to open my eyes again and I see him slamming his hands on the steering wheel as he drives. He lets out a long scream and slams the steering wheel again, and then he just starts sobbing. I can see his shoulders shake as he sobs, as he drives too fast for the roads around here.

"Reese, come on," Felix says, waking me up. Was I asleep? Are we still driving? My head and shoulders are in his lap, and he's tapping my cheek.

"What," I start to ask, but that's all I can get out.

"Reese! Oh my god, Reese, hi, please don't do that to me again!" He's crying and sniffling, not even trying to hold it in for my benefit at this point.

I want to ask him what I did to him, but I can't get anything out. I can't breathe. I reach my hand up to his face and he presses it to his cheek, his cheek that's wet with his tears. He lets out another sob.

"I…" I take in as deep of a breath as I can manage and say "I don't want to die," again.

"I know," he says through more sobs. "I don't know if you've seen yourself Snappy Jack, but you're a mess." He laughs softly and then cries again. "Your heart already stopped, I can't… I can't…"

"You can fix me."

"But you'll turn. You don't want that."

"But I don't want to die. Felix, I don't want to die. I don't want to die." I manage to just say 'I don't want to die' over and over again, I think mostly under my breath.

"I can still take you to the hospital if you promise not to flatline again. I can't do chest compressions and drive at the same time."

But I'm just saying "I don't want to die," over and over.

"I know," he whispers. "I know, sweetie."

Felix is still holding my hand against his cheek, and then he pulls it away from his face and kisses my palm.

"Are you sure?" he asks.

"I don't want to die," I breathe.

"Okay," he says, and lets out a deep breath. "Okay," he says again. He kisses my wrist, and then bites it. I don't even react to it, and let him drink however much of my blood he needs in order to do this. He holds onto my arm with both his hands as he drinks, and I watch him through a blurry haze that's getting blurrier with the second. The euphoric part of the feeding sets in, but it feels different this time. Instead of feeling like fairy dust in my veins, it just takes some of my pain away. The pain is a little less intense while his teeth are in my skin.

He takes his mouth away from my wrist and says, "I wish we were doing this under better circumstances."

Felix gently presses his wrist to my lips, and it's already slick with his blood. He must have broken the skin with his teeth for me.

"You have to drink it, Reese," he says gently.

I let my mouth open against his wrist and taste his blood as it seeps in my mouth. I can already taste my own blood in my mouth, so the metallic flavour isn't jarring. It's hard to swallow though, and I'm not sure if it's because I'm dying, or if it's just hard to swallow someone else's blood.

"Good job, keep drinking," he whispers. "That's it."

I start to pull my mouth away and close my eyes, but Felix puts his wrist back to my mouth.

"No, no, sweetie, you can't do that yet. Open your eyes. Look at me."

I open my eyes and let my unfocused gaze fall on him. I want to be able to make out his facial features, I want to be able to see his grey eyes, but I can't. He's just a blurry thing in front of me.

"Good. Good job, just a little more, okay? You need to have more."

I want to tell him that I can't, that I have nothing left. I try, but I can't even get a sound out. I can't even hold my head up even though it's resting in Felix's lap. I feel my head loll to the side and he taps my cheek.

"Reese, wake up."

I can't. I want to, but I can't.

"Just a little more. Please." He presses his wrist to my lips and I let the blood seep into my mouth. I don't know if I can swallow it anymore. "Come on, you can do it. You're so close.

We're so close, Reese. You said you didn't want to die, so you have to drink it."

I try to swallow it, I swear I do, but I can't. I can't breathe.

"Reese, please," he cries. "We're not going to make it to the hospital, so you have to drink more. Just a little more."

I close my eyes and feel my entire body getting heavier. It's less scary now, the thought of dying.

But then Felix starts to cry harder and that fear comes right back. I manage to open my eyes again and I try to say his name, but I can't get enough air to make a sound. He notices though, and looks down at me.

"Do you still want this?" he asks between sobs. "Do you still want me to turn you?"

All I can do is nod my head.

"Okay." He sniffles and takes in a breath. "Then you need to have some more of my blood. Come on, sweetie, you can do it. I know it's hard, and I wish I could do it for you, but I can't. You have to do it yourself."

It takes everything I have, but I take three more big swallows of his blood. Three more swallows and now I really can't breathe. I try to grab onto Felix's hand but I don't know where it is. I'm not sure I have enough strength anyway.

"It's okay, you can go to sleep now," Felix says to me, grabbing my hand and cradling it between both of his. "I know you're tired. You can sleep."

But I'm not going to die now, right? I want to ask it, but I still can't. I wish Felix could hear me thinking it so he could reassure me that I won't die if I fall asleep. That now I won't ever die.

He kisses my knuckles, my forehead, my temple.

"It's okay, Reese," he whispers. "I'll be here when you wake up."

PART FOUR

|

If I die, I'm not going to be able sit on Angela and Josh's deck with them in our rocking chairs and rub in their face that their dog loves me more than them. He would love me more because I would feed him secret human food when they aren't looking. Like pieces of my steak from supper, or my peameal bacon at breakfast. I would be his favourite human.

I wonder if I became a vampire if I could still sit on their deck with them. I wouldn't be old like them so maybe they wouldn't accept me into the rocking chair deck club. They would at least believe me about being a vampire at that point, because they would see that I hadn't aged a day over 30. Er, 30 and sixish months, I guess. But still. They would believe me but they would be insanely jealous and therefore still not want to be friends with me.

Is any of this even real?

Am I dead? Do I die first before coming back as a vampire? Is that what's happening? Did I do it right? Is there a way to do it wrong? Well, I guess if I did it wrong, I'd just die and I'd forever be the girl who got hit by a car while she was running and her shoes flew off and then she died. As if my shoes flew off. I think that's what happened, because Felix was asking where my shoes were, and the person who so rudely hit me with their car had already run away so no one could answer him. I certainly didn't take them off, so they must have flown off when I flew over the car. I must have flown over the car. Do you think I flew over it? Like in the movies? What do you think it looked like? I hope it looked badass. It probably didn't. I probably looked like a fucking tool.

‖

I'm pretty sure I've opened my eyes. The thing is, I can't remember what it feels like to have eyelids. Is that weird? I'm pretty sure they're open, but I can't see anything. Not even darkness. Well, maybe I can see darkness, I don't know. But I can't see anything at all. Are my eyes open? I blink a few times to remember the feeling of having and controlling eyelids, and they are definitely there, and when I stop blinking, they are definitely open. Am I lying down? I think I am. Should I roll over? Instead of rolling over, I move my arm.

Whoa!

Holy shit.

My arm has rubbed against something that feels like the most feeling I have ever felt. What has it touched? I want to squirm away from whatever it touched, but everything feels so heavy.

"Hey, sshh," Felix whispers. His breath is on the side of my neck, and I figure we're both on our sides and he's lying down behind me, but it feels like he's *everywhere*. His breath is so intense and hot, and my whole neck feels prickly now. And now my arm isn't the only thing that's feeling the most feeling, it's my entire body. It's like I can feel every fiber of whatever's touching me. The bedsheet, that's what it is. I can feel every piece of thread against my skin. "Just lie down for a bit," he whispers, lightly pressing my head back into the pillow. "Everything's going to feel really intense for a bit, okay? But I promise I'm going to help you through it, and it'll get easier. Okay?"

"Okay," I squeak, a tear escaping and rolling off my face and onto the sheets.

"Just try to go back to sleep for now, okay?"

"Okay."

"I promise you'll get through this."

"Okay."

The next time I wake up, I don't feel as heavy anymore, but I can still feel everything. I can feel every strand of hair on my head, my eyelashes on my cheeks when I blink, everything. The room is still completely dark and I wonder if Felix has done that for my benefit. I wonder if not even having overhead lights on just helps with the sudden sensory overload.

"Can you tell me how you're feeling?" he asks.

"I don't know," I say quietly.

"Do you regret what we did?"

"I don't- I don't know. I don't think so. I'm not dead... And I would have died if we didn't do that, right?"

"Yes," he says confidently.

"You're not just saying that?"

"Reese, you flatlined while I was driving you to the hospital and it took like seven minutes for me to restart your heart."

"Seven minutes?"

"Yes."

"I was dead for seven minutes?"

"And then you were dead for three days."

"What?"

He chuckles a little. "After. Um, before. I mean that's part of the turning process. Your heart stopped, you stopped breathing, and I just had to wait for everything to work its magic."

"And it took three days?"

"Yeah."

"So what, you just brought a dead girl to your apartment and slept next to her?"

"No, I brought her to your apartment."

"We're in my apartment?"

"Yeah, I had to make sure Hazel Grace and April May were taken care of."

"Oh my god, thank you."

"Of course."

I can tell that he's directly in front of me but I can't see him, so it feels a little weird to lean in to hug him, but I do, and he hugs me back. It feels different. It doesn't feel unsafe or anything, just different. I feel different. I still feel like me, but I also feel like something's off.

Probably the undead thing has something to do with it.

I keep my arms wrapped around him for a long time, and we breathe together, in sync.

"Felix, can you see in this pitch blackness?" I ask without pulling away.

"No, there needs to be some kind of light coming from somewhere in order for me to see. I taped the curtains down and stuffed the openings with blankets. The bottom of your door, too, so there's no light flooding in from the living room."

"Look at you thinking of everything. Feeding my rats and blocking all the light for me."

"I try."

"What do we do now?" I ask.

"Take it one step at a time."

"Alright." I slowly pull back from him and let my arms drop to my side. "What's step one?"

"Letting a bit of light in."

I suck in a sharp breath, and he puts a hand on my forearm. I swear I can feel his fingerprints.

"Not sunlight," he assures me. "Just the light from the living room."

"Okay."

"It's going to feel like a lot, but I promise it won't feel like that forever. Okay?"

"Okay."

"None of this will last forever."

"Really?"

"Okay, that was a lie." We both laugh and he continues. "The feeling of it all being too much. Of being able to feel literally everything. Smell and hear everything. The fact that it feels like you'll never be able to handle it, and that blood will be the only thing to calm it down. I promise all that will go away."

"How long will it take?"

"Let's just take it one day at a time. Everyone's different."

"How long did it take you?"

I can hear him stop breathing. I can almost *feel* him stop breathing.

"Felix?" I ask. "How long did it take you?"

"A few years," he says quietly.

"What!? A few *years!*? I can't take a few *years* to get over this! I have a family, Felix!"

"It's that or be dead! Then your family wouldn't have you at all!"

"But I can't wait that long." I start to cry and he pulls me into him.

"You literally have all the time in the world, Reese. You have all the time in the world."

"But my family doesn't. Angela doesn't."

"You can still see them before then. And we can make up a story about why you can't see them away from your apartment or something. We can make this work. We'll make it work, okay?"

I nod, but I cry harder. "I didn't want this," I say.

"I'm sorry. I'm so sorry. I'm so sorry, Reese."

"I would rather this than be dead, but this was one of the reasons I didn't want it before. Before I was going to die. It was one of the reasons I just wanted to keep growing old."

"I'm still sorry. I'm sorry you had to make this decision. I'm sorry that idiot wasn't looking where they were driving. Like they just fucking slammed into you!"

"Did you see it happen?" I ask.

"Yeah," he says quietly. "I saw you from my window."

"Did I look like a tool bag?"

"What?"

"When I went flying. Did I look like a tool bag?"

"What do you mean?"

"A loser? Did I look like a loser?"

"Did you look like a loser? Flying over a car?"

"Yeah."

"That's what you're concerned about?"

|||

Felix takes the blanket away from under and around the door, letting the soft living room light flood in. I can see that it's just a bit of a warm glow creeping along the floor, but already I can make out every object in the room. And it's weird because everything is still dark, but I can still see almost as if the whole room was lit up. I can't see the colors of anything because there's no light hitting most things, but I can still see everything. My dresser, the edges of my desk, my nightstand. Felix.

"Hi," I say.

He smiles. "Hi."

"How long do we sit here?"

"Until you feel ready."

"Okay, I guess I'm ready."

"Alright." He grabs my hand and leads me across my room to the door, and he opens it. I squint at the light, and tuck myself into him. "Just let me know if anything gets to be too much."

I nod and we walk into the living room, where the flooring changes to my big, plushy rug.

"Socks," I say quickly. "I need socks."

Felix disappears for half a second and reappears with a pair of socks for me. I'm afraid to even move in order to put them on; the carpet has so much texture. I can feel it between my toes, and on the soles of my feet, I can feel it as if I'm watching someone draw on my feet. I don't know how else to explain it. I think Felix understands what's happening in my brain so he picks me up and moves me to the couch, which isn't much better, but is a little better. He kneels down in front of me and starts slowly putting on my first sock.

"This is a lot," I say.

"I know. Do you have any tight leggings? And a tight long sleeve shirt? That'll probably help."

"How would that help?"

"They won't move around on your skin much, and it'll create a bit of a barrier between you and the stuff you touch."

"Oh, right, that makes sense. I have, um, I have a pair of compression leggings in my closet. I don't have a shirt like it though."

Felix nods and looks at his watch. "Just sit right here, I'll go buy you some new clothes."

"What am I supposed to do while you're gone?"

"You can do whatever you like. It might be easiest if you just sit here, though. I'm sorry."

He puts the other sock on me, kisses my forehead, and leaves my apartment. This is outrageous. I can smell Hazel and April. I can smell their pee even though I know Felix just cleaned out their entire pen. I hear them breathing. Hazel is breathing faster than April is. Is she afraid of me? Does she know? Oh my god, my rats don't know that I'm a vampire, what am I thinking?

I shake my head to try and get my stupid thoughts out but it makes me dizzy. I want to at least watch something on TV, but I'm afraid the screen is going to be too bright. Maybe it'll be fine. I don't know how long he's going to be gone for and I don't want to sit here just staring at the wall. The TV remote is on the couch cushion next to me. I don't even have to reach for it. I hit the power button without picking it up and the TV turns on. It's already open to Netflix and a preview of a new show starts playing immediately.

The colours coming out of the TV are so intense. Is that what red normally looks like? Is purple usually that... purple? It's like they're all electric, like there's some kind of colour static coming off them. I didn't realize colours could look more colourful than they already do, but there they are, being way more colourful than normal. I reach up to my face to take off my glasses and see if everything still looks the same when I realize that I'm not even wearing my glasses. I can see extra good without my glasses? I wonder if I put them on if it would make my eyes go back to how they were before and everything would look nicer and less, um, less. You know, just less everything. But I'm afraid to get up and walk around and touch more things and look at more things than I have to, so I select *Neighbourly* from my continue watching list. And then I pick up the clicker and try to change the brightness and contrast on my TV. I finally figure it out and bring everything down to a level that looks normal to me, but it's funny because I've put the settings all the way to the end of the sliders. As dark and as contrast free as it can go. But I can still make everything out perfectly, it's just not screaming at me like it was before. I turn the volume down to 2, and lie down on the couch.

I can hear Felix walking down the hall. I can hear his shoes rubbing against the carpet outside as he approaches. I can hear him touch the doorknob. *I can hear him touch the doorknob.* He comes right over to me as soon as he enters, and kneels in front of the couch.

"How are you doing?" he asks.

I just shrug.

"All the TV settings are super low," he whispers.

I just shrug again, and then I start to cry. He shushes me and gently puts his hands on my shoulders, gesturing for me to sit up. He pulls me into a sitting position and starts taking my t-shirt off for me. He unfolds the long-sleeved shirt that he got me, which seems to already have the tags pulled off, and he pulls it over my head. The fabric is smooth and slippery, so I don't feel too much texture against my skin. And it's a compression shirt so the entire thing is tight over my torso and arms. It's comforting, and when I lean back a little into the couch, there's already less feeling since the fabric isn't moving and rubbing on my skin. I stand up and he helps me take my pants off, and then puts on my new compression leggings. Everything feels about fifty percent better and I feel like I can breathe again. Not that I need to breathe. I'm pretty sure I'm still breathing though, even though I know I don't need to. I don't know how not to breathe. And I didn't actually feel like I couldn't breathe before, I was just using it as a figure of speech or a metaphor or whatever, but since I got onto the topic, I continued with it in the literal sense.

"I don't need my glasses anymore," I say eventually.

"No."

"But I like my glasses."

"When you get used to feeling things, we can get you non prescription lenses. You can still wear them if you like them."

I shrug and lean into him. I don't want to deal with this for a few years before it gets easier. What are we supposed to tell my family? Angela? My work?

"Did you call in sick for me?" I ask.

"What?"

"Work. I'm not at work. I'm going to get fired. What did you tell everyone? Did you tell anyone anything? What does Angela think? Has she texted me? She's going to think you kidnapped me!"

Felix tucks my hair behind my ear and pulls me into him for a hug. But he squeezes me so tight, so tight that it feels like he's trying hard to make sure I don't float away. I squeeze him back and then relax into his arms.

"Angela texted you a few times and I texted back pretending to be you. If she came over, she would have called the cops or tried to murder me."

"Why? I was here, she would have seen me."

"You were dead, Reese."

"Right."

He pulls away from our hug, but I pull him back, not ready to let go. He squeezes me again, and I wish I could stay like this forever.

"When you're ready," he says slowly, "I thought we could invite her over. Show her. She'll believe you when she sees it."

"What if she doesn't?"

"She will."

"Okay, but what if she doesn't?"

"Then we'll have to eat her. We can't risk her telling everyone that you think you're a vampire."

"W-what?"

"I'm kidding." He pulls back from our hug and this time I let him. "But you look different," he continues. "Your eyes are a different colour, and your skin is tighter. You look a little bit younger. She'll notice."

"I look different?"

"Not that different," he says quickly. "You still look like you. It's mostly your eyes that make a difference. If it bothers you, you could always get coloured contacts."

"What do I tell my family?" I ask.

"You probably shouldn't tell them anything. Just pretend that you're still mortal and go on with your life as normally as you can. Until you're comfortable with everything though, you might have to make up some excuse as to why you can't see them. Like say that you have some kind of terrible and contagious disease."

"Oof, okay."

"Also for now I told Angela that you're throwing up. She wanted to bring you ginger-ale and chicken noodle soup, but I told her that you didn't want to get her sick or for her to see you like this."

"You said all this pretending to be me?" I ask.

"Yes."

"What should I tell her now?"

"You can tell her whatever you want. I would make something up so she doesn't come over, though."

"What about work?"

"I would go with the terrible and contagious disease thing."

"Maybe I can work from home. I could totally work from home."

"Once I bring more stimulation into the apartment, you won't be able to work for a while."

"More stimulation?"

"Turn all the lights on, keep the TV at a normal volume and brightness, do things around the apartment, open the window so you can hear everything outside. I'll introduce it slowly so it's not as overwhelming as it could be, but it's still going to take some time to get used to it all."

"Can we start that tomorrow?"

"Yes, of course we can."

We spend the rest of the day researching long term contagious illnesses, and turns out there aren't really any. So we decide to tell my work that I have meningitis, and later we'll tell them that I've developed complications from it that won't be contagious, but will require me to still stay home. Then at least I can get long term disability and still get some kind of paycheque while all this stupid vampire stuff gets sorted out. We've decided not to tell my family anything. I just saw them for Thanksgiving and they live a few hours away, so there's no need to make anything up until the next time we would normally get together. So, Christmas. I'll have to say that I have the Flu or something.

The next morning, we get started with bringing in more stimulants, like turning on the overhead lights in all the rooms, and Felix not being careful with his movements or things he does around me. The noise and lights are so invasive that I sit cross legged on the floor, close my eyes, and stick my fingers in my ears. But then I smell something that takes everything away. I don't know what it is, it's something I've never smelled before. It has a warm, almost earthy scent, with a hint of savouriness. Anyway, it smells fantastic, and my mouth is watering as soon as I can smell it.

"Reese," Felix says calmly. I can hear him perfectly even though my fingers are still in my ears, but it's less intense, more like how it sounded when I was mortal.

I open my eyes to see him sitting in front of me with a glass filled with a dark, red liquid.

"Is that what smells so good?" I ask.

He just nods and starts to hand it to me, but when I take my fingers out of my ears and reach for the glass, he pulls it back.

"It's for me, is it not?" I ask.

"Yes, it's for you, but I want to warn you before you drink it."

"Warn me about what?"

"How you're going to act when you taste it."

"How I'm going to act?"

"It's not only going to taste good, but it's going to feel good. All the other stuff that's too overwhelming, it won't matter anymore. Just this will, and it will help ease that feeling. Which is both good and bad."

I'm not listening to him anymore. I can hear him talking, but I'm laser focused on the blood in the glass. I haven't even had it yet and I can already imagine what it's going to taste like. Even just smelling it, just looking at it, is making everything around me feel as if it doesn't exist.

"Reese, are you listening to me?" His voice is so gentle and comforting, it pulls me from my strange haze.

"Sorry," I say.

He smiles. "It's okay. This will take a while. I just don't want you to be scared of yourself."

"Okay." But as I say the word, I can feel something in my mouth. My gums hurt a little, and there's something else there, pressing into my tongue. I gasp and throw my hands over my mouth, terrified of what's in there.

"It's okay," he whispers. "It's because of the blood craving."

I want to ask if they're fangs, but when I go to talk, I can feel my tongue poke into them and I'm afraid. I can feel my eyes welling with tears, but I also still want the blood. It's strange, and I don't like it.

"You'll learn to control those too, okay? I know it feels weird right now, and scary, but just remember it doesn't mean you're going to kill anyone or anything. It doesn't make you a monster. It's just extra teeth."

I scoff, feeling so uncomfortable in my skin that I wish I could peel it off and run away. The only thing that's making me feel even slightly okay is the fact that Felix is here.

"They'll go away after you've had your fix. I would say try to drink it slowly, but I know you won't."

"I can try," I say, and feeling the fangs against my tongue freaks me out and I almost start to cry.

He shakes his head a little. "Nah. Just go for it. We can work on control another day."

"Okay."

He hands me the glass and I almost snatch it from him. I swear I meant to grab it gently, and I kind of did, but I also just kind of… grabbed it. The glass is in both my hands, and I look down at the dark red blood. It doesn't even freak me out that it's blood. It doesn't even freak me out that I want it. Which sort of freaks me out. Okay, so I guess I'm a little freaked out, but only because I'm not freaked out. Does that even make sense?

I put the glass to my lips and tilt it back, opening my mouth and letting the warm, thick substance slide over my tongue. And let me tell you, it's incredible. It's literally the most delicious thing I've ever had and I wish humans could understand how fucking fantastic this is. What the fuck. It's so good. I open my mouth wider and try to get more at a time, but the glass is already empty. How is it empty already? I lick the edges and try to run my tongue along the inside of the glass but the glass isn't short enough for me to get it all. I pull the glass away from my face and run my fingers along the inside, scooping up the remnants and then sucking it off my fingers. Oh my god. This is heavenly.

"Reese," I hear Felix say.

I stop and look over at him, the glass still in my hand, but almost completely clean.

"Can I have more?" I ask him. My fangs are still there, but I'm less freaked out by them now. I think just because the blood is all I can think about and it's like nothing else matters.

He nods once and gets up, returns in three seconds with a whole bag. Like a blood bag. Like the kind that I saw in his fridge that one time. The kind that are in hospitals, the kind that people get hooked up to for blood transfusions. The top has been snipped off and when he hands it to me, I see I can drink from it like it's a Freezie or juice pouch. I stick it in my mouth and gulp it back.

Oh my god. It's so good. It's warm and thick, and delicious, and I can feel it coat my mouth and my throat and everything else around me is softer. The lights aren't as bright, the sound of the heat coming through the vents isn't so loud, the people in the hall are quieter, it's like everything feels normal again. I squeeze the bag to get more faster, and I realize that as I drink from it and push the blood out of it, I'm moaning. I can't help it. I can hear myself doing it but I can't stop. It's so good. Nothing has ever tasted and felt so good in my life. It's taking everything overwhelming away. It's making everything bearable.

I empty the bag and try to squeeze it with my fingers and push whatever's left towards the opening at the end, like trying to get as much out of a tube of toothpaste. I get a little more, but it's not enough. Already everything is starting to feel like too much again.

"Here," Felix says, gently taking the blood bag away from me. I watch in a panic as he runs his fingers along it. What's he doing? There's still a little left, I need it. But then he tears it open and hands it back to me. I can lick the insides of the bag now. So I do.

"Can I have more?" I ask.

"No, that's enough."

And then I start to cry. Felix holds me and we both sit on the living room floor while I cry because I want more blood. Or maybe I'm crying because I think it's weird that I want more blood. Or I'm crying because everything feels intense again and I want it to go away. I have no idea why I'm crying. Being a vampire is complicated.

||||

"Okay, I want you try to and drink it without making love to it this time," Felix says a couple days later. This is the first time he's given me instructions or guidance on how to consume it, and I choke on some embarrassed laughter.

"What? I don't make love to it."

The corner of his mouth curls into a crooked smile. "Yes you do."

"What does that even mean?" I cross my arms, stubborn to admit that he's right.

"You know what it means. All your neighbours are probably getting sick of hearing you have sex so loudly."

"I'm not having sex at all," I counter.

"They don't know that! They think you're having the best sex of your life over here but you're just drinking warm glasses of O positive."

"I'm not... I'm not that... I'm not making *excited* sex noises."

He laughs and actually throws his head back. "Can you just try really hard to act like you're drinking a nice, creamy hot chocolate?"

"A nice creamy hot chocolate that's actually fucking fantastic blood."

He laughs again and hands me the glass. I reach for it, and he pulls it back again.

"Drink it nicely," he says.

"I don't know how," I admit. And right now all I want is to be able to drink the blood so that my fangs filling my mouth stop making me feel so out of place. "I don't understand how you do it," I add.

"It's easy, really. I don't want my neighbours to think they're overhearing me having sex, so I don't make sex noises."

"Fine. I'll try."

But he's still holding the glass a little out of my reach.

"What?" I ask.

"You're adorable."

"Thank you. Can I have the blood now?"

"Yes."

I don't drink it nicely. I try, I swear. But it can't be helped. I can vaguely see Felix over the glass, sighing, and looking defeated. He'll get me to the get the hang of it eventually, I'm sure.

"I have an idea," Felix says the next day.

"You're just going to let me drink the blood however I want for another week before we practice control?"

"You're hilarious."

"Am I? Because I was being serious."

"Do you want to get back to your life as soon as possible?" he asks.

"I did. But right now I just want more blood. I want blood and you all day long. That's all I need."

"That's sweet. But also that's kind of my idea."

I squint at him in confusion and he smiles, moving closer to me on the couch. He takes a sip of blood from his glass, swishes it around his mouth, and swallows it. I can feel my fangs sliding out of my gums and I'm jealous of Felix being able to drink without them coming through. But then he brings his mouth close to mine, and blows slightly on my lips, letting me taste the remnants of the blood on his breath. I breath it in and lick my lips, and then he kisses me. I can taste the blood on his tongue and I want to suck on it. I feel everything urgent taking over my body, but Felix pulls back a little and whispers, "Slowly, Reese."

I don't know why, but those words make me melt. I smile and nod, and kiss him gently, letting his tongue sweep over mine. He pulls away briefly to have more blood, but he leaves a little in his mouth this time, letting me have some the next time our lips touch. It's still hard to do this without making noises or being aggressive, but any time he feels me not being able to control myself, he whispers, "Slowly, Reese," or, "I thought you were a fan of moving slowly?" And I die all over again because he's so perfect and how is he so good at this?

I can't go any longer without Angela seeing me. It's almost Christmas and she knows I'm still off sick from work but also knows I'm absolutely not contagious anymore. Felix and I have been working on my control every day, and I'm mostly used to everything being so... *everything*. I haven't been out in the sun, and I haven't interacted with any other humans, but Felix says having my first human be someone I really care about will make it easier to control. Like he said when he explained it before, I can still enjoy how people smell, but I should be able to stop myself from eating them because I don't want them to die. Makes sense.

In theory.

"There's blood on the counter," he says to calm me down. "If it feels like it's too hard, you can have some of that. And you can do that without making noises now, so it probably wouldn't even freak her out to see you drink it."

"This whole thing is going to freak her out," I say. "What if I go all scary and fangy as soon as I see her?"

"Then it'll be harder for her not to believe us."

The intercom buzzes and we both jump a little with surprise. Felix gets up and buzzes her in without saying anything, and together we wait for her to knock on my apartment door. She doesn't know that Felix is here. She's going to freak out when she sees him. Hell, she's going to freak out when she sees me.

Felix opens the door and I stay hidden in my room. I'm afraid that I'm going to eat my best friend. I can't eat my best friend. My room is a safe place for now.

"What are you doing here?" I hear her say from the doorway.

"Can you please come in?" he asks her, sounding extra civil. It comes across as creepy to me, so that probably wasn't a good choice.

"Where's Reese?"

"She's in her room."

"Did you kill her? Have I actually been texting you for the last month and a half?"

"No, I promise you that she's the one you've been texting. As for killing her..."

"Oh my god, Felix, don't freak her out with a technicality!" I yell from my bed.

I can hear her gasp, and hear her feet on the floor as she's about to run to me, but then I can hear skin against fabric, and I know that Felix has stopped her from running to see me.

"You have to trust me," he whispers. "She's not herself. But everything she told you before, everything you were too afraid to believe, is true."

"What do you mean?"

"That night in November, that weekend after it snowed for the first time? Reese was hit by a car."

"What?"

"She didn't have meningitis. She was going for a run and someone was driving too fast and wasn't paying attention and went through a red light, and they hit Reese. It was in front of my apartment and I saw it happen, and I ran out to her right away. She was... bad."

"Oh my god," Angela says, cutting him off. "But I heard her. She's not dead, I heard her! Reese!"

"Listen to me," he says to her. "She was bleeding internally, she had broken bones, collapsed lungs, she couldn't breathe, and an ambulance never would have made it in time. Even if they did, our hospital isn't prepared for that kind of trauma. They would have had to airlift her to a bigger hospital and she would have died on the way. Hell, she stopped breathing in my car. I had to get into the back seat with her and give her chest compressions."

"What are you saying?" Angela asks slowly.

"I saved her life, Angela. By drinking some of her blood and then getting her to drink mine. By mixing our blood and her ingesting it, it um, it killed her. For a couple of days."

"And then what?"

"And then she woke up, and now she's like me. Sort of. She's like me, but I'm better at it."

"What?"

"Stop bragging!" I yell from my room.

I can hear Angela's breathing quicken, and can hear her footsteps on the floor again, and again I know that Felix has held her in place.

"Why won't you let me see her!?" she cries.

"Because she's going to look scary. She can't control her fangs when there's blood around yet, and you're the first person she's going to come near. We have to approach this slowly and carefully."

"Is she going to eat me?"

"I promise she won't eat you. If she tries to, I won't let her." I'm pretty sure he meant that as a joke, but it comes out really serious. "I'm joking," he adds. Okay, good. "She won't try to eat you."

"How do you know?" Angela asks.

"Because you're her best friend. Would you want to eat your best friend?"

"Probably not."

I snort at that, and then hold my breath because I can hear them walking towards my room. I can smell Angela through her pores or something, and already I can feel my fangs slipping out of my gums. I cover the bottom half of my face with my hands, even though I know my eyes look scary too. And then the door swings open, and there's Angela.

"Jesus fuck," she says immediately.

I laugh nervously, but keep the bottom half of my face covered.

"You really weren't shitting me, were you?" she asks.

"I was not shitting you."

"Can I come closer?"

I nod, but my hands are still over my mouth.

"Slowly," Felix warns.

She nods, and takes one step. Then another. Her heart is racing. She smells amazing. I want to bite her. I want to feel her veins burst open in my mouth and I want to drink her blood as it's still pumping through her body. But I don't want to hurt her. So I don't. I just think about it instead. I picture it clearly and it's amazing.

"Can I see your fangs?" she asks.

"They're scary," I say.

"If you could deal with it when you saw Felix's then I can deal with it when I see yours. I won't fully believe you until you show me, anyway."

I sigh and lower my hands. And then I raise my right hand back up to my mouth and lift up my upper lip.

"Holy fuck!" she screams.

I lower my lip and nod. "Yeah."

"Those are like, real ass fucking fangs! It's not just two fangs like in Dracula things, they're like, fucking everywhere."

"Yeah," I say again, laughing a little.

"Do they hurt?"

I shrug. "A little."

"Do you want to bite me?"

"A little."

"Fuck, eh? For real?"

I just nod.

"This is wild," she says.

"Yeah," I agree. "Tell me about it."

"Wait a second, what about that story about the blood drive in Felix's apartment?" she asks.

"We made it up."

"Are you serious?"

"Yeah," I say. "What else were we supposed to say? You obviously didn't believe me."

"True. What are you going to tell your parents?"

I shrug. "Nothing?"

"But it's almost Christmas! Can you handle Christmas with them? Also you look a little different. Your eyes are like this cool, smoky grey and you don't have any lines next your eyes when you smile." I've only just realized that I can't feel my fangs in my mouth anymore. Is my scary vampire face really gone? I run my tongue along my teeth and smile, but don't tell Angela that I've never been able to do that without having any blood, so that I don't freak her out.

"I'm going to tell them I have the flu," I tell her.

"They'll try to come visit you if you tell them that."

"I'm going to tell them not to. That Felix is staying with me and taking care of me. I'm an adult, I can spend Christmas away from my parents."

"Okay."

"Are you going to tell Josh?"

"I don't think I have much of a choice," she says easily. "If you want to keep being our friend, hiding it won't end up working out. So you're going to have to show him your fangs and stuff.

But then you'll be able to be yourself with us. I mean, as long as you don't like, randomly shove your face in our necks and smell us and stuff. Or eat us."

"Is Felix invited?" I ask quietly.

"Of course he is. I'm sorry I didn't believe you before."

"It's okay, I get it."

"I mean like, imagine someone just telling you that their boyfriend is a vampire. Like that's the silliest thing I've ever heard."

I laugh a little. "I know."

"You have to tell me one thing, though," she says.

"What's that?"

"Can you promise me that he did actually turn you because you were dying?"

"Yes."

"For real? That's not another story you made up because you don't want me to judge you? Because if for one second you think I'm okay with my best friend just letting a man she's known for five months and only dated for three, turn her into a vampire because they think they'll love each other forever, then you are sorely mistaken. I do not approve. That is rushing into this whole immortal thing way too fast, and I think that-"

I cut her off. "Angela. I promise. I never actually wanted to be a vampire."

"Really? That's weird."

I roll my eyes. "I wanted to be able to grow old. I didn't want to fight the urge to eat people. And all… the other stuff. I promise I didn't do this for love. I was actually dying."

"But did Felix know you didn't want this?" She turns towards Felix. "Did you know she didn't want this? Because that's a dick move right there. Like I wouldn't have wanted her to die either, she's my best friend, but if she didn't-"

I cut her off again. "I asked him to do it. I didn't want to die. I was scared."

She takes a deep breath. "Well okay, then."

I smile at her and she smiles back.

"So you got by hit a car, eh?" she asks. "That's badass. Did you go flying?"

I know my friends are throwing me a surprise party. I know it's just going to be me, Josh, Angela, and Felix, but I know they're trying to pretend like nothing's happening. Because I can hear literally everything. Felix knows that I know, because he knows that I can hear everything, because he too, can hear everything, but he's playing along. We're both playing along for Angela and Josh's benefit, really, because they've done so much to plan this. It's sweet how much they want me to still be able to do human things. I put on the dress that I ordered for the occasion as soon as I heard Angela and Josh whispering about it, and look at myself in the mirror.

Thirty-One. Technically. Kind of. I've been mostly alive for thirty-one full years, but this birthday feels weird. For one, because I look younger than I did last year, and two, I don't have to shove tissue under my armpits to soak up my anxious sweat. Because I don't sweat anymore. It's fantastic, really. Too bad you can't experience it.

I wait until it's fully dark out and then head down to my car. I take the stairs because I'm still afraid of being stuck with a stranger in the elevator. I'm not afraid of biting them or killing them, but I'm not sure I could control my vampire face, so just to be safe, I take the stairs. If I pass someone there, I can just keep going. Felix is apparently working, but I know he's not. He's been at Angela and Josh's since before I woke up, to give the appearance that he's at work. I heard them whispering about it every time I used their bathroom. They really should have texted each other or written notes, but I never said my friends were smart. Just sweet.

The three of them yell surprise when I walk into their house, and I start to cry because I wasn't expecting there to be cardboard cut-out people all over her living room and kitchen.

"What's with the cardboard people?" I ask.

"We wanted it to feel like it was more of a party for you. Felix did it, but he didn't tell us about it."

I smile at him. "Of course he didn't."

"So, are you surprised!?" Angela asks.

"Yes," I lie. "I had no idea you guys were planning this. I thought we were just going to chill and watch movies or something."

"Why are you wearing a dress then?" Angela asks, raising an eyebrow.

I hold up a bag with sweats in it. "I was going to get changed after I made you take birthday pictures of me."

"Sure." She smiles and gives me a hug. "Come do shots."

"Okay."

We do a shot together and then Felix comes over to me. "Happy birthday, Reese."

"Thanks. Except it isn't technically my birthday."

"It's not?"

"Well, no, I guess it's my birthday. This is the day I was born. But I'm not older this year."

"You're not?" He scrunches his eyebrows. "How is that possible?"

"It's complicated," I say, smiling at him. "But it's also kind of my first birthday. Because it's my first time turning thirty again."

"Turning thirty *again*? How is that possible?"

"I said it was complicated," I say with a little laugh.

He smiles. "Alright. You wanna do a shot together?"

"Yes. Do you know what's in a Snappy Jack?"

"I don't think that's actually a shot."

"Okay, you're right, I can't find anything online about a shot called a Snappy Jack and I've looked multiple times over the last year. It's very frustrating."

"Yes, it is frustrating to be wrong."

I hit him in the shoulder and we both laugh.

"Why don't we make it a real shot?" he suggests.

"Why didn't we think of this last year?"

"Because you were determined to convince me that it was already a real shot."

"Right, yes, of course."

"Okay so the first ingredient is obviously Jack Daniel's," he says, pouring some into a shaker.

"Obviously," I agree.

"What other ingredient should we use?"

"Something snappy."

"Obviously," he says with a smile.

And then he winks at me.

Acknowledgements

I need to thank Laura Kulson first, because not only did she read the first draft and give me excellent feedback on major scenes, but she also came up with the cover concept, did the artwork for the cover, *and* came up with the title! My only input was putting Thirty in brackets. I don't know how she does it, but she's incredible. Also I'm not sure if she knows this, but she's going to read the first drafts of all my books until one of us dies.

Sarah Jane Wetelainen read the second draft of my book and also read the final draft for typos which was incredibly helpful. I want to thank both SJ and Laura for allowing me to run synopsis and playlist ideas by them and ask for help more times than were probably acceptable. SJ basically wrote the last two lines of the synopsis as well, so she is also amazing for that.

A couple people helped me with Josh's character and the dessert he makes, but said that no acknowledgement is necessary. I think it's necessary, so I guess I'll say thank you without mentioning their names.

I also need to thank my TikTok followers for their support and excitement surrounding this book and the TikTok series I based off it. Even though TikTok didn't show this series to as many people as normal (which can be disheartening, especially when you're literally planning on publishing a book out of it), the people who did see it, loved it. Everyone's love for it helped me to be excited about this book. I was nervous about this book (as I am most of the time before publishing a book) but this time it felt different. I tried my best to do a different take on a common genre and I was nervous that I hadn't succeeded. That maybe I just *thought* I had, and that I was the only one who liked this story. But even with less views than my previous skits, it had just as much love. All the people who saw it left kind comments sharing how much they enjoyed it and wanted to see more, or how excited they were to read the book. And that means more to me than you know.

Listen to the Spotify Playlist!